FRAGMENTS

FRAGMENTS

BY MAGDALENA AND ASHE STEVENS

Published by aNOUNymous Inc.

This is a work of fiction inspired by true events and the authors' lived experiences. While drawn from real-life people, places, and situations, the narrative has been fictionalized and dramatized for storytelling purposes. Some names, characters, businesses, events, and locations are either the product of the authors' imagination, used with permission, or presented fictitiously. Any resemblance to actual persons, living or deceased, is purely coincidental unless expressly acknowledged.

No generative AI was used in the creation of this novel or its cover. The authors do not consent to the use of this work in any form for the training, fine-tuning, or development of artificial intelligence models.

Content Warning:
This novel includes themes of trauma, emotional abuse, mental health challenges, and other mature subject matter. Reader discretion is advised.

TheAuthorCouple.com
aNOUNymous.com

Cover and interior design by Coverkitchen

The cataloging-in-publication data is on file at the Library of Congress
LCCN: 2025913942

ISBN:
Hardcover 978-1-7379524-0-4
Paperback 978-1-7379524-2-8
ebook 978-1-7379524-6-6
Special edition 978-1-7379524-8-0

First Edition Published 2025

VALISE OF MEMORIES

"Our choices are the essence of who we become."

*My little girl, alone on a soft, grassy mountaintop
with the earth cool beneath your bare feet and wild
chamomile whispering to your thoughts—I write
this for you. Know that your solitary dance won't
last forever; the world will one day catch on to your
unique rhythm. This is my offering, the understanding
that society never gave you but should have...*

My emotions feel like a crumpled piece of paper. Raindrops drum against the large window behind me. I glance at the clipboard on my lap—a reminder of why we're here. The date on the form, June 9, 2023, is just another day for most. But for me and my daughter, it marks the beginning, or perhaps the end, of a long journey. I can't run from this. Not today. Not when Ruby needs me to be more than her mother. Not when she needs me to be her strength.

Phoenix finds my hand. Warmth threads between our fingers. Leaning in, he murmurs, "You're okay, Lena. It's going to be fine." His breath is a soft whisper that anchors me in the eye of my emotional storm.

"Any suicidal ideations, Dr. Hartley?" Dr. McKenna asks, her tone cutting through the silence as she looks over her glasses at me. I avoid eye contact, scanning her office instead. The walls, a chronicle of her career, are lined with diplomas and awards. Years of dedication to psychiatry. Her mahogany desk, etched with signs of wear, stands as a quiet witness to the countless people that have found clarity in their lives while sitting across from her. She waits for my response, her expression patient and understanding, framed by her stylish gray bob and chunky glasses.

As a fellow physician, I respect the depth in her eyes. Eyes that have confronted immense sorrow yet still carry a glimmer of hope.

A breath.

The words are there, somewhere—lodged behind my ribs.

"Not now, but there was a time..." A pause. My eyes catch a flaw in the pattern of the rug. I hypnotize myself with it, as if it could lead me to the right words. Tears well up in my eyes, blurring the room's fine edges.

"It's imperative for an accurate diagnosis that you share with me everything you can recall. Are you able to talk about it?" Dr. McKenna's voice carries a gentle firmness.

Another breath.

My past is a wooden valise, overstuffed with moments I tried to forget—postcards, ticket stubs, memories smeared like old photographs. And now I'm prying it open, unsure what will fall apart in my hands and what will remain intact.

"Please, go on, Dr. Hartley. I'm here to help you." Dr. McKenna removes her glasses and sets them aside along with her pencil, leaning forward—a motion we doctors use to signal our undivided attention.

Phoenix is watching me. His fingers pulse gently against mine—twice—a Morse code signal. Dot-dash. My husband and I speak a rare language where gestures convey more than words ever could. A spark of encouragement spreads through my body.

I peel my gaze away from the safety of the rug and manage a fleeting look at Dr. McKenna. The eye contact drains me more than it should. I take a drag of air, like a cigarette. My tears pull back, as if deciding to stay. The answer she is trying to prod out of me stays too.

"The strength I'm finding now is for our little daughter, Ruby. I'm here for her." The words come out stronger than they feel inside of me. "I don't want her to grow up thinking she's a weirdo. As I did."

Ruby's laughter—the most beautiful sound in the world—echoes in my memory. It's followed by another sound: low, heart-wrenching sobs after she returned from school last Tuesday. I rocked her gently to sleep that night. Sticks and stones, I told her, but I wasn't sure I believed this mantra myself. The cruelty of children leaves marks. How could other kids bully her, treat her as an outcast, when they should be celebrating her uniqueness?

She is so kind. "Don't step on the roly-polies, mommy," she says on our hikes. Pure light. I often fear that the alienation she's experienced might dim her bright spirit.

"I don't want Ruby to feel adrift in our society. I need to understand myself to understand her." I finally lock eyes with Dr. McKenna. She keeps leaning forward, quiet, waiting for me to respond to the question every psychiatrist has to ask. The question—Any suicidal ideations?—reverberates in the quiet. Unanswered. It unlocks a door I had once slammed shut.

One more breath, through pursed lips.

And I force myself to venture back in time.

"You have to understand, Dr. McKenna, I haven't always been on the right path. I once was a naive twenty-year-old model stepping out of a taxi in Paris. It all seemed like a glamorous destiny..."

CHAPTER 2

FASHION STORM

"We leave footsteps on the shores of time for future selves to trace."

"**M**ademoiselle, réveillez-vous!" calls the taxi driver. His voice, raspy and cigarette-tinged, drifts over the front seat as if from a distance. I sway with the vehicle's movement, my body sliding across the plasticky leather. A turn nudges my head gently against the tinted window.

His muffled, "Regarde... something... tour," seeps through the haze of my semi-consciousness. Catching my confusion, he points to the window and switches to English. "Eiffel Tower!" I squint toward where he gestures, my sleepy eyes straining to trace the landmark's ascent. Its summit dances just out of reach, lost in a swirl of motion and shimmer of morning light. The world outside is a watercolor painting, its details smudging into the edges of my dream.

I exhale slowly, and it feels like I'm stepping onto a grand stage under the weight of a thousand eyes. For the first time, I'm breaking free from my silent, submerged life in New York City—where my screams were smothered, unheard, as if trapped underwater. My husband (though I question the fit of that title now) already seems like a part of another life. Here in Paris, freedom is touchable, breathable. You can see the blue of the sky as the birds touch it with their wings.

"Voilà! We are here!" The taxi abruptly stops, jolting me back to reality.

"Let me help you with your luggage." The driver gets out, opens the trunk, and reaches for my suitcase. In front of me looms a grayish four-story building, its windows and doors adorned by ornate arches. A large entryway, framed by May's pink blooms, buzzes with activity. On the sidewalk, a security guard directs what seems to be a traffic jam of fashion models, queuing outside the elegant building. I pay the driver, then sling my backpack over my shoulder. Both hands are needed to wrestle this enormous suitcase over the curb.

"Are you here for the casting?" asks the doorman, his French accent unmistakable. The way he dropped "h" in the word "here" makes me grin, even though I suddenly feel conspicuously foreign. How did he know I don't speak French?

"Yes," I reply, noting the gigantic line of beautiful young women spilling out from the entrance and stretching half a block to the right. Their stares follow me and my unwieldy luggage, sending a flush of heat across my face. Gripping the handle of my suitcase, its wheels stuttering across the pavement, I start toward the end of the line. With each step, I realize: this too is a form of freedom.

Resigned to the indefinite wait, I prop my luggage against the building's aged mortar and peel off my orange hoodie. The air carries the scent of chestnut blossoms and the multilingual chatter of the models, underscored by the rich buttery aroma from a nearby café. This tapestry of Parisian life tugs a smile to the surface—almost. Glancing at my Nokia, I'm greeted by eleven missed calls from my husband, a digital echo of a life momentarily left behind. I slide the cellphone into the abyss of my denim pocket. I'll deal with him when I'm mentally ready.

Half an hour later, the line snakes up a dark wooden staircase, each step lit by a vintage copper lamp. Whispers ripple through the line as my suitcase thuds against the first step.

"Are you...sure?" The doorman's hand pingpongs between me, the stairs, and my suitcase. I offer a forced chuckle, quickly swallowed by the tide of giggles. As my suitcase squeaks in protest, I catch flashes of conversations.

"It's for Italian Vogue."

"Yeah, I shot with Meisel last month."

"My agent says McQueen might fly me to London for a fitting."

Every name-drop sharpens the edges of my outsiderness. I don't belong in this glittering world. At least not yet. It still feels surreal. How did a small-town girl from Poland end up here, lining up next to Vogue cover stars?

I was a senior in high school, still figuring out how to pronounce "focus" without people laughing (because it sounded like "fuck us"), when an agent from Elite Models stopped me in the buffet line at Whole Foods.

Back then, I was just a recent transplant with dreams of one day becoming a doctor, more intrigued by textbooks than catwalks. My mom had left for the U.S., the kind of thing people used to do during communism. My dad and grandpa, both revered architects, were left to raise me.

Neither of them put much stock in appearances, especially mine. "Millions possess beauty—it alone leads nowhere, my little love... But this," my grandpa would say, tapping my forehead like an eggshell, "this will open the world to you." College in the U.S. is a dream that results in an astronomical cost, so I leaned into modeling as a way to finance my dreams. I didn't expect to love being a model...but it sucked me in. The way photographs tell stories. The stillness before the camera. The way I can be just...anyone.

I was always mesmerized by Linda Evangelista's work. She's a true chameleon, becoming someone different in every shot. To me, being a model is art.

Around me now, portfolios flutter open like passports—stamped with runways, campaigns, the names of photographers I've only seen in magazines. I don't have any of it. Not yet.

At the top of the stairs, still catching my breath from dragging my suitcase up seven flights, I sense her leaning in behind me. Her blond hair grazes my shoulder.

"You just got here, huh?" There's no judgment, just curiosity.

"Yeah. Straight from the airport." Our eyes meet. We both look exhausted.

"It gets better after a few weeks."

Her nod and faint smile say the rest. She knows this life—what it costs. Here, beneath the beauty, we're all carrying the same doubt. Even in designer shoes, we're just normal women, aching for validation.

"Next!" calls the casting director, his head peeking through the doorway. In a swift move, I shape-shift. Hoodie cinched into a belt, I swipe the sweat from my lip. My fingers comb through my pixie cut. I can't help but notice how it sets me apart from the flowing ribbons of long hair that define early 2000s fashion.

"You can put your luggage here," he says as I come inside, gesturing to the far corner of the room. "Can I have your book?"

"Yes." I fumble through my backpack for my portfolio. He strides to a table where four women are seated, his fuchsia high heels click-clacking across the wooden floor. After a quick flip through my portfolio, he places it in front of the older woman seated farthest to the right. "She's got that Linda Evangelista edge, with a touch of Elizabeth Taylor's softness," he says, glancing back at me. "What a look." The compliment flares in my chest, briefly eclipsing the anxiety coiled tight beneath it. I step forward. The woman gives me a once-over, then turns to my portfolio. The others seem to hold their breath. Despite the glow of her skin, the cobweb of lines around her mouth and eyes betrays her age. She's likely in her sixties—seasoned, discerning. It's clear she's the one steering this ship.

"Lena. Hmm…" she murmurs, still focusing on my photos. "Nice name. Where are you from?"

She studies the shots through her oversized red eyewear, holding it like a magnifying glass. The color against her all-black outfit adds a bit of softness to her edge.

"I'm from Poland," I say, remembering Grandpa's rule: always honor where you come from. I skip the part about my U.S. citizenship—no need to give them a reason to stereotype.

"Pologne! Bien. Do you speak French?" Our eyes meet in a moment that feels like a silent conversation. Her look isn't judgmental, but not exactly warm either. Like she's weighing something, maybe sifting through my expressions.

"I don't. I speak Polish, German, and English," I say with a hint of pride.

"Hmm..." She swivels to the others and shoots off a string of French. I stand there, bemused, for what feels like forever. They're clearly talking about me, in a language I don't understand, on purpose. And I catch none of it. It's almost comical, like I've stepped into a foreign film with no subtitles. I'm out of the loop yet somehow still in the center of attention.

"Lena, try this on." She reaches for a dress on the rack and hands it to the casting director, who passes it to me. I guess walking over would be too much effort. With a subtle nod, he points me toward a makeshift changing area behind the clothes rack—barely private.

"You will need help to zip up. Let me know when you're ready," he adds. The black dress, heavy as a fisherman's net, fights back as I shimmy it over my hips. Sequins and feathers, intricately stitched into the fabric, scrape against my bare legs. French murmurs drift from the women. What an odd disconnection—I feel like a Queen Anne doll, stripped of anything human. Just a living mannequin meant to show off the dress. The director zips me up and turns my back toward the four-person audience. I wonder if my back tattoo adds an edge to the dress or counts as a fashion faux pas.

"Magnifique! Well, let's see you walk." Red glasses flips her hand with authority. As I walk toward the table, the sequins scratch out a soft melody, and the feathers tickle my ankles with each step. I stop and strike a pose, imagining she's a photographer at the end of a runway. She whispers something to the director in French, and he promptly takes a Polaroid of me. Once I've changed back into my clothes, he dismisses me with a wave.

"Thank you for coming," he calls before leaning out the door with a loud, "Next!"

On my way out, I lock eyes with the blond. My brows lift and my eyes pop, almost involuntarily, but just enough for her to get the hint. Her lips twitch into a nervous smile. Message received.

As I descend the stairs, suitcase in tow, my phone rings. I reach for it, but the suitcase wheel catches on a step. It happens too fast and yet in slow motion. And I can't stop the bag from falling with a series of theatrical thuds. The girls waiting in line can't contain their laughter.

"Hello?" I answer, trying to pick up my suitcase with one hand.

"Hi, honey. I can't wait to finally meet you in person. I'm waiting at the model's apartment with your key. But first, I've got good news and more good news. Which do you want to hear first?" The spirited voice of my agent, Rex, fills the line. Before I have a chance to respond, he adds, "You're confirmed for the Glamour magazine shoot tomorrow, and you've booked Balmain!"

"What?" Shock makes me breathless. "Really? I booked Balmain? But I've only just left." The laughter in the stairwell dies instantly.

Stepping into the warm spring Parisian air, a wave of triumph washes over me. My first day in Paris, and I've already secured two prestigious jobs. The sensation is surreal, like stepping into a dream I had never fully allowed myself to imagine.

At the curb, I extend my arm, trying to hail a taxi with the effortless expertise of a New Yorker. Yet, Paris is not New York, and the taxis, seemingly indifferent to my urgency, glide past, their off-duty signs flickering in the afternoon sunlight.

As I persist, my phone rings again, slicing through the hum of the busy afternoon.

"Hello?" I answer, the effort to flag down taxis dividing my attention.

"There you are. Thought my wife ran away or something." The irritation is obvious.

"Hi, baby. Sorry, it's been non-stop since I landed. I went straight to the casting. And—I got it! The Balmain show. Plus a Glamour shoot tomorrow."

The words spill out too fast, unfiltered. I should've rationed the excitement, fed it to him in smaller pieces. But it's too late now.

"Balmain and Glamour, huh."

A pause. Heavy with unsaid criticism.

"Too busy for me already. Or has the city gone to your head?"

"It's just been…hectic, Tomek. I didn't mean to ignore you."

The guilt seeps in on cue, like it knows the script better than I do.

"Busy, right."

He exhales. The sound is sharp and cold, as always.

"I guess you're a star now, too bright to remember the little things—like your husband waiting on the other end of a silent phone. But sure, tell me about these glamorous jobs. Are they funding your college dreams now? Or are they paying you just enough to leave me?"

I shut my eyes tight for a brief moment, gathering my composure.

"I was overwhelmed, okay? I just landed, I feel like shit, and I had to run straight to a casting." Hoping for a flicker of empathy, I add, "It's relentless—being constantly judged, scrutinized. It's not just walking in a dress for a few minutes. It takes a toll on my mental health."

"Mental health," he echoes, his tone laced with dismissal. "Meanwhile, I'm here, handling everything by myself, while you're off in Paris, indulging in your aspirations, your vanity."

"But we agreed I could do this—to finance my education, to become a doctor. It's not some high life I'm living here." The words escape me just as the faint scent of freshly baked bread from a nearby boulangerie wraps around me. My stomach tightens.

But it's the other kind of hunger, the hunger to be heard, that aches deeper.

Tomek doesn't believe that hunger deserves to be fed. Not mine, anyway. Only he matters. It's his world, always...and I'm supposed to feel lucky just to exist in it.

"And I'm not indulging. My diet's been nothing but protein bars and ramen noodles. Which has helped me tuck away nearly a hundred grand in the past ten months." I remind him.

His scoff is sharp enough to cut through the phone line, puncturing my short-lived bubble of happiness. "A doctor? Really, Lena? You need a functioning brain to become a doctor—stick to being a mannequin."

The line goes dead. Hunger replaced by a knot in my stomach. His words, always designed to erode, remind me of the delicate balance I navigate being married to him. But...I wonder. Maybe he's right?

I take out the map from my backpack. My finger traces the lines to the model's apartment. I decide to walk the eight blocks to clear my head, or at least try.

The suitcase is heavy, my past dragging behind me. A sadness settles in before I even have the time to process the argument. This brief escape from Tomek won't last. Why am I doing this to myself? Why don't I just leave him?

I met Tomek at eighteen, shortly after moving to NYC for modeling.

Dolce & Gabbana was hosting a runway fundraiser in the Hamptons, and I was one of the models. He was a guest. A decade older, handsome, magnetic. A financier from some big firm in the city. It's no surprise I fell for him so quickly, naively marrying him less than a year later. He swept me into his world, where grand gestures of love-bombing slowly turned into something suffocating. His charm, once dazzling, became a thin veneer over a cage, each bar forged from criticisms, commands, and the chains of isolation he wrapped around me. Friends, once close, faded into the background. Their warnings—"Lena, can't you see he's manipulating you?"—were lost beneath my belief that this was true love.

Rage. Apologies. Rage again.

I lived on eggshells, always trying to be enough. To not provoke the storm. Each episode cut deeper into my self-worth, leaving scars no one could see—undermining who I once was. His love was no longer a sanctuary, but a storm. Unpredictable and destructive. And now, walking alone through this city of light, I wonder not just about his love...but my own worth.

My feet ache. A spoon clinks against porcelain, and the street around me comes into sharp focus. Piano notes are drifting from a charming café, where lovers curl into each other and wisteria claws its way up the building—both dreaming of greater heights. The purple blossoms stretch like fingers, striving to transcend the roots that hold them in place. My suitcase bumps over relentless cobblestones, its weight growing unbearable. All the burdens I carry. Everything I think I need (but refuse) to let go. The wisteria, though confined, stretches for the sky. But unlike the wisteria, I possess the freedom to walk away from what holds me down. I remind myself: I'm not a flower, I don't have to bloom where I'm planted.

Glancing at my map, I realize the models' apartment is just steps away. The classic gray cobblestone façade comes into view as I turn the corner. Large windows and ornate details hint at a century-old story. Despite the daylight that bathes the street, the hallway hoards its shadows. It's impossible to tell where the walls end and doors begin, except for a flicker of something metal. My eyes struggle to adjust as my fingers skim the cool, uneven wall in search of the doorbell.

Suddenly, the door swings open. "Hi, honey!" A middle-aged man with a blond shag fills the doorway. "Let me help you with this," he says, grabbing my suitcase. His voice needs no introduction.

"Jesus, what did you put in here? This bitch is so heavy!" he yells out as he moves toward the room on the left. "Oh, by the way, I'm your agent, Rex. Sorry, totally forgot to introduce myself." He chuckles, almost breathless, as he hefts the weight.

"Books." I cackle. "Too many!" I follow him to the room. "Ah, and it's so nice to finally meet you."

"Pleasure is mine." He shoots me an over-the-shoulder glance. "Books, huh? It sure feels like a dead body."

"I wish!" The thought escapes before I can catch it. Rex drops my suitcase on the floor near a small twin bed by the window, next to two other beds—a trio lined up against the wall like in a dollhouse, with a few inches between them. My eyes are immediately drawn to the one covered in a jumble of hastily discarded clothes. The windows are dirty, with flaking paint on the old frames. Outside...a chestnut tree is in full bloom. Beauty framed by the ruin. The poetry of life, I guess.

"This one's Josionne's." Rex gestures with a flourish toward the chaos. "She's from Brazil. An absolute sweetheart. You'll love her."

My attention shifts to the wall above her bed, a collage of Gisele Bündchen's magazine tear-sheets and Vogue covers, each affixed with tape. A mural of dreams and ambition.

"Ah, the Brazilian inspiration wall!" Rex says admiringly as he catches me examining the collection. He's that rare mix of flamboyance and fierce tenderness—instantly likable.

"Here's your apartment key. Guard it with your life," he says with a playful wink, his mascara-clad blue eyes sparkling. I accept the worn yellowish key, hesitating to sit on the bed's stained mattress just yet.

"Oh, and here are the details for tomorrow," Rex continues, pulling a sheet of paper from the back pocket of his jeans. "Your shoot call time is at nine a.m. You should wrap up by two or three, then Balmain at four. You're also invited to the afterparty hosted by Madonna—make sure you're there. It's a great opportunity to get yourself seen. All the addresses are right here. I've got everything laid out for you."

"Wow, Madonna?" I say, and immediately regret how forced that sounded. Celebrity name-dropping in this business is just...no. Rex doesn't need to know how I really feel. So I add, "I love her! Really—thank you, Rex."

"You got it, darling! Get some rest; you have an exciting day tomorrow," he says, exiting with the same energy he arrived with, leaving a trace of warmth behind him.

After a long, rejuvenating shower that washes away the afternoon's fatigue, I settle for a simple meal of a protein bar and an apple from my backpack. Sitting on the wide windowsill, I eat slowly, watching the Parisian afternoon unfold through the crusty window. I find myself weaving narratives for the people who pass by: who they are, where they're going, what they do for a living. It's a game born from countless hours of feeling alone among the crowds.

Time slips by, unnoticed, until the setting sun begins casting long shadows across the wooden floor. Unpacking, I line my favorite books along the window's parapet. Each one, backlit with the orange sunset, is a tender reminder of Grandpa Stach. "Always find beauty in everything. It will ground you, no matter where you are," he'd say, his voice deep and soft. Thoughts of visiting him in Kraków, in his beautiful apartment filled with books and plants, so close yet so far, nudge at my mind. He has always been my life's magician, teaching me how to manifest my dreams.

I roll out my purple sleeping bag across the bed, a ritual that feels like a hug from the past. It's more than just fabric. It's a cocoon of memories from camping trips with Grandpa. Each fold a story, each crease a shared moment of wisdom. I slip into it. It grounds me in a way nothing else can. Not in this foreign city. Not right now. I close my eyes and drift away.

The tranquility of the early evening is shattered by the sudden ring of my phone. "Hello?" I mumble, barely awake, feeling the cold air nip at my skin.

"Hey, hun. I just had a really bad day, and I took it out on you earlier. I love you." Tomek's voice comes through, tinged more with self-pity than remorse. There's a pause, as if he's waiting for me to immediately forgive him. "But, look, I'm not the one enjoying a glamorous lifestyle in Paris."

"Tomek, I'm wrapped in my sleeping bag, lying on a mattress that's seen better days." I pause, running a hand through my hair, feeling the grit of paint flakes against my scalp. "And I'm picking paint out of my hair because the window frame next to my bed is probably a century old. 'Glamorous' isn't the word I'd use to describe this."

A failed plea for understanding. He won't hear the discomfort in my tired voice.

"Well, you wanted to do this, so don't start complaining now," he retorts with a hint of venom. I can picture him, pacing in our spacious NYC living room, his frustration searching for an outlet.

"I'm not complaining—just telling you how it is." I clutch the phone tighter, wishing that just for a moment he could see the world through my eyes.

"Sure, you 'tell it how it is.' Meanwhile, I'm over here, busting my ass at work all day. For us! And I come home to nothing but a moldy sofa." His voice rises, and I imagine him gesturing to the hollow space around him. "Even my mom can't believe how you've been acting," he adds, the mention of his mother making my heart sink a little more.

"Tomek, I can barely keep my eyes open." I sigh, looking at the cracks in the ceiling, as if they could interject in my defense. "I really don't feel like arguing right now."

"No one's arguing with you, Lena. You're just too sensitive, always taking everything so literally." His disdain drips through the phone. "It's impossible to have a normal conversation with you."

"Listen, I've been up for over twenty-four hours and have a big day tomorrow." My voice is weary but firm. It's easier to find this amount of courage when we aren't arguing in person. "Two important jobs, and then I have to go to a party hosted by Madonna." I brace myself for his reaction, knowing full well I shouldn't have mentioned it. But I was never a good liar, so I hope for the best with the truth.

"Party? What party? Are you getting paid for it?" His tone sharpens, accusatory rather than curious, and I can feel his judgment as if he's right beside me.

"No. But I have to go. My agent said it's important for networking." I muster the most reasonable tone I can between thoughts of losing my shit altogether.

"You're married! You're not going to any party to strut your ass around high-fashion society!" I can almost feel his spit on my cheek as he shouts through the phone.

"Babe…" I begin, my voice softer now, an attempt to reason with the unreasonable.

"Don't 'Babe' me. How dumb can you be? You're being utterly disrespectful!" His verbal assault is so tangible, I have to hold the phone away from my face, his anger almost radiating through.

"I'm not trying to be disrespectful. I'm trying to be successful." My determination swells despite his verbal bombs exploding in my ears. "If you keep screaming, I'll have to hang up."

"You make me scream! You're the storm in our marriage, always causing chaos." His words are a projection of his own behavior. "You're a selfish bitch!"

The line goes dead with a harsh click, followed by a long beep, leaving me in silence. A silence that isn't just the absence of sound, but the echo of every harsh word between us.

CHAPTER 3

TOUCAN'S SKY

"Sometimes we cannot feel our wings."

The samba beat bursts from a boombox, coaxing my heavy eyelids open.

A silhouette of a young woman is dancing. A morning breeze sneaks through the grimy window, making my face tingle. It triggers an unstoppable yawn—one that feels too vulnerable, especially this close to someone I don't know. Sunlight pours through the parted curtains, and I squint just as she leans over. She's backlit in golden light. Her dark, damp hair brushes against my face with a fresh zing of citrus. It's an oddly welcome burst of life in our otherwise stale room. "Wakey wakey, roommate!" Her melodic Brazilian accent slices through the drumming boombox. Josionne.

She sways, electric, as if the morning belongs to her. A wide, infectious smile spills across her high cheekbones—bright against her smooth brown skin. I grin back before I realize I'm doing it. A smile triggered by invisible threads of joy, spun from her dancing fingers. "Shit. What time is it?"

I bolt upright. A tightness seizes my throat. Frantically digging through my sleeping bag, I unearth Rex's crumpled note—and my heart pauses at the nine a.m. call time.

"7:19 a.m.!" she declares. I sigh with a ragged relief. Her laughter mingles with the samba. Both buzz against my skin like summer fireflies.

Rummaging through my suitcase, half-tangled in clothes, I blurt, "I'm Lena."

She beams. "I know! Rex mentioned we'd be roommates. I'm Josionne." She spots my portfolio and picks it up. "Is this your book?" she asks, thumbing through the pages.

I nod and smile, flattered by her interest. With the grace of someone who belongs in front of a camera, she reclines on her bed, her long legs bridging the space between our beds. "These are stunning." Josionne traces an image, as if committing it to memory.

"The contrast of your green eyes and dark hair against your skin—it's striking. You have this timeless elegance, like a young Elizabeth Taylor." Her words are not just a compliment but a recognition of something deeper—something I don't see in myself. Many of us models are blind to our own beauty.

"Thanks." I blush. Her observation sparks a flicker of warmth, a reminder of self-confidence buried deep under the weight of my current life. She sees past the photos, past the model.

A connection forms between us, in the quiet space between admiration and shared dreams.

"Sorry about the music. It helps me get into the zone before castings," she says, reaching to turn down the volume. "I'll be heading out soon, in case you want to catch some more sleep." She pulls on green khakis and a cropped white T-shirt with the fluid ease of someone at home in this foreign city.

"Actually, I've got a photoshoot myself," I say, threading my legs into my jeans, smiling more genuinely than I have in weeks. "Mind if I tag along to the train station?"

"Sure!"

Outside, Paris is fully awake. The city pulses with the rush of cars and footsteps of people in a hurry to start their day. The sweet comfort of fresh chocolate croissants, enjoyed moments earlier at a charming café, lingers on our tongues as we march toward the Metro station.

"So how old are you?" she asks, once we swipe through the ticket barriers.

"Twenty. You?" I lean over the tracks, trying to spot the incoming train.

"Sixteen." She twirls like a kid.

"Jesus, you're only sixteen?"

"Yup. Been here six months." She lifts her chin, side-eying me with pride.

"You're just a baby." I shake my head. Modeling pulls us in young—she's still older than most.

"Nah-ah. Not a baby. I'll buy my mom a house soon. I've almost got half."

"A house, huh?" I smile.

"Yeah. A beautiful house in São Paulo." She gestures through the air as if casting a spell.

Under the round Metro lamps, her onyx eyes catch the light—and something in them tugs at my heart.

"I'm saving for college. I want to be a doctor," I say.

"Beauty and brains." She squints, her face inching closer to mine. "I can see that." She bumps me playfully. "I'm so happy you're my roomie. My big Paris sis!"

In her confident smile, I glimpse the girl I once was—full of hope and untouched by life's harsher truths. Like a toucan, she's vividly free, soaring toward her dreams with wings unclipped—no strings, no cages, just boundless sky. In this moment, I both envy her and feel a fierce urge to protect her.

I reach for her hand, making sure she feels the weight of my words.

"You've got this magic in you. Don't let the world dim it, okay? Promise me."

The words come out impulsively, meant just as much for her as for my younger self.

She pulls me into a tight hug, her long arms wrapping around me like a Bronzino figurine, her chin resting on my shoulder. The bustling world around us fades, replaced by the warmth of a new friendship that feels like Grandpa's home in Poland. To the passing crowd, we must look like lovers saying goodbye.

A gust of wind from my arriving train sends her curls flying. She is a whirlwind against the stillness of the moment.

"Go catch your dreams, my big sis!" she whispers, pressing a kiss on my cheek.

Seated now on the scratchy, upholstered subway seat, I catch a final glimpse of her. She waves, her smile as bright as the ceramic tiles lining the wall behind her.

As the train lurches forward, my hand rises in a wave almost of its own accord.

Happiness and sadness braid themselves through my chest, like the intertwined trees in my Bieszczady Mountains. My reflection in the window catches my eye. I allow it to hypnotize me. The thought of the bright soul I've just connected with tugs a soft grin to my lips, soon overshadowed by the sudden intrusion of Tomek's image. His words from last night slice back into my consciousness. I close my eyes, summoning the memory of Josionne's smile, as if performing an exorcism to drive him out. In my mind's eye, a toucan takes flight, soaring free.

Flashbulbs burst like distant stars around me, the aggressive staccato of the camera's shutter echoing my racing heartbeat.

The journey to the studio blurs in my memory—I must have zoned out.

"Oh, oui, chérie! Just like that! Part your lips slightly. Yes! hold that pose!" The photographer's hoarse voice echoes, his thick French accent reverberating through the cavernous, sunlit studio. His fingers juggle both cigarette and camera.

Barefoot, I stand on a three-foot wooden box at the center of a swirling fashion scene. If only my beloved grandpa could see his introverted little girl, now a modern princess, towering over the Ville de l'Amour. The dress—adorned with a high white collar, an intricate feather pattern, and sharply contoured shoulder pads—surpasses anything I ever imagined wearing.

Growing up in the Bieszczady Mountains, I was a short-haired tomboy, seldom seen in dresses or makeup. Yet, here I am, ensconced in a seven-foot-long gown, a cocoon from which I'm emerging, transformed. The makeup artist has the same contagious energy as Rex. He smiles and winks a lot, bopping to the beat of the music. Between takes, each delicate sweep of powder under my eyes makes me feel more like a butterfly. Ready to unfurl, to fly.

"Chin up, now look away. Yes! Beautiful, that's it, Lena!" The photographer's commands are ringed by cigarette smoke billowing from his lips. Once again, the flashing lights envelop me in their warm glow.

His cues uplift me. There's a strange comfort in not seeing his eyes, hidden behind his giant Canon lens.

Eye contact is almost painful. Each gaze too weighted, too full of unspoken things I can never fully decode. Eyes are a kaleidoscope of emotions—their depth, the stories they tell. It's all too much, too distracting. But the camera is different. I adore the camera's eye. It's cold, detached, free of messy human intricacy. It offers a safe space. And I can become anyone I imagine, a trait that makes me a good model.

The remainder of the photoshoot is a succession of dazzling outfits and ostentatious poses, each piece of clothing freeing a different character within me. When the flickering of the camera fades, the studio falls into silence.

"Great job, darling!" the photographer exclaims, planting air kisses on my cheeks before bidding me au revoir in his signature rasp. Within the quiet of a changing room, I peel away the layers of extravagant attire and slip into my worn-in jeans.

Retreating into my introverted shell carries a bittersweet tang. I find myself yearning for the loud, colorful characters I embody before the camera; without this creative outlet, I feel both diminished and invisible.

The life of a model is a relentless sprint. Castings, gigs, flights, and the perpetual shuffle of living from suitcase to suitcase. Darting from the studio, I engage in a necessary dance, alternating between wiping away layers of makeup and nibbling on a baguette I just got on the run—my sad little attempt at sustenance. The backstage of the Balmain show is an organized frenzy. Models, poised like elegant statuettes in their prep chairs, are transformed by the makeup team into breathtaking embodiments of living art.

In the midst of all this, a familiar voice cuts through: "Ah, there she is!" The woman with the red glasses, who had exuded all business at the casting, now beams at me. Her smile bridges the gap between the stern image I remember and the warmth she now radiates. With unexpected gentleness, she takes my hand and guides me through the backstage maze to a tall man in a crisp suit and a pale-yellow tie, standing with an air of quiet authority. "Oscar, meet Lena, our season's discovery," she declares. The realization that I'm being introduced to Oscar de la Renta, the legendary maestro of haute couture at Balmain, sends a jolt of disbelief through me.

"Beautiful," he says, scanning me with his piercing dark eyes. The word, simple yet laden with sincerity, wraps around me, flushing my cheeks with pride, like the heat from the first sip of a rich red wine. This unexpected complement awakens a sense of validation within me, a feeling I didn't realize I was yearning for. In a reflex, I smile, my hand discreetly brushing away the crumbs of my hasty meal from my mouth.

"Come, darling, Andre is waiting for you," Oscar says, gesturing toward an empty prep chair. An Asian man with the sweetest dimpled grin greets me, pointing his makeup brush like a wand—a fairy about to cast his spell. Red glasses lady's radio hisses, and she says something in French to Oscar, who nods. "See you on the runway," he says, before disappearing in the rushed backstage crowd.

As I settle into his chair, the backstage cacophony—a blend of voices, footsteps, and the clinking of hangers—somehow fades into the background. Andre's brushes sweep across my skin, each stroke a pleasant distraction from the sensory chaos. I focus on the cool metal of the chair beneath me, trying to ground myself. When Andre is done, I open my eyes to a reflection that seems almost foreign—a Balmain haute couture model instead of the usual tomboy. The new mask fits surprisingly well. I always feel the characters modeling brings out in me. Like reading, they're my escape into another world.

"Wow. Thank you, Andre!"

"Ah, don't even mention it, sweetie! You're absolutely gorgeous, and it was my pleasure to work on such a canvas," he replies, waving off my compliment with a flourish of his hand.

"We're all mirrors for each other, aren't we?" I muse, catching his gaze in the reflection.

He squints back, his dimples deepening into a genuine smile. "Exactly. We help each other reveal the parts of ourselves that are hardest to see."

As I step away to change into my first outfit, the chaos pulses with a different rhythm, one I'm becoming a part of.

The black chiffon of my dress grazes its fingers against me, tingling as I stand in the runway's shadow. Lined up, newcomers and supermodels alike, we wait for the music to kick in, the lights to flash, and the crowd's buzz to quiet down. A chorus of deep breaths weaves through us, mine among them. Around us, stylists primp fabrics into perfection as makeup artists bestow final blessings with their brushes. The woman in the red glasses orchestrates our procession like a maestro, her gentle nudge ushering the models ahead of me with a hushed, "Go."

The music's beat throbs in my chest, and a voice buzzes in French through her walkie-talkie, signaling my turn. She nods and says, "Lena. Go!" Feeling a nudge at my back, I step into the spotlight.

Catwalk lights burst. Warmth rushes up my face. It's not embarrassment, but that breathless thrill you feel at the top of a rollercoaster. The audience fades into the background, leaving just me, the music, and my synchronized steps across the pristine floor. Endorphins dance across my skin, raising each hair on my arms—I'm floating, buoyant, gliding toward the light. Every so often, I wonder if this is the feeling one gets in the "tunnel" described in near-death experiences. Reaching the end of the runway, I strike a pose, enveloped by the staccato of camera flashes and a symphony of whispers and applause. Just as I'm about to turn, in the pauses between flashes, I see him. The only face without a smile. Clapping slowly. Almost mockingly. Tomek. Unmistakable. At the far end of the room. The gravity of his stare turns each step toward backstage heavy with the weight of his unspoken words. Suddenly, my buoyancy vanishes. I feel like a toucan that has run out of sky.

LOVERS' LOCKS

"His victim is always guilty."

In the taxi with Tomek, the Parisian evening loses its luster, fading into a pale echo of yesterday's radiant daydream. Rain blurs the city. The wipers beat rhythmically, a melancholic soundtrack that seems to muffle more than just the noise outside. Why did I choose to go with him instead of attending Madonna's party? Why do I let him be this relentless sinusoid of my life? The ups and downs. The cycle of happiness to despair. So fucking exhausting. I rest my forehead against the cold window. It's sobering. My eyes trace the raindrops, trying to guess which way they'll fall. Are our lives like that—shaped by chance? Or do we truly have the power to choose our direction? Tomek's hand lands on my thigh. His touch is colder than the glass, even more sobering than the window.

"I love you, Lena," he claims, but his voice, which used to feel soft like cotton blooms basking in summer light, now lacks tenderness. His words don't match the hard pressure of his fingers, digging into my skin, almost hurting. With him, words say one thing—his touch says something else.

"I love you too," I whisper. "But it's hard. So fucking hard to always feel like my dreams...like I don't matter." My words sound hollow, as if only spoken inside my head. Maybe they are. Can it really be love...if someone only loves the idea of you? I don't know.

Our hotel room at the Four Seasons is enchanting, bathed in the glow of the light that sneaks in from the street. The large window, draped in gold-beige tassels, frames the Eiffel Tower flickering in the distance. She's a tall, tapering heart that sets the pulse of this city. On the balcony, hot-pink flowers burst against the rainy grayness. They remind me of Grandpa's apartment, and I smile for just a second.

My gaze lands on a large black package with a red bow, conspicuously placed at the center of the king-sized bed. Tomek smirks.

"Let's just say it wasn't the best deal for a stock guy, but my wife is worth it." His voice carries tenderness I haven't heard in months, despite the smug expression. A flicker of hope. Maybe we can find our way back. Back to how we once were. Truly in love. Genuinely happy. His words make me giggle as I swing around the doorframe to peek into the lavish bathroom. "Nice! I'm hungry. Will you feed me?" His laughter fills the room like upbeat music. I almost forgot how it sounded.

"Only if you wear this," he says, his eyes crinkling with amusement as he hands me the black box. I flop onto the bed, fingers nervously peeling through the layer of decoration to flip it open, before a scarlet Versace dress spills into my lap.

"Tomek, this must have cost a fortune!" Our eyes meet in the mirror. His face is lit with that boyish grin I haven't seen in forever. I can't help myself. "What did you do, sell an organ on the black market?"

He chuckles. "Shh, don't worry about it. You're worth every penny." He seals it with a kiss, final and firm. No room for questions.

"At least my makeup is already perfect," I say, shrugging off the price tag as the gown's silk skims my skin—like an intimate whisper only I can hear. As we stand before the rustic mirror, Tomek's muscular arms envelop me. Our eyes meet in the reflection. His are full of something...maybe adoration, maybe lust. Or a bit of both. They trace my entire silhouette. His lips find the back of my neck, soft as the feathers of a hummingbird. This is the love I miss. The love we used to know—before it frayed. Before it tangled, like forgotten yarn.

"I hope this moment lasts forever," I whisper to our reflection, though I think it's more a wish to myself. Suddenly, my stomach growls like an angry wolf.

"My lord, this model is seriously hungry," Tomek jokes. "Let's go get dinner." He twirls me towards the door.

Downstairs, we slip through the black-gilded iron doors into a restaurant that practically breathes opulence. A middle-aged maître d' leads us down a hallway lined with potted palms. The hallway opens into the pulsing heart of the restaurant, where violet and fuchsia tulips—so fresh they might've been flown in from the Netherlands this morning—spill from tall crystal vases at the center. Above, a grand chandelier is casting rainbows across the ceiling. As we move past the kitchen toward our table by the window, I smell it, the intoxicating blend of truffles and tulips. And I can sense all the old-money eyes around us—sharp, appraising. Like they see through the dress. Through me. And then I feel it. That familiar sting of otherness. I don't belong here.

"Good evening, sir, madame. Welcome to Le Cinq," says a waiter, who carries an uncanny resemblance to Vincent Cassel. He pulls the chair for me.

"It's a rare pleasure to see such youthful energy grace our establishment. Madame, your radiance tonight perfectly complements our ambiance. May I suggest a wine that is equally captivating?" His smile softens the pomp of his words, making it feel strangely sincere.

"Thank you, you're too kind." I blush, as I sit down, returning a smile that surprises me with how natural it feels. "I'll trust your recommendation for the—"

"Actually, we'll take a bottle of the 1989 D'Oliveira Bual Madeira," Tomek cuts in, his voice booming across the table. It startles me, as the waiter flinches mid-nod, his mouth snapping shut. A beat of awkward silence follows as he recalibrates his surprised expression into a polite smile.

"That's a great choice." He glances at me. I'm so embarrassed, I hope the makeup hides it. "I'll be back with your wine in a moment," he adds, and walks away. I glance down at the menu. The obscene price tag of the wine glares back. Tomek's gaze bounces between me and the waiter's retreating figure. I scan my husband's face, searching for the trigger. Even though I have learned to read him, I am still never sure. What set him off this time?

Tension hangs like fog over our empty china plates. I mentally rewind the scene, combing for what might've lit Tomek's fuse. I extend my hand across the table, but he recoils, folding his arms like a barrier. Did I do something wrong?

"Are you okay?" I ask, voice low, threading between the clink of silverware and the chatter of nearby conversations.

"Of all the waiters, we get a Parisian Casanova hitting on my wife," he mutters, rolling his eyes and flicking his hand in a theatrical wave.

"Seriously, Tomek? You think I'd swoon over some rehearsed lines from a waiter?" I lean in, keeping my voice just above a whisper. Tomek always does this. I've become numb to it. But I guess, here, in Paris, it surprises me. I look him dead in the eye, trying to get through his thick skull. "This is a Michelin star restaurant. He probably says that to every woman who walks in."

"Yeah, right. I saw how you smiled at him," he snaps, his eyes flashing with accusation. I drop my gaze to the plate, as if the fine china could shield me.

"Here's your bottle of the 1989 D'Oliveira Bual Madeira." Our unwitting Parisian Casanova returns with the wine. A short cork pop, and he pours us a glass. I don't look at him and retreat into tracing the cool rim of the plate with my fingers. Endless circles. The clatter around me fades. For a second, I fade too.

Lost in a maze of what-ifs and could-have-beens, I wonder (for the hundredth time this year) where the line is. The line between trying so hard to be loved and losing yourself.

The smell of fresh caviar and an intricately arranged appetizer being set beside me snaps me back to reality. I don't remember ordering anything.

"Have we decided on the mains?" Casanova asks, flashing a grin of whitened teeth. His voice sounds far away, as if I'm in a well. I glance up for a second, still tracing the plate with my finger. Then my eyes drop, back to the safety of my hands. Tomek mumbles something—probably our order. I sit frozen, thoughts churning in a storm of things I wish I could yell out.

"Look, I'm sorry." Tomek's hand closes over mine, halting my nervous plate-tracing. I lift my eyes and meet his, even though it takes effort. There's a softness in his gaze—unexpected, maybe even real. "Let's enjoy this beautiful dinner, okay?" he says, voice dipped in sugar that almost tastes genuine. A thread of hope tugs in my throat.

"Okay." I nod. That shadow of a smile I thought was gone sneaks back in, unexpected but welcome. I eye the miniature cupcakes topped with black caviar pearls.

"These look irresistible," I say. "And I'm starving."

The cupcake bursts with flavor, absurdly good. Tomek's eyes nearly leap from their sockets as his eyebrows shoot up. "Oh my God, so good," he mumbles through a mouthful. His expression makes me giggle—one of those uncontrollable giggles—and I nearly send a spray of unchewed caviar across the table.

Back in the hotel room, I can't shake the weight of that dinner bill—enough to feed a family for a month. Still, I surrender to the mellow buzz of the city outside. The warmth of wine buzzing through my head softens the sting of the evening's earlier crack. Tomek's hands find a surprising gentleness—one I haven't felt since we first met. As he pulls me close, his feather-light touch carries the faint scent of caviar, tulips, and his lingering woodsy cologne. Is that tenderness under his light eyelashes, or am I just tipsy enough to imagine it? His fingers trace my waist and hips. A sensation so disarming and familiar. For a moment, I let myself believe in this illusion. This is what I crave from him. From myself, even.

As his lips meet mine, the world blurs into an orchestra of all his whispered promises. They are so vivid that I almost hear him speak them again. Maybe I'm just a little drunk. His hands move with a care that conceals all the arguments we've ever had. He is so gentle as he deftly undoes the zipper. And the waterfall of my dress cascades to the floor.

"Can't we always be like this?" I breathe it into his lips before I know I've said it.

The sudden ring of my phone slices through the silence like a siren, cutting off our kiss before it gets a chance to land. I catch a flash of irritation in Tomek's eyes as I pull away.

"Seriously?" he says. His head tilts in disbelief. I dig through my backpack. The ringing is growing louder, annoying, more insistent.

"It's my agent," I say. Tomek's face hardens. His face shifts, a triptych of frustration, resignation, and finally, anger.

"You're unbelievable," he mutters, brushing me off with a dismissive hand gesture before collapsing onto the bed. Arms flung wide, he sighs, puffing out his cheeks like a tantruming child. Juggling the yelling phone in one hand, I slither into the robe.

"Hello?" I say, stepping onto the misty balcony.

"Hey, hun, where are you?" Rex's voice comes through a pulsing backdrop of loud music. "The party's nearly over—we've been waiting."

"I'm so sorry, Rex. I can't make it," I reply, nervously toying with the tassel of my robe. He sighs. It's the same sound of resignation that echoes my husband's earlier frustration.

"Attending these events is crucial if you want to break into the industry."

A shiver runs through me, part rain-damp balcony, part guilt for letting my agent down.

"I know, it's just..." The excuse dries in my throat, so I choose honesty instead. "My husband's in town."

Silence follows, longer than is comfortable for a phone call. Just the thump of club music pulsing in the background.

"Look, I get it, but these invites are rare. I could've invited another model." Rex's voice is serious yet gentle, missing its usual cheerfulness. Now I'm silent. Searching for the right words. Trailing my fingers along the cold railing. Knocking loose raindrops, one by one.

"It won't happen again," I promise, heading back inside.

Tomek's on the bed, flipping through a magazine he's not really reading. His jaw is clenched. His expression is darkening into a scowl.

"It's okay. Just be at the agency first thing tomorrow." Rex's tone softens. "YSL wants Polaroids of you."

"Oh my God, absolutely." Relief rushes through me like a warm tide. A second chance.

As I put down the phone, I meet Tomek's stare. Icy and boiling at once. A wintry volcano ready to erupt.

"What the fuck is this?" Tomek explodes, grabbing my portfolio and hurling it across the room. It hits the floor at my feet, flipping open on impact. A familiar photo stares back at me—black-and-white, tastefully lit nude. For a moment, the room seems to pause with it. And I freeze, shuffling responses in my mind like tarot cards.

"It's art," I finally say. "You can't even see anything."

I gesture toward the image: me on a plush armchair, legs crossed, one arm draped just right. Nothing vulgar. My gaze, directed over my shoulder, seems to challenge the viewer. The scene carries a sense of female strength and vulnerability. It's elegant and composed, the kind of photo you'd find in a fancy New York gallery.

"That was for i-D Magazine, shot by one of the best photographers in New York." I emphasize the last part like it will somehow make all the difference.

He says nothing. The red anger simmers to the surface of his cheeks.

I yank on my clothes quickly, portfolio now pressed against my chest like armor. Breath is shaky.

"This is bullshit! You might as well be working at a brothel," he scoffs. Each word is soaked in venom.

"You know what? You're full of shit! I haven't done anything wrong!" My voice is more forceful than usual. Perhaps a bit of the wine's courage. "I'm so sick and tired of your constant put-downs. I'm fucking exhausted!"

"You better watch it," he hisses, taking a step toward me. The veins in his neck bulge like braided cords.

"Or what?" My voice holds. Heart punches against my sternum.

Then I feel it—a sharp pain. I'm fully sober now. A single drop of blood blooms against the white of my T-shirt. That's it. The moment it all breaks. I break with it. Tears follow, not from shock, but from the sudden clarity.

"Oh my God, Lena." It sounds almost like a question. "I'm so sorry, baby..." Tomek's tone snaps to remorse. It's the same tired line. We've rehearsed this too many times.

"See? You push me to this. You make me a monster."

I don't respond. Not to that. I just wipe my bloody nose and the tears burning at the corners of my eyes. My hands move fast, frantic. I gather what's left of my dignity. My thoughts scatter like confetti caught in the wind.

"I can't believe you hit me," I shout, voice shaking. "You swore—on your mother's life—you'll never hit again!" I yell, not looking for, nor expecting, an answer.

He reaches for me. Too late. Like a cornered animal, I grab my backpack and slip past him, darting toward the door before he can grab hold of me.

"You are a monster! And I wish I never met you!" My voice breaks. I grab my shoes and slam the door behind me. The sound echoes through the hallway with the finality of a gunshot.

I run down the corridor, into the elevator. My heart is pounding as I cram my feet into my shoes and count the floors out loud like a calming spell.

Three. Two. One. Each number slows my frantic breath.

Outside, I bolt through a maze of wet Parisian streets. The city glows with puddled light, but I don't look back at the shadows. The shadows that stretch behind me, long and reaching—like they're trying to pull me back into what's now my past.

The key to the models' apartment slips from my trembling hands, clattering loudly against the floor. Memories of how I arrived here escape me as I whisper prayers for Josionne, my sweet toucan, to be inside. My fingers fumble with the key again. The effort is punctuated by sobs that I can no longer hold back. When the door finally swings open, darkness wraps around me, my heart racing against the silence. I slam the door shut and lock it.

As I turn on the light, the emptiness hits. My gaze is involuntarily drawn to the mirror. A yellow sticky note in the center reads, "Big sis, off to London for a job. Back Friday. —Josionne," its edges framed by drawn hearts. As I peel off the note, tears blur my vision, her cheerfulness mocking the pain spreading across my skin. A sad girl stares back at me from the mirror—a large bruise emerging on her cheek, dark purple spreading beneath the streaks of tear-smudged makeup.

"Fuck," I say to her. "Fuck," she echoes back.

Shivering, I slip into my sleeping bag, with shoes and clothes still wet from the rain. I curl up, trying to find comfort in my grandpa's hug that still lingers somewhere in this fabric. My eyes shut tightly as if to block out the world. Block out this mess. The sobs that escape are my only lullaby, rhythmic and raw, spreading through my body harder than any melody. And the sleeping bag holds me with a kindness and gentleness that I rarely felt from Tomek.

The ring of the phone abruptly pulls me from deep sleep. Seeing Tomek's name flash across the screen triggers a wave of nausea. I send his call to voicemail. My feet are heavy as I shuffle to the bathroom. There's a part of me that hopes the bruise has disappeared, or that the events of last night were just an ordinary nightmare. But I know neither is true.

I splash my face with cold water in an attempt to reduce the swelling, my eyes locking with my reflection.

"It's not that bad," I whisper to myself, beginning the careful application of full-coverage foundation to hide the green-purple. Each touch of the makeup brush feels like a ghost of Tomek's hand, striking me again. Yet, with each deep breath, I reassure myself of the strength that remains in me. Maybe it has even grown since last night.

"You'll be okay."

"You'll be okay."

"You'll be okay." I nod to the green-eyed girl in the mirror, then stride to my room and press Play on Josionne's boombox. The lively samba rhythm erupts. And I dance. Every step defiant, every move giving me strength—giving me back to myself. "You'll be ok," I whisper again.

Walking has always helped me think. I'm a hiker at heart. Something about movement loosens the knots in my mind. So today, I walk to the agency. Let Paris do what it does—infuse the morning with a little magic. The cool air kisses my swollen cheek. Old cobblestones click beneath my tennis shoes. It feels like the city is humming old love songs just beneath my feet.

"Hello, gorgeous!" Rex calls the moment I step in his office. He's already reaching for a Polaroid camera.

"Hi, Rex. How are you?" I ask, trying not to sound nervous. Wondering if the makeup is holding. But when he steps closer, I see the shift in his eyes.

"Darling," he says, brows folding in concern. "What happened to your face?"

"I had too much wine last night and..." The lie stumbles out, thin and brittle. "I tripped."

"Oh, sweetheart." His voice drops, warm and connected. "You really should see a doctor. That looks serious."

"I'm okay... Is it that noticeable?" I ask, blinking fast to keep tears from rising. But I already know the answer. He hesitates.

"I'm afraid it won't heal in time for us to shoot Polaroids for YSL," he says gently, touching my shoulder. "They were hoping to book you for their next campaign. Shoot's in a few days."

"They can't wait?" I ask before I can stop myself.

"I'm afraid not, darling."

His words follow me long after I leave. Out on the street, Paris is bustling and indifferent to how I feel inside. My phone won't stop buzzing—Tomek's name lighting up again and again.

I keep walking. Not sure where I'm going. Just away. Eventually, I stop on a bridge tangled in padlocks. Thousands of them. Love, rusted shut.

The sun glints off the metal and stabs my eyes. Some locks are etched with names. Some with little notes. Vows. Memories. Wounds. Second chances.

I lean on the railing and look down at the Seine. Its surface sparkles, pretending nothing bad ever happens here.

Are they still together, all these lovers? Did the locks outlast the love? My chest tightens. My mind goes blank. A thought seeps in. Maybe Tomek is right.

Maybe I am broken. Maybe I bring out the worst in people, including myself? My mind's all over the place. Like a spiderweb someone brushed against, now just a tangle of broken threads clinging to themselves. These thoughts have always been there, but now they're slipping out, unfiltered. If no one loves you, are you even real? Is existing without love...living?

I grip the railing. Let the sound of the river pull me in. Would anyone notice if I disappeared?

My foot shifts—just an inch forward. I step over the railing. And then my phone rings.

Its shrill tone slices through the moment like a blade.

If it's Tomek—I swear—I'm jumping.

GRANDPA'S PANSY

"Your soul is an accumulation of all your experiences."

"Lena?" Dr. McKenna's voice is faint. Phoenix's warm fingers thread through mine. I slowly flutter my eyes open. The room comes into focus in pieces, like someone turning up the light one dimmer notch at a time. I fight the fog still clinging to my thoughts. Dr. McKenna leans in. Her bushy eyebrows lift—sympathy written plainly across her face. The back of the leather couch bites through my hoodie, colder than I expect.

Somewhere nearby, a hint of lavender—probably from a hidden diffuser, tucked between the stacks of books and scattered notes. I turn my head and find Phoenix. His eyes are glassy.

"Do you need a moment?" Dr. McKenna asks, her voice barely louder than the soft rain tapping against the window behind her.

Strange California weather—June gloom, as we call it. I answer her without words, my eyes speaking before my mouth does.

"No, I'm okay. I need to continue," I say, steadying myself. A single tear slides down and rests beneath my chin. I take a breath, feeling anchored by Phoenix's hand.

"For my daughter," I add.

"Let's pause here." Dr. McKenna's chair squeaks as she leans back. She folds her arms and adds, "You were dealing with a classic narcissist."

Her words hang in the air like an unwanted smoke signal, carrying a memory I know all too well.

"I blamed myself so much in that marriage," I admit, eyes dropping to the pattern on the rug beneath me. I count its threads in silence.

"That's more common than you think," she says. "People like you, empathetic, open, often get tangled up in a narcissist's web."

She pauses. I meet her gaze. She looks at me like I look at Ruby sometimes when kids push her away at the playground.

"They twist the story," she continues, quieter now, "until you start believing it's your fault. But it's not. None of it is. You were a victim, Lena. Full stop."

Phoenix's breath brushes my neck, soft and slow. He exhales, arms tightening around me.

"I've never heard this story," he murmurs. His voice vibrates against my skin. There's so much life in it despite the worry. It reminds me of Josionne's samba boombox. It gives me the same sensation.

The room seems to hold its breath. When I meet his gaze—those fiery hazel eyes—there's a quiet storm in them.

"It was…" But the words stick. The memories are too heavy, pressing down before I can finish the thought.

His eyes soften. A smile reaches them before his lips even move. His hand finds the small of my back, tracing gentle circles. Quiet encouragement.

"It was a very dark time," I finally say. "But it feels cathartic to speak it now." Each word is slow. Careful. Like setting down something fragile.

Dr. McKenna leans forward slightly. "So, did you jump?" Her question doesn't just land in this quiet office—it echoes back through the years, hitting that night like a bell.

Suddenly I'm there again. Back in Paris.

My phone rings, sharp and urgent. I fumble with it, heart in my throat. A Polish number flashes on the screen. Relief. Not Tomek.

The plastic is cold against my cheek. "Hello?" I whisper.

My feet inch back from the railing, retreating from its chill as if some invisible force is guiding me away.

"Hi, Lena! I just got a new phone." My grandfather's voice crackles through the line. His voice is melodic, heart-steadying, like the records of Edith Piaf he plays in the morning. It's the voice that sang lullabies when I was five and too scared to fall asleep alone. The same voice that told me true stories of nightingales nesting in the rose bushes, just outside the window of my childhood home.

"Hi, Grandpa." My lips flutter. The Seine glitters below, blurred by my tears as it reflects the spring sky above. I picture his hands planting flowers in his large balcony pots, glasses slipping down his nose.

"My love, you sound sad. What's happened?" he probes. His intuition has always been sharp.

Tears fall freely now. I see the Wisła river. The way we used to feed swans with dried up bread.

"So much. I've made so many bad choices," I confess, each word quivering as if mirroring the trembling leaves along the riverbank.

"There's always a way back, my little flower." His voice softens. "You just have to take the first step in the right direction." His words cut deep—a cut not to cause pain, but to free me. I inhale deeply. The air carries a quiet sense of change. I turn away from the bridge. And I start walking.

"I think I need a break from modeling...from this life," I admit, feeling a weight lift with each step.

"Then come visit your old guy. I've got books, the plants... and a bowl of żurek waiting," he says. And I can practically see the fogged-up window above the stove, the smell of white borscht curling through the house.

Returning to the models' apartment, I start to pack, the cheerful beats of Josionne's samba filling the room. I write a brief note for her: "I had to go, not sure if I'll return, but I've left you all my books—words that have inspired me. Love you. Be brave, and always fly high." I draw a few hearts like the ones on her note and stick mine on the mirror.

My reflection meets my gaze—bruised cheek and all—yet, in my eyes, there's a fire. No longer a victim. Now, I am a warrior. Stepping away for a bit. Will reach out when I'm ready to return. Key's under the door, I text Rex, and don't wait for a reply. Just close the door and slide the key underneath.

My oversized suitcase drags me down the stairs. Each step feels like the past, pulling me in the wrong direction.

"Fuck it," I declare to the empty stairwell, wiping the sweat from my lip. The valise of my past, with all its weight and unwelcome memories—stays here, in Paris. I leave it leaning against the stairs and march toward my new life—for the first time in years, feeling weightless.

As the plane's wheels lift from the ground, the air claims its mass. The low hum of the engine vibrates through my seat. A comforting monotony. I take a sip of the bitter airplane coffee. Leaning my forehead against the cool window, I watch the lights of Paris fade into the distance. But soon, the avalanche of emotions overwhelms me, and tears carve countless paths down my cheeks. Sometimes finding your way back to the right path is painful. It's a sobering calculation of wrong turns taken, of time and fragments of life seemingly wasted.

Meeting Tomek had felt like escaping a fire only to plunge into boiling water—a different kind of pain, but equally scorching. After my mom left for the U.S. when I was six, my dad raised me, and I spent every summer and school break at my grandpa's in Krakow. Whenever I could, I asked to stay with him. My dad always let me go—reluctantly. Sometimes I wondered if, after waiting nine years for my mom to return, he was just afraid of losing me too. When my parents finally divorced at sixteen, I was torn between them. I never wanted to live in the U.S., but everything changed when my dad remarried. His new wife made life unbearable, constantly stirring up conflict: "You'll do what I say. I'm your mom now," she'd snap. "But I have a mom," I'd cry, only for her to sneer, "Oh yeah? Where is she? Far away. She left you." My dad's wife was the kind of witch Disney villains are modeled after. By the time I was seventeen, I couldn't take it anymore. My grandpa would have taken me in, but as a minor, I had no say—my dad refused to let me go. So I had no choice but to move in with my mom in the U.S. It's no surprise that, in all my vulnerability, I later fell into Tomek's arms, desperate for the love and affection he initially gave me—a temporary balm for my aching heart.

As I drift off, caught between dream and reality, I see her. The little girl with long dark curls, smiling, stretches her hand toward me. To her, I promise silently: I'll teach you strength, show you love that reaches beyond the emptiness of words.

Kraków's Old Town Square is glimmering after a rainfall, the lamplight catching in puddles, skipping across the cobblestones like tiny dancing fairies. The buttery scent of something freshly baked drifts from a café, pierogis maybe, and my stomach growls. Shit, I haven't eaten anything since yesterday. As I pass the Sukiennice square, its merchants closing the stalls for the day, I spot an old man surrounded by pigeons. Some bold enough to perch on his arm, pecking at bits of bread from his palm. Some flap their wings as they fight for their turn.

Just ahead is Grandpa's building. Three stories of warm, weathered brick. A typical Krakovian tenement that has out-lived many wars and still stands with a quiet kind of pride. The city renovated it recently, giving it a fresh coat of warm, peachy paint. Above the charming indie bookstore is a row of windows, most of them dark—their residents turned in for the night—but one lit up. I already know which one is his. He's up, waiting for me. I smile, because of course he is.

He opens the door before I can knock.

"My flower," he beams. His silver mustache lifts with his smile, turquoise eyes glimmering under the hallway light. His lush gray hair is slicked back, like he got ready for an important meeting. Even though he was born as a simple farm boy, he has so much class.

I smile through sudden tears.

He pulls me into a hug. It's the kind of embrace that stitches you back together without asking what broke you. This is what home feels like.

But then my stomach growls, loud and shameless.

"A-ha! Someone's hungry," he laughs. I laugh too, and that's when the scent hits me—żurek. Sharp and garlicky. I catch a hint of vinegar, pig skin fried to a crisp. The smell alone could feed me for months. The air here is always rich with something he just cooked.

Grandpa's apartment is its own little universe. The space is more of a jungle-library than a living room. Floor-to-ceiling bookshelves line almost all the walls. Dark oak, worn smooth at the edges, houses everything from old maps to first editions of

Polish poetry. Even the cabinets have been repurposed to hold more books. Classics, philosophy, handwritten notes, and some of his architectural designs rolled up and crammed between the books. And then there are the plants. Ferns, ivy, orchids, even a small dragon tree in the corner. He makes anything bloom like it takes no effort.

The kitchen is just as I remember. A round table with four mismatched chairs, tucked beside the window that overlooks the square.

I wrap my hands around the bowl of żurek, breathing in the sharp vinegar and crisped-up bacon. One bite and it hits—salty, sour, comforting. The warmth of the soup spreads through my body, chasing away the wet chill I brought in from the streets outside. Steam curls up in white ribbons. Mingling with the kitchen light, it looks like some kind of old magic. Grandpa pulls up a chair beside me. The floorboards groan under him—an old house's way of saying hello.

His eyes fall on the bruise.

"Everything okay with Tomek?" Grandpa's eyes pierce through me as if he can already read the answer in my mind. I pause, spoon suspended midair, caught between the warmth of now and the weight of yesterday. He just waits. His eyes hold safety, even when the world is cruel. My spoon finally drops into the bowl with a soft clink. I breathe in, letting the warmth settle somewhere deeper than my stomach. Edith Piaf hums from the radio. "La Vie en Rose"—one of Grandpa's favorites. Fitting soundtrack for my story.

"I'm so broken, Grandpa. I wasted so much time. Tomek...
he was a dead-end street. He showed up in Paris and we...fought."
My tears drip into the zurek. I don't even try to stop them.

"Come," he whispers. His wrinkled hand reaches for mine.
His touch is always so warm. We move through the narrow hallway. Beksinski's haunting paintings are sprawled across the only
book-free wall. Grandpa once studied architecture with him at
Kraków Polytechnic, long before Beksiński became a global phe-
nomenon. Grandpa's slippers whisper against the wooden floor
as we make our way to what used to be Grandma's office before
she passed away when I was just a teenager. One painting always
pulls me in—a woman striding through a stormy sky, torch in
hand, her red cloak snapping in the wind. A crow flies beside her.
Pure feminine energy.

Though many find Beksinski's work unsettling, Grandpa
and I have always been drawn to its raw, dystopian beauty. There's
something strangely real—almost tactile—about the worlds he
conjures. Distant yet intimately familiar. Grandpa leads me into
Grandma's old office, once her sanctuary. Here, the past still
breathes in every corner. The room is still meticulously arranged.
Shelves lined with surgery textbooks, an archive of her life as a
cardiothoracic surgeon. My fingers trail along the cracked leather
spines. All the covers are worn smooth—she used them a lot. He
stops in front of a cluster of framed photos. A little window into
the world we all once shared. "I took this one," he says, smiling,
pointing to a photo of little me in Grandma's white coat, a stethoscope hanging from my neck, eyes lit up with wonder. "Remember this?" He gestures to a shot of me clutching a trophy from

my eighth-grade biology competition—my grin nearly wider than my face. Next to it: my high school diploma. "Honor roll," he murmurs, swiping his hand across the glass. His voice carries a quiet pride. From the desk, he lifts a book of my poems, each page pressed with a dried four-leaf clover. "Your words," he says, thumbing through the pages, "meant as much to her as all your medals and diplomas." I smile through tears. "Ah, that day in the mountains," he chuckles. "You and I found a whole field of these bright-green plants." The memory squeezes more tears into my eyes before I can stop them. Grandpa twists the side of his mustache as his lips stretch into a smile. "You must have picked every four-leaf clover," he says, grinning. "We laughed that it'd be enough luck for the whole family."

"Sometimes I wonder if my luck's just...run out. Like I used up all my four-leaf clovers," I murmur, more to myself than to him, as I peel one loose and gently twist its stem between my fingers.

"You make your own luck, sweetheart. Your own dreams," he says, sweeping his hand around the room—from the photos to the anatomical models. "Your grandma always believed you'd follow in her footsteps," he adds softly. "And so do I." My gaze finds a black-and-white photo of Grandma during the Second World War. Her light hair spills over her shoulders, framing those piercing eyes. A leather bag crosses her chest. Next to it, an old newspaper clipping reads: "A Woman Behind WW2 Przemyśl Prison Break." She served in the Home Army, the largest underground resistance in Nazi-occupied Poland. Stories of her cunning and bravery, how she picked the code name "Hyacinth"—feminine in Polish, masculine in German—to confuse the enemy, were the bedtime stories of my childhood. Grandpa honored that legacy in her tombstone: a marble hyacinth, snapped in half to symbolize strength and sacrifice. Below it, the words: "Soldier of the Home Army."

"Ah, my beloved Maria. My Hyacinth." He takes the photo gently off the wall, cradling it. "She was, pardon my French, one hell of a badass."

Coming from a man of his elegance and intellect, the word "badass" makes me laugh through my tears. "She sure was." My voice catches as I say it. Noticing the shimmer in his eyes, I pull him into a hug.

"So are you," he murmurs into my hair. "Don't forget where you came from. You have to always find your strength." He pulls back, face lit up with mischief. "No man should ever raise a hand to a woman—or clip her wings when she's trying to fly. If it weren't for this blasted arthritis," he adds, raising a playful fist, "I'd give him a piece of my mind."

The next morning, sunlight nudges me awake, buoyed up by the scent of English breakfast tea. Through barely opened eyes, I spot Grandpa on the balcony. He is framed by his jungle of flowers, watering can in hand. He's not just watering them. He recites poetry like a true plant whisperer, completely in his element. Outlined by the morning sun, he moves with that same quiet grace he's always had. Mozart plays softly from the old radio, weaving through the breeze that smells of wet petals and last night's rain. When I get up, my gaze lands on a white dress with embroidered blue flowers, laid gently on the armchair near the bookshelf. He must've noticed I had nothing else to wear. That quiet thoughtfulness warms me. My fingers brush the linen, and I know—it was hers. It even smells how I remember Grandma, gently floral and powdery. I slip it on, feeling a mixture of gratitude and awkwardness—it's whimsical and more old-fashioned than anything I would usually choose to wear.

"Good morning, Dziadziu," I greet him, my fingers delicately grazing colorful pansies.

"Good morning, my flower," he says, cheekbones lifting, eyes crinkling as he sets the watering can down. "Remember this little one?" he asks, nodding toward a pot spilling over with pansies. Warmth rushes through me as the memory blooms. "I found a single pansy when I was seven," I say, smiling. "It looked so lonely. Someone must've tossed it aside."

He strokes the petals with care. "I talked to it every day until it grew roots," he says. "And now look what we have." He gestures to the wooden pots along the edge—bursts of yellow, pink, and purple overflowing from every one.

Laughing, I admire his green thumb. "You could make a stone bloom."

He twists his mustache, eyes twinkling. "Nah. It's just love. Love makes everything bloom."

"You're something else," I say, shaking my head. His words are like daily quotes one writes in a journal.

He shrugs, eyebrows lifted like he knows it. "I'll go get us pastries."

I kiss his soft, wrinkled cheek. "Oh...and thanks for Grandma's dress," I add, giving him a little twirl.

"You look beautiful in it," he says, lifting the watering can again. "When you get back, I have something else for you. Something she wanted you to have."

My sneakers pad across damp cobblestones—a single beat within the soft hush of Kraków's Old Town Square. The hub unfolds in a serene ballet of unhurried people, their paths weaving like koi fish in a still pond. What a contrast to the frenetic pace I've known elsewhere. You can smell freshly baked pretzels from the nearby cart vendors. There's one at almost every corner. The bread aroma mixes with the earthy scent from the rain-kissed stones, evaporating in the sun. I breathe it all in. This energy that dissolves the demons of my past. Around the Sukiennice, merchants call out, their stalls bursting with color and clamor. Life hums here. St. Mary's Basilica rises with quiet majesty, its spires catching the light. Locals and tourists drift through its open doors, drawn by faith, or maybe a bit of stained-glass magic. Then the trumpet call—Hejnał Mariacki. Every hour on the hour, it screams through the calm, loud enough to startle a flock of pigeons into the sky. I pause and close my eyes. I let the sound permeate me. The trumpeter ends his final note suddenly, mid-breath. That abrupt silence (legend says it honors a bugler who was shot mid-note during an Ottoman siege) wraps the city up with a note of quiet defiance. I feel it wrap around me too. This city, with its unrushed rhythm and stubborn spirit, mirrors my own slow return to peace. I hear Grandpa's voice from the night before. Remember where you came from. I carry those words with each step. A small mantra. A way home. A way back to myself.

With fresh, still-warm pastries cradled in a paper bag, I wander past St. Mary's again. Incense and melted wax drift from the open doors. I stop. It's been a long time since I felt a spiritual pull, but here it is.

Inside, I step into a hush so complete you can hear flies buzzing. Here, silence is sacred. Morning sun filters through the stained glass, laying a soft mosaic of light and shadow across the basilica. The altar, a masterpiece by Wit Stwosz from the late 1400s, glows in a kaleidoscope of blues and golds. Its wooden figures, almost lifelike, seem to breathe under the dance of color. I light a candle. A quiet offering for Grandma, flickering alongside centuries of whispered prayers as the basilica slowly empties. The morning mass just ended minutes ago. For a breath or two, I find peace between all the echoes of devotion. People prayed here for centuries. You can feel them, hear them almost. Just as I reach the heavy wooden doors, a hand—warm but deliberate—closes around mine. I spin around. She stands there. An old woman with a web of time etched across her face, her eyes a faded blue. The intimacy jolts me. She cups my hand. There's something about her foggy eyes, the way they seem to see right through me. Two silver braids escape the edges of her black scarf. She looks like she stepped out of a story—an Old World babushka who knows too much. Her fingers trace mine, papery yet warm.

"Lena," she whispers. "I bring a message from Maria."

My grandmother's name startles me. I freeze. Babushka's brows lift, tuned to something I can't hear. Her face tilts slightly, like she's catching the weight of my breath, its sound. She's clearly blind.

"You are meant to be a healer," she says slowly, like the words are being fed to her. "You'll find happiness with a spiritual artist. Walnut eyes. Together, you will welcome a daughter. She will gather the scattered fragments of your heart and make you whole."

"Walnut eyes?" The words fall out of me. My heart is pounding so hard I can hear it.

"Yes, walnut. The blue-eyed one was a mistake," she exhales, her breath grazing my skin. Of course, Tomek's face flashes in my mind.

A voice breaks through—sharp, annoyed. "Mom, for heaven's sake."

A sleek blond woman—mid-fifties, maybe—swoops in, nervously linking arms with the babushka.

"I'm so sorry," she offers, eyes darting between me and the floor.

"It's okay." My voice barely makes it out.

She tries a smile. There's too much unsaid in it for it to truly feel warm. As she steers her mother toward the exit, I catch her whisper—"You promised you were done with the fortune-telling."

But the woman stops, turns her head toward me like she knows I'm still there.

"Remember," she says, her eyes moving side to side rapidly, "walnut eyes."

The warmth from the pastry bag in my hand contrasts sharply with the chill of the moment. I step into the light pooling from the basilica door. A long shadow spills over my feet. Eyes closed, I whisper it like a spell:

"Walnut eyes. Spiritual artist. Healer. Daughter?"

THE WHISPERS OF FATE

"Don't fear the darkness—it reveals the light."

I clutch the now cold bag of pastries to my chest like a shield as I head back to Grandpa's. Hair stands on my arms. A leftover magic from Babushka, I guess. Growing up in Poland, I learned to approach fortune-telling with a mix of awe and caution. It's not just empty mysticism. Sometimes underneath it hides the truth. I remember when my mom went to one. The woman told her she'd move to America—back when getting a visa under communism felt as likely as flying to the moon. Few months later, she sat on the edge of my bed and used my teddy bear to break the news. "Mommy has to go to America," she said in the bear's voice, its little arms moving with hers. She promised toys—lots of them. But even as a kid, I knew toys were just placeholders. No doll or plush pony could fill the space she'd leave behind. I wanted her, not toys. Before I could fully understand, I was at Warsaw airport, watching a plane disappear into the clouds. She was heading to Chicago. And I was squeezing my dad's hand, aching for one last hug. One more smell of her long, dark hair.

"Grandpa, you won't believe what just happened," I say, breathless, kicking off my shoes with adrenaline.

"I'm all ears," he says, curling his mustache like he always does when something interesting's about to happen. I set the pastries between us. He pours the tea.

"I went to St. Mary's to light a candle for Grandma," I say, "and this elderly woman stopped me." My voice lifts, still caught in the spell of it. His eyes widen. He nods for me to go on.

"She told me my future," I say, pausing to sip the steaming tea. "She said I'll be a healer. That I'll marry some spiritual artist. And we'll have a daughter."

He takes a bite of his blueberry pastry. Crumbs cling to his mustache as one brow arches, teasing me before I even finish.

"Didn't need a psychic to figure that one out," he chuckles. We laugh together between the bites. Outside, the street murmurs through the open window, blending with the quiet strings playing on Grandpa's radio. He leans in, and for a second, the light catches his eyes. They shine. He's still just a boy, behind all the wrinkles.

"I spoke to your mom today." He lifts his tea, pausing just before the rim. "She wants to see you." Another beat as he scans my face.

I choke slightly on a bite I didn't finish chewing. Tea helps, but not enough. Thoughts rush in. Too many at once.

"Her door in Chicago is still open," he says.

"You still talk to her?"

He meets my gaze, soft-eyed.

"Not often," he says, shrugging. "But today, yes." He glances at the tea. "Grace might not be my daughter, but she's your mother. She's still part of this family."

Grandpa always reminds me that life isn't about taking sides. We're just two people, sitting in this kitchen, trying to make sense of things.

"You know…" I say, chin resting in my palm. "She and I are so different."

He just nods. Nothing dramatic. Just understanding that needs no words. "Maybe it's not such a bad idea." I look at him. He takes a loud slurp of the tea. "Chicago's got good schools. I've thought about it before. It's just…you know how my mom is." Grandpa nods without a word. Looking at him as if he holds all the answers I add, "Chicago might be the fresh start I need. Divorce and all."

"Hmm, divorce. Good, good," he says.

"I'm doing it," I say, with a grin breaking through. "The psychic said he has walnut eyes, remember?"

"Walnut eyes it is," Grandpa says, chuckling. Our laughter trails off. There's a bit of bittersweetness under the surface. A goodbye that both of us know is coming. He doesn't say it right away. Just leans forward, the corners of his eyes folding deeper.

"You could also stay here with me and my flowers. You don't bother me, and Krakow has good schools too," he says finally. "It would mean the world to me."

"I know, Dziadziu." The words catch in my throat. My mouth curls into a smile that's not really a smile. "But it's probably better for me to go," I say, even as the words come out heavy. "There's more for me out there." It hurts to say it. "We'll visit each other, right? I'll come back. You'll come see me," I say quickly, trying to sew the distance shut before it even begins.

"Whatever's best for you, my flower," he says. He nods, even though it clearly pains him. I hug him, chin tucked into his shoulder. I don't want to let go yet.

After breakfast, I finally work up the nerve to call my mom. Even though we haven't spoken in ages, I somehow crave her reassurance. A little girl in me still wants my mother's love. The phone rings...and rings. Too long. Shit, what time is it in the Windy City? My heart flip-flops. I glance at Grandpa's balcony—flowers blooming like they don't know what it means to hesitate.

"Mom?" I blurt, barely breathing. The word leaps out before she can say anything.

"Hi, darling!" Her voice is bright—a mouse-like peep. "It's so good to hear your voice. Are you okay? Grandpa told me what happened. I always knew that guy was no good." Classic Mom. She spills it all at once, like she's been holding her breath for years.

"It's a mess," I say. My voice frays at the edges.

"It's okay, Lena." Her voice drops to that softer, soothing pitch I remember. "There's a room here waiting for you. For as long as you need."

I can picture it already—overflowing with her trinkets. Ceramic cats, glittery frames, clay angels from Poland, bright beaded chachka. No corner spared. Everything is covered. Mom's chaos, that was strangely comforting in my childhood, though my dad was always annoyed by it.

"Thanks, Mom," I say. Guilt flashes through me. I hate how I have nowhere to stay and have to rely on her.

"Do you want me to book the ticket?" she asks. Her eagerness practically hums through the phone—compensation for being absent in my childhood.

"No I got it, Mom. I've saved quite a bit modeling. But thank you for offering," I say proudly, knowing I have a hundred grand sitting in my account.

After we hang up, I just stand there. The light filtering through Grandpa's balcony bathes his flowers in gold. I watch the petals sway, feeling the weight of what's coming on my chest like a dumbbell. Do all journeys hurt this much? Chicago means a fresh start. A chance to fix things with Mom. Maybe even find myself again.

But leaving here. This quiet, book-filled place that smells like soup and old wood. The place that has Grandpa in it. It feels like diving off a cliff.

I check my phone. A whole row of missed calls from Tomek.

Do new beginnings ever really erase our scars? Or do we just learn to carry those scars better?

"Lena." Grandpa's voice cuts through my thoughts. I turn, and he's already reaching toward me, his hand outstretched. "I told you I had something special for you," he says, guiding me into Grandma's old office.

A small, timeworn wooden box sits on the desk. It's etched with delicate flowery patterns by mountain village artists from Southern Poland.

"Go ahead, open it," he nods. As I do, the hinge lets out a tiny squeak—a sound straight from my childhood. Inside: Grandma's emerald ring, cradled in velvet. The sight of it floods me with so many memories.

"Grandma!" I'm back in her arms—me, a small kid—twisting that ring three times on her finger, convinced it made wishes come true.

"I thought I was a magician," I whisper. My laugh tangles with a few tears.

"She believed in your magic," he says, voice warm, "and so do I." He smiles, his eyes bright with our shared memory. I slide the big oval stone onto my ring finger. It glimmers in the sunlight. Something shifts. That ache in my chest softens into strength.

"It fits like a glove," Grandpa chuckles. "Even your fingers are the same size as hers. She always wanted you to have it."

"Thank you," I whisper, wrapping my arms around his neck. I kiss his cheek, breathing in the faint trace of his cologne.

"One day, I'll pass it on to my daughter."

Grandma's ring casts rainbows on my hand as I step outside. Her strength is now my own. And a bit of inherited magic.

I breathe in Kraków's afternoon and make my way to the travel agency. It feels right. Like I'm finally stepping toward something new, something entirely mine. I picture myself in a white coat. I don't dwell on the how, just trust the will be. What the babushka said. And then there's him. The one with the walnut eyes I haven't met yet. I already see flashes of him. Feel his touch.

The travel agency is quiet. Posters of beaches, church spires, and pyramids line the walls. A sweet older woman types in the details for a flight to Chicago next week.

"What a steal," I say, feeling excitement rise with each tap of her keys.

Once everything's set, she lifts her gaze and asks, "How would you like to pay for this reservation?"

"Can I use debit?" I pull out my blue Chase card, trying to sound casual. My chest tight for no reason.

"Absolutely," she says. Our fingers brush for a moment as she takes the card. The beep is sharp. Wrong. It slices the quiet in half.

"Declined?" I blink, heat rising to my throat. My mind races—$100,346.76, a number of money in my account that I know by heart from my last ATM withdrawal in Paris.

"There must be a mistake. Could you try again?" I look at her, trying not to throw up. She nods slightly, her expression melding professionalism with a hint of annoyance, a softer cousin to the French eye roll I've become acquainted with. She swipes again. Same long, jarring beep. Same fucking no.

"I'm deeply sorry, ma'am. It's still declined," she says. "Would you like to use another card?"

"I'll be right back," I whisper, already backing toward the door, avoiding eye contact. The chime behind me sounds louder than it should. Outside, Kraków buzzes—colorful, unbothered. It clashes against the way I'm coming undone. I stumble, barely dodging a fall. Dialing the number on the back of my Chase card takes several attempts, my fingers trembling with each failed try.

"Yes, hello? There's been a mistake," I blurt out, the words tumbling out awkwardly, the card slipping in my sweaty grasp as I relay the account number to the representative.

"Ma'am, your account currently shows a balance of two cents."

"That's impossible. Could you double check, please?" I repeat the digits, hoping for a different outcome, my voice steadying into a chant of desperation. "There are charges from Paris—Versace, the Four Seasons, Le Cinq. All on the twenty-third. Then two large withdrawals today," the agent says. Every word takes another bite of my hope.

"Withdrawals? By whom?" My voice cracks, a lump forming in my throat as tears threaten to spill.

"The withdrawals were authorized by the joint party on the account, Tomek Kowalczuk."

Dr. McKenna's sharp breath pulls me from the horrible drama of my past. I blink, disoriented, back in her office, with the comforting weight of Phoenix's hand on my back.

"Oh no, he didn't!" she gasps, briefly breaching her neutral physician tone. A rueful smile twists my lips.

"He did." I nod. A laugh bubbles up—brittle, even to my ears. It's a strange sound, part disbelief, part remembered pain, but here, in this space, it carries a quiet defiance.

"After I filed for divorce, he was trying to chain me down with my own money, hinting that I could have it back if I just dropped the divorce," I explain, my gaze drifting to a gray smudge on the wall next to a diploma.

"Unbelievable." Dr. McKenna slaps the desk lightly. It's almost cute, the way her anger peeks through. Female rage and solidarity.

"Yeah," I say, letting out a bitter chuckle. Phoenix just sits there, stunned. He's never heard the whole story. "Then Tomek would reappear—flowers in hand, begging for forgiveness."

Dr. McKenna sighs and leans in, resting her cheek in her palm. "Monsters often come with flowers, don't they? And financial control—that's classic abuser behavior," she says. The room quiets as the air fills with the faint lavender scent of her diffuser. Hearing her name the abuse I endured is more validating than I thought it would be. She looks at me with renewed focus. I know this look. It's when the human spirit overtakes the clinician. And suddenly, you're no longer a doctor. You're a human healing another human. Making them bloom free for the first time.

"After everything—even the Paris bridge—most people would've crumbled. But here you are. A doctor. A wife. A mother. You've kept going, even after he tried to clip your wings. What kept you moving forward?"

"I have this insane focus," I answer, followed by a hollow laugh. "When I want something, it becomes...like an obsession."

"Lena doesn't just knock on doors. She makes a door if there isn't one there to open," Phoenix says, looking at me, giving my hand a squeeze. We all chuckle.

Dr. McKenna makes a note, then gestures encouragingly for me to continue.

"So I went ahead with the divorce and let that money go. It was the price of my freedom, I guess. And when the FBI started asking questions about Tomek..." I pause, rolling the drawstring of my sweatpants between my fingers, seeking a moment of grounding.

"FBI?" The word hangs there. Phoenix and Dr. McKenna both stare at me, shocked.

"Yeah," I say, still toying with the drawstring. "Insurance fraud. A hit-and-run at a gas station. God knows what else. All of it after I'd already closed that chapter."

Dr. McKenna shakes her head. "What in the world," she murmurs.

"I left just in time. It's like someone was watching over me," I say, and sigh a little. "Maybe there's a reason for everything."

Dr. McKenna, still absorbing the story, leans in. "So, how did you find your way to Chicago?"

The rain tapping the window fades, replaced by distant church bells in Kraków. My chest tightens, not from the sterile air of the office, but from the memory. I'm back with Grandpa, tears streaming down my face as I tell him about the travel agency. My college savings—gone. Dreams shattered before they could even take shape, thanks to Tomek's betrayal.

Grandpa's hands, warm and comforting, encase mine. No words needed, just his quiet love.

"This is just a log on your path, Lena," he says, his voice steady. "It's there to test how much you want this dream. You'll leap past it." His wisdom carries the weight of lived experience. Born to tomato farmers in a small village and raised during the

Second World War, Grandpa was the first in his family to break the mold—earning a college degree, becoming a celebrated architect, and eventually, a revered architecture professor. His journey always inspired me. Now he reminds me that no obstacle is too great when you have the drive. The passion. The purpose.

"Thank you for being my light in this shadow," I murmur, wiping my eyes with my sleeve. "I love you so much, Grandpa."

"Hold on," he announces, lifting himself with a humble strength. The familiar shuffle of his slippers against the aged wooden floor echoes as he moves away. A moment later, he reappears in the dim hallway, framed by the eerie beauty of Beksinski's paintings. A yellow manila envelope rests in his hand, folded like it's hiding something not yet ready to be shared. He settles next to me on the couch, the room's lush plants standing guard as he places the envelope in my hand.

"I don't need this," he says, nodding toward the envelope, urging me to look inside. I untie the string. The paper feels coarse under my fingertips. Inside: a bundle of dollars. So much work. So much of his sacrifice.

"Grandpa, I can't take this," I whisper. A tear, my own, lands on the envelope. His smile warms me.

"I'm old, and I've lived my dreams," he says. He cups my hand. "But you, my dear granddaughter, you're on the cusp of something remarkable. I feel it, deep in the marrow of my bones." He places the envelope in my hand.

It suddenly feels heavier. I glance at Grandpa. A map of his life is etched in the lines of his face. Each wrinkle is a pathway he once walked. Each one shows the joy. Or the sorrow. The resilience. My eyes well up with a river of tears ready to breach. His belief in me—like glue—fills the cracks in my heart that Tomek had fractured into pieces.

Without a word, I lean my head against his shoulder. His presence wraps around me like a cloak woven with threads of hope and strength.

In this moment, I understand that his gift is not just money. He passes me a baton in the marathon of chasing dreams. I have to run like those who came before me. My hand grips tighter against the envelope as I nod in determination.

"I will make you proud one day," I whisper.

His arm encircles me. "I'm already proud, my love. Now, let's get you to Chicago."

As Grandpa's words echo in my head, the memory begins to fade, like mist dissolving under the morning sun. The barely perceptible weight of the envelope transmutes into the weight of my own hands in my lap. The warmth of his generosity is replaced by the physical presence of Phoenix's arm encircling me.

I blink. Grandpa's apartment fades—plants, books, Beksiński's paintings, replaced by Dr. McKenna's neutral walls. The transition is jarring but somehow makes sense. The past and present are never separate. They breathe through each other like lovers. Existing inside us, all at once.

Dr. McKenna is watching me, her gaze kind and patient, an invitation to return from my journey through memory.

"And how did you two meet?" she asks, her voice grounding me in the now.

I draw in a deep breath. There's the same twinkle in Phoenix's eyes—the one Grandpa had when he knew I needed grounding more than advice. I bump his shoulder playfully, then glance at Dr. McKenna. A grin comes, seemingly unguarded. And I say, "Finally, a story that will make you smile."

WINDS OF CHANGE

"Learning to walk with the spiritual rhythm of the universe."

The garage door groans as it lifts. That familiar squeak that grates in my ears. I pull in. Same old sight: towers of food cans, stacked past what the shelves can hold, spilling into every corner. It's a post-communist relic: my mom's need to stockpile, just in case. Seasonal trinkets peek out, waiting for their next holiday. For the moment when they can shine again. I have to step around the overflow, careful not to knock anything down. It has the vibe of the backstage at wonderland: gaudy, excessive, over-prepared. This chaotic welcome has become an everyday ritual since I've been living here. Mom thrives in this kind of mess.

After kicking off my shoes, I hurry upstairs, narrowly evading an ambush by the Melaleuca packages sprawled at the entrance. With a quick adjustment of my backpack, I maneuver the bulkier package upstairs. My arms are shaking, but I'm determined. If I don't help, someone's going to the hospital today.

"Mom?" I inquire under my breath, breaching the quiet.

"Over here, Lena," she says from the kitchen. She's by the open porch window, soaked in pinkish-gold Chicago sunset. She's an island of calm, puffing on a cigarette with nonchalance like she didn't just clean two houses. Behind her, the garden bursts with life, a vivid stretch of color that seems almost offended by the wisps of smoke floating through the air. It's an amusing contradiction: the serene trinket-loving gardener wrapped in a shroud of smoke, her blooms thriving in silent protest.

"Ah, thank you. Just put it here," Mom says, nodding toward the table. Her smile pierces through the haze. Melaleuca whitening toothpaste.

The rich aroma of red borscht with mushroom dumplings—my favorite—competes with the menthol scent of her Capri cigarettes. A steaming bowl is waiting for me on the table. Almost like I'm at Grandpa's.

"Thank you. I'm starving," I utter, planting a kiss on her cheek, holding my breath to dodge the smoldering vapor.

The first taste of the spicy beet soup momentarily distracts me, offering a much-needed break after a day of studying.

"So, the FBI was here about twenty minutes ago." She lights another cigarette from the bud that's almost done burning.

"Again?" I choke out, caught off guard, a dumpling nearly lodging in my throat.

"Yes, again." Her voice is tired, annoyed. The smoke swirls from her nostrils. She looks like an angry dragon.

"Jesus." I put the spoon down and start pacing. "It's been five years."

"I assured them you have no idea where Tomek is, and they should just leave you alone." She dismisses the matter with a wave and takes a deep drag of her cigarette. "I told them you're a college student, in need of peace. You've suffered enough because of that...asshole."

I sit in the chair. Speechless. I'm too hungry for this shit. She stares at me as I devour dinner.

"Mmm, Mom, this was divine," I say, pushing away the bowl with a satisfied sigh, letting the shadow of that man fade for a moment.

"So how did your biochemistry exam go?" She puts an iced bottle of sparkling water beside me. I chug it down.

"Good. I got a hundred and two percent," I say as a loud burp escapes on the last syllable.

"Extra credit. Nice!" She smiles. "You're my smartest daughter."

I laugh because I'm her only child.

"And you're my favorite mama." I joke back as I put my plate and empty glass away.

"Your work clothes are on the bed," she says. "I just washed them."

"Thanks! Love you." I give her a juicy smooch. My clothes are neatly folded on the bed, smelling like a fresh summer beach somewhere in California. The scent is always slightly different, impossible to reproduce. Mom is a laundry chemist—always mixing different fabric softeners.

"Ok. Heading to the gym, then off to work," I say.

"Drive safe, my sweets," Mom says, a bit of concern in her smoky voice as she lands a kiss on my cheek. She leaves there a hint of mentholated nicotine, and a touch of the warmth I longed for in my childhood. Better late than never, I suppose.

I slide into SLY, my $1400 beat-up white Nissan Sentra. Named after the first three letters on his plate. The irony's not lost on me. SLY, like me, is persistent, enduring, and has a bit of that off-beat charm. We've become quite the team on the Chicago streets. The drive to the gym gives me time to think. Trees blur past the windows. Maybe they're leaving the past behind too. The city's rhythm matches my own. Fast. Focused. Like I'm finally going somewhere on purpose. Mom and I are closer now. We laugh a lot. Well, she does, at least. It's not perfect, but the old stuff doesn't sting like it used to. We've stitched our lives back together.

It's been five years since I landed in Chicago. I'm in my third year of college—art history major, pre-med minor. My last stand of rebellion before med school. Grandpa's manila envelope helped me get SLY and manage tuition until I landed a bartending job at one of Chicago's trendiest nightclubs. Our weekly calls keep me grounded. Despite occasional waves of loneliness, my focus never wavers.

The cycling studio's dim lights feel like a break. It's where sweat turns into something useful. I find my pace on the bike. One, two. One, two. Latecomers hustle in, filling the room. There's the repetitive clicking of shoes locking into pedals. The best class of the day: Angela, at 7:30 p.m. She's more than an instructor; she's a force, known for turning a workout into a meditation about life.

As the class nears its apex, Angela's voice cuts through the music and the symphony of breaths. Clear. Commanding.

"Come on, give me your best! What are you fighting for? See it, go for it!" Her clarion call resonates with a deep part of me.

I close my eyes and pedal harder. The bike fights me, like everything I've had to push past to get here. Sweat beads at my hairline as my lungs demand more air. Images of my dreams unfold: a successful career, a life of independence, the laughter of a child. Yet, an unexpected vision intrudes, gentle, but insistent. It's him. Walnut eyes. Features chiseled from the stone of my deepest desires. His presence in my mind's eye isn't a distraction but a mysterious and comforting signpost. My future. Despite physical exertion, it's the thought of him that accelerates my pulse. Where is he now? What path will lead me to him? Lost in the rhythm of my imagined future, I whisper to myself. Or to him, "Where are you, walnut eyes?" The bike disappears under me. So does the room. But I keep pedaling—through dreams, through doubt. It's not just Angela's voice driving me now. It's him. That strange pull toward someone I haven't even met yet.

Out of the shower, I breathe deep. Try to hold tight to what I'm chasing. I still live out of my backpack. Everything I need, always with me. It's the last echo of that old model life. A whirlwind that feels like someone else's story now. This is a new chapter. I lean over the gym sink, squinting into the harsh mirror light. A swipe of smoky shadow. Mauve lipstick. Another mask. Another version of Lena. Then comes the uniform: red corset, black fishnets, cabaret skirt. It's Saturday night. Show time at Visage.

Visage lives in the thick of River North, right where downtown pulses hardest. At night, it owns the whole block. It's the newest hotspot in Chicago's nightlife scene, with lines stretching over the entire sidewalk. The walls are decked out with fashion shots. The black-and-white silhouettes of Kate Moss, Gisele Bundchen, and Linda Evangelista are staring down at me. Everything's sleek. Stylish. Just the right amount of pretentious. Models work the bar, the floor, the VIP tables. That's how I got hired. It's the kind of place where people come to be seen. And probably to look at us too.

Niko, the owner, air-kisses my cheek like always as I walk in. He's head-to-toe Prada again. No surprise there.

Eliza hired me, even though I had zero bar experience. "You look the part," she said. "We'll teach you the rest." She's the manager. A boss lady, in every sense. She also happens to be dating Luc, the guy I'm always paired with downstairs. He's fast, funny, and safe—meaning there's no weird tension between us. We just work well together. And Eliza likes me because I don't try to sleep with him.

The place glows with fiery leaf-shaped lamps by the VIP booths. I step inside, ready for whatever chaos the night decides to serve.

Behind the bar, Luc is already bouncing around with his energy drink. He flashes that Abercrombie boy smile.

"Ready to conquer the night, eh?" he asks, his French-Canadian accent softening the word 'conquer' into something almost charming. His smile is infectious.

"Always," I say, attacking ice chunks with a metal shaker, prepping my station for a long night of mixing drinks. "Especially with you as my wingman."

We laugh. That light spontaneous laugh that makes this place, for a moment, not feel like work.

Eliza appears like she always does—gliding in as if she owns the air around her. Her long platinum blond hair flows down her back, shining like glass. The straightness of it, the color, the whole vibe—somehow it gives away her Korean roots before you even see her face.

"Hi, my love," she says. Her luscious lips leave a bit of gloss on my cheek. I secretly wipe it off while she scans our setup.

"Lena, do me a favor," she says, nodding toward Luc. "Make sure he's still upright by the end of the night." He nearly chokes on the drink.

"I got you, girl," I shoot back, smiling. She winks, and then throws Phillippe and me a warning look. "I can see you on the camera." And we all laugh. This is our rhythm at Visage.

Luc gives me a glance, half challenge, half smirk. "Bet you a hundie I'll outring you tonight."

"You're on," I whisper, already grinning. "But you'll lose. Again."

Eliza claps once, sharp as a whip crack. "Okay, focus, kids. Chicago Bulls is in the back tonight. Couple of film people too. Let's be tight."

Her tone is firm, but the trust she holds in us softens the edge. We know what to do.

As she walks off, Luc leans toward me, nodding at the bottle service girls getting briefed by Niko near a glowing VIP table. They look majestic. Long, flowing, perfectly blow-dried hair. Tight-waisted corsets. Barbie limbs in heels. Each more polished than the next, like they stepped out of the black-and-white photos on the walls. It reminds me of those casting lines in Paris.

Somehow, I always end up in places I barely belong.

"You should think about bottle service," he says, polishing a bottle until it gleams. "Tips are insane."

"I couldn't," I say. "There's something about this." I tap the bar. "Feels safer. Keeps me on this side of the madness."

"You know you're weird, right?" He chuckles, shaking his head.

"Weird and broke is better than drunk guys grabbing my ass all night," I say. It's a joke. But not really.

Luc wiggles his butt, laughing. "I'd do it if I could."

In minutes, Visage's bursting at its seams. Lights strobe. The bass takes over people's bodies. They crawl up to the bar in an endless line. Like ants. Each time louder and drunker. We keep pace—vodka Red Bulls, espresso martinis, whatever's trendy this week. Luc and I fall into rhythm. And like clockwork, once the buzz hits a certain level, they start buying us shots. That's when we go undercover. The fake sambuca comes out. We filled it with water before the night began. Nobody ever wants sambuca. It tastes like cough syrup. But it looks like we're partying, with our shots on the house. Everyone is happy. I reach for the empties, but a delicate manicured hand beats me to them. She lifts one and smells it.

"That's so smart," says the brunette in the black spaghetti strap dress. She's tiny, but her voice cuts through the noise. Her dark eyes sparkle with a little mischief, tucked behind a sweep of mascara.

"What is?" I lean in, taking the glass out of her hand. She flicks her bangs and pulls me close, cupping my ear like she's about to tell me a secret.

"That sambuca trick—so you don't end up passed out behind the bar halfway through the night." She laughs, her voice a melodic whisper cutting through the chaos.

"Unless someone asks to light it on fire—then we're screwed." I laugh, the sound catching somewhere between the bass drops.

"I would." She chuckles. "I actually like it. Can I have two shots of the real one?" I pour the sambuca and light it up. The blue flame flickers across her gorgeous face as she slides me a fifty and nudges the other shot forward.

"Cheers!"

The warmth of licorice spreads down my throat. She knocks the empty glass on the bar top.

"Hey...you're in my bio class at UIC." She squints like it's just clicked.

"I am?" The question slips out as I blink. Her face clicks into place. The club lighting rearranges her into that version I remember—quiet, focused, always at the back of the lecture hall.

"I always see you in the library. You're like...smart-smart." She grins. Her words float between the beats. "And fucking beautiful."

I feel all the sambuca now rising to my cheeks. She pulls out her phone and hands it to me.

"What's your number? We should study together. I'm always at Caribou Coffee in Glen Ellyn."

"No way! That's three blocks from my place," I say, tapping my number in with fingers still cold from the ice.

I hand it back. She looks at the screen—"Lena?"—and grins. "That's a beautiful name. I'm Anya." She secures our new-found bond with a text. Then a tall, blond figure wraps around her, pulling her away. She gives him a quiet, knowing smile. Like they've said something without saying a word. "Okay, I gotta go. Caribou tomorrow? One p.m.?" Her voice cuts through the noise of the fading crowd.

"Sure!" I yell back to make sure she can hear me. She waves, then blends into the night as I resume my dance with the martini shaker. The crowd thins. Visage exhales. The dance floor echoes with leftover memories.

The music keeps whispering secrets into the air. Every night at the club dies the same way. Eliza throws us a nod. Luc and I slap a high five over buckets brimming with tips. I stand, motionless, hypnotized by the glare. In that moment, all the vibrant souls I encountered glimmer in the dimming light, like night rainbows arching across the canvas of my life's sky. Ephemeral. But burned in my memory.

These past few months, the Caribou Coffee near my mom's house has turned into our quiet corner of the world. Anya and I always grab the same spot: the old beige loveseat that's molded to me by now, right by the fire but facing the window. Outside, fall paints everything in strokes of yellow and orange. Our table, cluttered with textbooks and sticky notes, feels like an island in a sea of coffee aroma and murmured conversations.

Anya's right there across from me. Sometimes she draws me out of my study bubble with a joke. Other times, the only thread connecting us is the synchronized rhythm of our iPods.

"What's up?" I look up from my organic chemistry textbook, catching Anya giggling at her laptop screen as if it were telling her a secret. She leans over the top of it, whispering, "I'm chatting with this guy on MySpace."

"MySpace?" I echo, intrigued, a little confused.

"Of course you wouldn't know," she teases. "You're always living in your own world. You need a distraction now and then or your head will explode." I look at her, my eyes crinkling with a smile. That's how she shows her love. With sass. Her infectious optimism, and the way her brown eyes sparkle, remind me of Josiane's child-like wonder.

Without warning, she scoots closer. "Watch this, bestie." She grabs my laptop and types in myspace.com like she's about to hack a governmental website.

"You're going to love it. It's full of artists and weirdos. Perfect place for you." She dives into setting up an account for me.

"What should your username be?" she asks.

"Lena?" The suggestion hangs in the air for a second. "Wow. Original as fuck." She rolls her eyes, dramatic. I giggle. "Okay, okay, hmm...what about 'Magician'?"

"'Magician'?" She tilts her head.

I nod slowly. "I always thought there's something magical about being a doctor. Especially in osteopathic medicine. Healing with your hands. It's like you're a magician." My thoughts drift to the holistic approach that drew me to the Doctor of Osteopathic Medicine program. Learning to heal not just with our knowledge but also with our touch was the main reason I decided to apply only to osteopathic schools. Magician feels like a name I've always carried. My dreams encapsulated.

"That's perfect." She beams. "It's so you. Magician." She taps each letter with a deliberate click. "Now, we showcase some of your magic with those stunning photos of yours." She dives into my files like she's seen them a hundred times. When she picks the profile photo, it stops my breath.

It's the one where I'm staring straight into the lens. Alex took it. Alex the bouncer from Visage, with dreams bigger than the nightclub. The one who sees people better through a lens than most do in real life.

In that image, my short hair forms a wild halo around my face. Cheekbones carved by shadow. Eyes lit with a smoky allure that would make Marla from Fight Club nod in approval.

"This! You're the embodiment of a magician here," Anya announces.

I lean in, captivated by the version of myself staring back from the screen. There's something raw there. Untamed. Something I rarely let myself acknowledge.

"Wow, Alex really captured something, didn't he?" I murmur, a mixture of awe and a newfound appreciation for his skill swirling within me.

"So much passion in your eyes. Just gorgeous!" Anya does the chef's kiss. Her laughter spills out—light, affirming—filling our cozy corner and sealing the choice. It's more than a photo. It's a piece of who I am.

"A real-life magician," I whisper, my eyes closing for a moment, envisioning the possibilities.

Anya adds herself as my first friend and shows me how to navigate the site. We set the background—a sepia-toned angel painting I found on Google Images. The angel's looking up, breaking away from the ropes binding her wrists. It feels like a mirror. A spiritual being caught mid-breaking free. This image illustrates a journey of strength and growth, a symbol of the solitude I've embraced since leaving my abusive past. Yet, it's not just about breaking free; it's about yearning for a deeper connection. Not just to be loved, but to understand and love myself. Like her, I have the strength to rise. I just need to remember. Unleash it. Like Grandpa said.

"Man, you're weird," Anya says, eyeing the finished profile. "But that's why I love your wild brain." She squints at me under the shadow of her bangs, half-serious, then cracks up.

"Better weird than ordinary." I nudge her shoulder playfully, maybe a little too hard. She teeters dramatically on the loveseat. We can't stop laughing.

"Oh wait, you need a theme song. What do you want it to be?"

"'Miss You' by Trentemøller," I say without thinking. A song I accidentally downloaded from LimeWire a few months ago, along with his Radiohead remixes. That nostalgic, raindrop melody is playing in my head before she even opens the search bar.

"Moody." She smirks. "You'll attract some emo artist with this." Then her eyes flick to the clock.

"Oh shit! I gotta go, late for my date with Mark." She scrambles to shove her laptop and books into her corduroy bag, then plants a quick kiss on my cheek before dashing out.

"See you tomorrow, best friend!" I yell out as Anya sprints from Caribou Coffee.

"Love you, Lena! See ya!" Her voice fades into the busy street.

"Love you!" I yell back, just as the glass door closes behind her. Hope she heard it.

Left in the quiet, I plug in my headphones. Trentemøller's music wraps around me. A cloak of introspection. Soft, nostalgic, full of space to think. I keep on personalizing my page. Under political beliefs, I add: "God has no religion." It's something that's always lived in me, even with my Catholic roots. For my location: "Rhythm of the Universe." It's how I've started to see my life. I'm a feather in the water—guided by the current. A little nod to *The Alchemist*, which I just finished reading.

This moment, typing out my chosen identity in the buzz of a coffee shop, becomes its own kind of sanctuary.

The echo of Anya's laugh lingers. The warmth of our weird friendship still hangs in the air.

She accepts me in all my complexity. And she was right—this MySpace thing is a wonderful distraction.

With every click, every choice, I'm carving out a space that feels like mine.

A digital spell. A footprint. A vision board for the magician I want to be. I add all the artists I can find.

Most are from Los Angeles—a place I've never been, but somehow already dream of. Eyes closed, Trentemøller looping in my ears, that familiar vision returns. The man with the walnut eyes. His gaze, piercing yet soft. A flame that warms without burning. This dream figure, with his exotic allure that defies categorization, speaks of a connection that transcends the physical. It's spiritual. Internal. Wordless. My heart races. Will our paths ever cross? Outside of dreams? Outside of babushka prophecies?

A flicker on my screen pulls me back.

A pop-up: friend request.

OXx FIREneedsAIR xXO.

I frown, intrigued, hovering over the profile picture: John Lennon's "Imagine," framed by colorful flowers woven into a peace sign. He's listed as male. Location: Mother Earth, California.

Sixty thousand followers. Bio:

"My grandmother, Vincenta, taught me that no prayer goes unanswered."

He's marked as seventy-seven years old. I can tell he's significantly younger, his age evidently a symbolic play on numbers. Every photo is from behind. No face. Just a lean, muscular back inked with intricate tattoos. Deserts. Temples. Oceans. Foreign streets. His theme song plays softly through the page: "Sound in a Dark Room" by Telefon Tel Aviv. Hypnotic. Intoxicating. Like his photographs. My breath quickens. Each photo feels like a spiritual breadcrumb left for someone like me. Every caption, a line of poetry. Every image, an offering of art. And his tattoos. Stories he's lived, which I try to decipher. It feels like I'm back on the parapet in Paris, people-watching—my favorite game.

Where has he been? What sorrows have his eyes seen?

Then one photo stops me. He's kneeling in front of the Egyptian pyramids.

Arms outstretched, as if surrendering to something ancient but becoming free at the same time.

His bare back faces the camera. Chinese characters inked down his spine. Symbols of his travels, both outward and inward. Stories never told out loud. The caption reads:

"fill your vessel...signed, phoenix hartley."

HEARING DEAD LANGUAGES

"You can't silence destiny."

Months have slipped by since the crisp autumn days gave way to the bite of a Chicago winter. Now, as the city shakes off its chill, St. Patrick's Day bursts onto the streets in a riot of green. A loud, joyful proclamation of spring. Anya and I, arms looped, march down Hubbard Street. The lights of the sky-scrapers cast a soft glow over the green-clad crowds. The streets are filled with laughter, drunken conversation, and the occasional cheer from a nearby bar. Some guy is catcalling girls in crop tops.

A classic Windy City soundtrack. "I'm so glad the MCATs and all those applications are finally behind us," Anya says, her red heels tapping a confident rhythm on the sidewalk.

"Me too. Now we just wait for interviews," I say as we weave through the alcohol-infused crowd.

"I hope we both get to stay in Chi-town." Anya grips my arm tighter. I nod, just as a chill off Lake Michigan sweeps under my skirt.

"Why did I ever think this skirt was a good idea?" I mutter, shivering.

"Stop it. It's not that cold," she teases, rolling her eyes.

"Beauty is pain." I laugh.

"Look—we're here." She points to O'Callaghan's, a bustling Irish pub with a dark green facade and a gold-lettered sign that promises warmth and tall pints of Guinness inside. Anya leads me through the crowded doorway, her fingers laced with mine as she scans the sea of heads for Mark. Inside, the pub is a stew of sound and smell—spilled beer, fried wings, the tang of whiskey, the clink of glasses, loud conversations, and the heat of too many bodies packed into too small a space.

"Anya! Babe, over here!" Mark's voice cuts through the clamor. He waves us over to a reddish four-top tucked into the corner—the one we nearly missed. He greets Anya with a movie-scene kiss. Her tiny body floats off the floor, red heels shining as one of her knees lifts behind her.

I can't help but smile at their ridiculous cuteness. Then I see him.

Austin.

Dark-haired. Fit. He's leaning back casually, with a near-empty Guinness sweating beside him.

The guy they've been trying to hook me up with for months.

"Hey, sweetheart," Mark says, pulling me into a half-hug.

"Hey." I say, managing a polite smile.

He nods toward Austin. "Look who's here."

"Hi." I extend my hand. But in my mind, I roll my eyes, just like Anya. Austin's grip is colder than expected and damp—probably from that glass of beer.

"Nice to see you again," he says. His handshake lingers a moment too long. I wipe the wetness off on my skirt. His green eyes meet mine. There's flirtation in them. Warmth, maybe. But it doesn't land. The sentiment is one-sided. Anya sees it. The lingering eye contact. And she throws me a subtle told-you-so look over her shoulder.

Laughter flows like the drinks. Quick. Easy. My indifference to Austin aside, the four of us are already lost in O'Callaghan's warm, chaotic hum. We're tipsy before we even notice, and I'm laughing at his stupid jokes.

Austin is a lawyer. Same firm as Mark.

It's not hard to guess he played football. That green T-shirt hugs his chest just enough to hint at the athlete underneath.

What surprises me is his humor. He's actually funny.

His laugh is easy, open. It bubbles up between the clink of glasses and half-drunk stories spilling around us. He's the kind of guy women salivate over in romance novels. But I'm not salivating. Her voice returns. The babushka in Kraków. Walnut eyes, remember...

Austin's are green. Deep emerald—just like his T-shirt. Just like this whole St. Patrick's Day vibe. Emerald in the candlelight. Catching flickers, shadows. Giving more away than he probably means to.

His every glance comes with a hair swipe. Like it's part of the ritual. His eyes keep finding mine. There's sharpness there. Curiosity...maybe nerves? Even with the warmth. Even with the laughs—I hesitate. I let him in for a second. Just a flicker. That's all he gets.

After the pub, we all end up at Mark's sleek Gold Coast penthouse. It's in a renovated six-story mid-century building with a sliver of lake view. Inside, it's textbook bachelor pad. Open layout. Giant windows. A leather sectional and flat-screen TV orbit a pool table like it's the nucleus of the place. It probably is. The bedrooms are made for nocturnal souls—dark, hushed, perfect for sleeping off late nights. My boots knock against the wood floor. Anya's pumps echo a bit faster. The light flips on. I'm blind for a second before my eyes adjust to the golden glow of ceiling floodlights.

"Make yourself at home," says Mark, nodding towards the couch. He scoops Anya up. Her lean legs hanging over his arm. Their giggles disappear into his bedroom. The door shuts.

Austin heads for the pool table but stops midway and looks back at me. Shit. Just me and him now. And all that uncomfortable silence. I flop onto the leather couch and instantly regret my outfit—my skin sticks to it like tape.

He breaks the rack. The crack nearly startles me. I avoid his eyes, but he's looking. I feel it. I grab the remote, flip through channels aimlessly until National Geographic pulls me in.

"What does your tattoo mean?" Austin finally breaks the silence.

"Which one?" I shoot back, even though we both know he means the one on my wrist. The back one's hidden beneath my turtleneck.

He sits beside me. "You have more?" His eyes drift, part curious, part undressing me.

"Yeah..." I say, eyes persistently on some show about ancient Egypt.

"I was asking about the one on your wrist." He scoots a bit closer. I shoot him a side glance. The kind that could freeze a lake—he immediately scoots back to where he started.

I raise my wrist. "This one is my lucky number."

He scoots closer again. "May I?" He reaches out. With a gentle touch that belies the boldness of the act, he traces the ink on my inner wrist.

"What number is it?"

"Nineteen. Babylonian numeral," I say, turning slightly to meet his gaze. No frozen lake this time.

"Unusual choice." His eyes flicker with amusement.

"Maybe. But randomness isn't really my thing. This number...it follows me." I pull my wrist away. "I'm superstitious."

Seeking a shift in conversation, he tries another angle, "You're very artsy."

"Art and science." No elaboration.

"Ah." He frowns, confused.

"I'm getting a BA in art history, and then I'll be off to med school," I say.

"That's cool. I'm just a lawyer guy. Not really artsy," he says, stating the obvious. His words just hang there. I let them. The allure of his green eyes fails to hide what's missing underneath. I hate eye contact. But I stare. At his eyes. Eyes are like kaleidoscopes—everyone's soul spins in its own shape. Some more complex than others. Austin isn't complex. He's a handsome, nice, shallow guy. There's no intricate arrangement here. No rainbows. Just the most basic design. As he inches closer, the space between us shifts subtly. His muscular thigh presses against mine, the fabric of his dark denim forming a flimsy barrier between us. His leg feels hot, feverish, even through his jeans. "You're fascinating." His tongue flicks across his lips. I notice because I always look at people's mouths when they talk. "And your eyes—so cat-like," he adds, whispering.

"Thanks," I say, shifting my eyes to the screen. He's closer now. I can feel the heat of his breath on my neck as his arm wraps around my waist. We lock eyes for a second. His hand lands on my thigh. Warm, like the rest of him. It startles me. And then I notice. The unsettling...tiny piece of dirt under one of his fingernails. Beer from O'Callaghan's bubbles up to my throat. I disengage from his hold.

"Excuse me..." Quick. Icy lake gaze. "I have to use a bathroom." And my boots thud along the floor, breaking up the soft notes of Sade coming from Mark's bedroom.

I curl up on the bathroom floor, knees to chest, back against the cold wall. A strange kind of solace. My eyes close. A gentle sway carries me into the comfort of my thoughts.

I drift, letting my thoughts rock me. I'm a boat on the water, I tell myself. My mind slips to the MySpace artist—his inked back to the lens, standing before vast, aching horizons.

Each photo felt like a page from a silently screaming journal. A soul's quest mapped across the canvas of the world. His hands collecting memories like art pieces. A knock—more a bang than a tap—pulls me back.

"Lena?" Anya's voice cuts through the door.

"She's been in there, like, twenty minutes." Austin's voice follows, tinged with annoyance.

"Are you okay?" Anya's voice softens. I unlock the door. She slips inside and shuts it fast behind her.

She looks at me, eyes searching. "What happened?"

I have no answer.

"Nothing. I just... I want to go home." My voice is small, folded into the discomfort of the moment.

"Ok. Let's go." She scoops me up.

"Thanks." I hug her.

"You're weird as fuck, but I love you," she says.

"I know." Our hug grows tighter.

As we leave, Mark is frozen. Austin stares at the floor. Both open-mouthed. Neither will meet my eyes.

As she shuts the door, she whispers, "Caribou tomorrow, okay?"

I nod, silent, as the taxi glides into motion. Downtown shimmers on the water off Lake Shore Drive. The skyline ripples across the lake. Distorted yet beautiful. Weird. Just like me. Anya's silhouette disappears into the lit entrance of Mark's apartment building as I release a breath I had been holding for too long.

The hush of Mom's house wraps around me as I ease through the door. The kitchen glows with the soft under-cabinet light—she's awake. She's in her usual spot by the porch door, left slightly ajar. Her cigarette smoke does a slow waltz in the dim light.

"Couldn't sleep," she says, like it's news. Her weary smile carries both resignation and welcome. I slump onto a barstool across from her, the weight of the night distilled into a single, eloquent, "Eh."

Mom raises an eyebrow—her silent way of asking for the story behind that sound.

"Anya's boyfriend brought Austin," I say, tracing the rim of the island, eyes fixed anywhere but hers. Still, I catch the twitch of a smile as she exhales a slow stream of smoke.

"Oh, the lawyer guy," Mom says—sleepy voice, but that flicker of excitement gives her away. I know Austin ticks every box in her head.

"Yeah. The one I don't feel any spark with," I say, head in my hands, eyes drifting to the moonlit night beyond the porch. My fingers brush the screen of my laptop, still sitting on the counter where I left it.

"You're thinking about that MySpace artist," she says. Her intuition, as usual, cuts right through me.

"How do you know?" I lock eyes with her.

"I'm a witch. I always know." The puffs of smoke do make her look a bit witchy as she says this. "Mystical MySpace Man," she says. Her accent lands on every wrong syllable. I smile, just slightly. A flutter rises in my stomach, warmth spilling into my cheeks at the mention of the Mystical MySpace Man.

"Lena Grace." She only says my full name when things are about to get serious. "Life's not always about sparks," she says. "Look at me—worrying about bills, taxes, the mortgage. This isn't Poland. In America, we live to work. It never ends. Work, stress, sleep, repeat...until you die." She rubs her temples like she's trying to erase the thought.

"I get it, Mom," I say, though part of me is still resisting her bleakness. I stare out into the night. Somehow, the darkness feels less suffocating than the future she just mapped out.

"This Austin...he seems like a good catch. Maybe give it a chance?"

"I just... I don't know, Mom. It didn't feel right," I mutter. My voice knots in my throat. My shoulders tense—caught between her expectations and my own doubt. She sighs and stubs out her cigarette. The gesture says what she doesn't. She's resigned to everything. Fuck it.

"Honey, you're divorced and twenty-seven. Sometimes you need to see beyond those sparks. You've been through enough—don't make another mistake." Her words hang there. Love, wisdom, motherly concern. All of it.

Yet, my mind keeps drifting. Back to the MySpace artist. Back to the soulful photographs that speak beyond words. Connection that feels real, even through the screen. How do you explain that your heart feels tethered to someone you've never met? But I'm stuck in some digital delusion? Maybe I'm stuck in some digital delusion. After a long pause, I lean forward as she lights another cigarette.

"Maybe you're right, Mom." I nod.

"I am," she says, inhaling deep. The cigarette tip flares orange. "Austin might be just what you need."

I toss and turn all night, restless. Dreaming of the MySpace artist's face. In my dreams, his features are clear. Strange, how that contrasts with the mystery he leaves online. By morning, I'm a mess. Sweaty. Tired. And more lost than ever, despite what Mom said. Later, back in my usual seat at Caribou—indented perfectly to me—I cradle a white mocha for comfort. I scroll through his page, searching for...I don't even know what. Proof for Mom that she's wrong? Austin's dirty fingernail invades my mind. What the fuck? I shake my head to erase it as the door swings open. Anya finds me in seconds. She slides into the seat across from me, urgent concern all over her face.

"What the hell was that with Austin last night?" she demands, her bag thudding on the table, her gaze piercing mine for answers. I just stare.

"You literally traumatized the guy."

I exhale and cover my forehead, shielding my eyes from her look. "I fucked up, I know." My voice cracks with regret. My pulse picks up. My cringe-worthy exit replays like a blooper reel.

"Girl!" Anya slaps her own forehead.

"It's not like I'm not trying, you know? It's just...you've both been pushing Austin onto me for months. He's got everything—looks, brains, money, a hot career. Mr. Perfect on paper."

"Exactly. Thank you." She throws her hands up, emphasizing her point.

"But there's just no spark for me. It's like running into a wall every time I try to feel something."

"Woman, what's wrong with you?" Anya shakes her head, baffled.

"He had a piece of dirt under his nails," I whisper.

"For fuck's sake." Her face disappears into her hands. A long sigh follows before she looks up at me again.

"Why am I like this?" My voice is on the verge of tears. The question just hangs. Neither of us has an answer.

"Look, I get the whole mystery artist from MySpace, but you need a reality check."

"You sound just like my mom," I mumble, peeking at her through my fingers. She gently takes my hands.

"And she's not wrong," Anya asserts, squeezing my fingers as if to anchor me back to her version of reality. "Austin's a good friend of Mark's. We could hang out together," she says, trying to make it all sound easier. I manage a smile. More like a grimace. The absurdity hits me—comparing life with Austin to a man I've only known through a screen.

"You can't get over this faceless MySpace artist, can you?" she says.

A light chuckle escapes me. More a reflex than a response. I shrug off her rhetorical question. Anya's curiosity takes over, and she flips my laptop around.

"What's his name?" she inquires, her fingers poised on the trackpad.

"Phoenix," I say. A flutter rises in my stomach just from the name. "Even his name carries a hint of magic." A warmth spreads through me as I say it. Anya's brow furrows as she scrolls, looking for anything to feed her skepticism.

"A wild artist from LA? 'Fill your vessel'—sure, it's poetic. But can he offer anything real?" Her voice carries the same seeds of doubt my mom planted in my mind last night. Her question hangs unanswered as she scrutinizes Phoenix's profile, adding with suspicion, "He doesn't even show his face."

"He's faceless on purpose. It's about his art, the message... not his ego," I say, fierce despite her doubts.

"I bet he's just ugly," she muses, raising an eyebrow, a playful challenge in her voice. Suddenly, her hand shoots to her mouth, a gasp locked behind it.

"Holy shit," slips through her mouth. Her shock is written across her face as she bounces her gaze from me to the screen.

"What is it?" I lean in.

"Oh girl, wow!" Anya's head bobs in disbelief.

"What?" I nearly launch across the table trying to get a peek.

"He's not ugly, that's for sure," she says, her eyes scanning the image. "And no longer faceless." She turns the laptop slowly toward me.

The image hits me with such force that I reel back. My gasp is swallowed by silence. For a moment, my palms press against my eyes. Then I stare at him. Captured in pixels. His eyes. The kaleidoscope. "Fuck," escapes me in a whisper—a shockwave rippling through me.

Phoenix is rising from crystal blue water. Droplets trail down his chiseled jawline. A caption reads: "speaking in dead languages..." His dark brows frame the intense gaze of fiery brown eyes. A stare so penetrating it seems to reach out from the screen, demanding attention, commanding presence. Now, FIREneedsAIR makes perfect sense. I look at Anya and whisper, more to myself than her, "Walnut eyes."

FOLLOWING DOTS...

"Do you quiet your soul's yearning for safety?"

I stare at the screen, my heartbeat echoing in my ears. Each second elongates like a shadow stretched by the setting sun. My mind races. Through his eyes, I travel—every place he's seen, every moment he's captured. It all pulses through me, breathing life into pixels. I'm pulled into his mystical orbit. Impossible to leave. The gravity's too strong. I draw the laptop closer, as if shrinking the space between us might make the connection real.

"I need to be the first to comment," I whisper. It's our unspoken ritual—he always leaves the first trace beneath my photos. A digital dance. Our connection. Anya leans in, eyes sparkling. Her smile gives away an excitement neither of us fully understand. I tap fast. The words tumble out. They've been simmering inside me, just waiting for this moment. I hit send and turn to Anya, scanning her face for a reaction.

She studies me with a look of complete bewilderment.

"'The heart on fire,'" she reads over my shoulder. Sarcasm drips from every syllable. "Really?" She rolls her eyes.

"It's our language," I say, mostly to myself. A smile touches my lips. "He'll understand. His heart shows in his eyes." I lock eyes with her, toying with the cord of my iPod. I whisper, "Fire needs air."

"You're an absolute original." She shakes her head, giggling. A loud pop pings from the screen.

"Oh shit! I just got a message," I say. "It's from him."

Anya leans closer, her wide eyes glowing in the screen light. My fingers move across the track pad. I hope she can't see how much they're shaking.

Phoenix writes: **Lena, if it is not too intrusive, may i ask what you think of my art? flight—phoenix.** A wave in my chest hits. Like I'm on top of a rollercoaster.

Anya's eyes pop. "Everything's lowercase except your name. Who is this guy?"

I shrug. She shoulders me playfully. "Some wild artist?"

mesmerizing, I reply, keeping my response lowercase to echo his informal style. My cheeks burn. I keep hitting refresh. Over and over again. Anya leans back, theatrically slapping her forehead. "Girl, you're so gone."

A pop. Another message. :)

She leans to see what it says.

"That's it? A smiley face? He's a minimalist, I guess."

"You don't get it. A smiley can say a thousand things," I say, imagining him at his computer. Far away. Connecting my soul.

Just a couple of strokes on the keyboard. Just a little smiley face. But my heart's doing gymnastics.

Anya's laughter breaks the tension. "At this rate, you'll both still be flirting into your sixties." She winks.

Another message from Phoenix flickers onto the screen, brief and to the point: **what's your number?**

Without missing a beat, I reply: **19.**

Anya's reaction is immediate. Her booming cackle turns all the heads in the coffee shop. We even earn a stink-eye from the lady across the table, startled out of her thick fantasy book.

"What?" I shrug.

Phoenix's next message pops up, just: **lol.** Anya giggles, pointing to the message as if it is her answer too.

"He meant your phone number, not your lucky number, silly," she says.

I bury my face in my hands. "I'm such a dumbass."

"Just a tiny bit." She laughs.

A message from Phoenix, with his phone number, flashes on the screen.

Before I can react, Anya grabs my laptop, declaring, "Give me this." She swiftly types in my number and hits Send, sealing the deal faster than my flushed face can protest. My phone rings with Phoenix's number immediately, each trill amplifying the heat in my cheeks. Hesitating only a moment, I send the call to voicemail. It's not so much shyness but the strangeness of talking on the phone with someone I haven't met in person. Anya waves her hand dismissively with a chuckle, her head bobbing in amusement.

"You're such a dork," she says, hugging me. "But I freaking love you. You're gonna drive this guy crazy."

"Love you too," I murmur back, glancing at the clock. "Gotta go to work." I shut the laptop screen. Phoenix locked underneath. The poetry I can't wait to revisit later.

"See you later!" she yells as I rush out—almost getting my backpack caught in the door. Always so clumsy.

As I drive to Visage, "Sound in a Dark Room" by Telefon Tel Aviv pulses through the speakers. Each beat brushes against my skin, leaving goosebumps—like what I imagine Phoenix's touch would feel like. It's as if our yearnings are synced, flickering between distant cities. I feel this strange, otherworldly tether to him. Is it odd? Or just me? Somehow, it feels like he holds the answers to the puzzles in my heart.

I glance out of the window. The passing scenery blurs time with the familiar rhythm of these drives. The cool, crisp air of March has melted into the sticky warmth of summer. The shift almost startles me. Funny how time slips by when you're not watching. The road to Visage is still the same. The same rhythm. The same song. Sometimes sameness feels like comfort. Predictable. Safe. I still imagine Phoenix's touch. Still feel the pull. Months have passed, yet everything feels unchanged—except the world outside my window.

At Visage, I take my place behind the bar. Luc greets me with his usual kiss on the cheek. I try to mask my nerves, glancing down as my phone buzzes with a new message:

i tried calling you, but it went to vm.

I type fast: **Sorry. Hearing your voice over the phone would feel surreal. I'll wait until we meet in person.**

As I set up my bar station, chipping at ice blocks with the shaker, my thoughts drift to his voice—the voice I've never heard. What does it sound like?

Through Visage's house beats and flashing lights, I try to imagine it. Hear it.

Something rich. Soulful. Intense—like the gaze I've memorized from his photo.

I picture his voice weaving through the noise, threading between the beats like silk. Warm. Enigmatic. A voice that lives in the quiet spaces between words.

Hypnotized by the music, the lights, and the swirls of my own imagination, I spend the night mixing drinks with a perma-grin plastered on my face.

"What's his name? You've been smiling at your phone all night," Luc teases, shaking his cocktail tin like a maraca.

"Phoenix," I say, my voice dipped in daydream.

"If he makes our Lena this happy, I'm all for this Phoenix dude." He elbows me playfully.

My smile stretches even wider when I spot Anya weaving through the crowd toward my side of the bar.

Right then, my phone lights up.

I snatch it off the bar and lean toward her. She clocks the way I move—her eyes ping-ponging between my phone and my face. She knows.

"What did he say?" she asks, brow arched.

I flip the screen open. My eyes flit across each word. Then—

My hand flies to my mouth. A gasp escapes.

Anya, caught somewhere between panic and glee, grabs my Motorola.

"Shut up!" she yells.

The phone slips and clatters against the bar top. Anya's eyes practically pop as she shoves her bangs back with both hands.

Luc freezes mid-shake and leans over, gossip antenna fully extended.

On the screen:

i'm coming to chicago to see you. how's next wednesday?

Luc lets out a low whistle. "This Phoenix—" he says, pausing dramatically, then flashes me a wink and a thumbs up before the shaker resumes its maraca rhythm.

Anya pulls me closer, her hand cupping my ear so her words cut through the nightclub's chaos.

"Wow. Maybe you're right about this Phoenix. Let's see if he actually shows up—or if he's just full of shit."

She steps back, scanning my face for a reaction. But I'm lost in a smile, basking in the glow of the moment, my imagination already tracing the outlines of what might be.

Visage's hypnotic lights blur, and the music softens, signaling the end of the night. I tally my tips, fingers moving through bills with half a mind.

Out of the shadows by the bar, Alex steps into view. The bouncer turned photographer. The one who captured me as Magician—the girl who now stares at Phoenix from a MySpace profile picture.

"Lena, we're still on for tomorrow at noon?"

"Yes," I say, excitement flickering through me at the thought of creating something beautiful again.

"Great. Eva's off, so she's looking forward to doing your makeup. See you then."

He vanishes as quickly as he appeared.

Back home, finally alone in my bedroom at Mom's, I reread every text from Phoenix. I trace the shape of each letter, imagining the cadence of his voice. I study his photos again, tucking them beneath my eyelids like wishes. Hoping my dreams will know where to find him.

The next day, I'm at Alex's studio on the west side of Chicago, where summer sun pours through wide windows, the glare dancing across white floors. I always cherish shooting with Alex and his wife, Eva. Our sessions feel like an exploration of light, makeup, and unbridled artistry.

"Hold it," Alex calls from behind the lens, his focus as intense as mine. "That's it!" His voice bursts with quiet electricity. I hold the pose. He circles me slowly, searching for the angle. The shot. The moment stretches—held in focused silence, broken only by Ibiza-style house beats and the muted click of the shutter. The window light frames me like a spotlight. Out of the corner of my eye, I catch Eva. Her hands come together in a soft, appreciative clap—face glowing with quiet joy. "Now, turn your back to me—I love the tattoo," he says. Sunbeams play in my eyes as his camera clicks in rapid bursts. My bare back, etched with wings, tells its own story as I glance over my shoulder. A gaze past the lens into something unseen. Into Phoenix's eyes. I find them somewhere in the fiery sun.

"I love shooting with you. You make it about the art," I say to Alex, who moves fluidly around me, eyes scanning for the best angles.

"You're my muse. Ford loved our last shoot. Are you sure you don't want to sign with them?" he responds, a hint of pride in his voice.

"I'm okay. I'm heading to med school—this just tickles my creativity," I say, then add with a smile, "You're a great photographer. You let me be free in front of the camera."

I'd missed modeling—the process of creating visual stories. Shape-shifting. Light and mood. Alex is the only photographer who truly captures me—not the characters I've portrayed in the past, but the essence of who I am. Maybe it's because I feel liberated now. Years removed from Tomek's abuse and the boxed-in feeling that used to follow me everywhere. When I was with Tomek, I could never truly be myself in front of the camera, always shadowed by the fear of his jealousy and judgment. Now, I can fully stretch my wings. Now, every click of the camera, every burst of light, feels like shedding another layer of that old, confined self. In front of Alex's lens, I'm not just posing. I'm declaring my freedom. My rebirth. I'm ready to step into the light of the future. The light I once found blinding.

"Holy shit. I think we got it," Alex says, scrolling through his Canon, eyes locked on the shot we've just captured. I walk over, white tank clutched to my chest, and lean in to see the shot. Eva smiles, eyes wide. "Holy shit," she echoes. I stare at the image. "Wow. I look like a phoenix rising from the ashes." A strong woman gazing into the distance, wings inked across her back like a battle cry. Is this really me now? The new me? "I think this is one of the best shots I've ever taken," Alex murmurs, brushing his fingers over the camera. "The light catches your eyes just perfectly." Pride warms my cheeks. A flush of something electric spreads through me like wildfire. I feel like I could take flight. Then my back pocket vibrates. My Motorola lights up with a message from Phoenix: **i can't come on wednesday anymore, :(i have to work.** And just like that, the studio's charge drains. My smile fades. Alex and Eva clock the shift. I start explaining. The MySpace crush. The long-distance almost-love. Oversharing? Maybe. I don't care.

Another message. My heart stutters.

why don't you come to LA? it reads.

I yank the white tank over my head, hands shaking with a jolt of energy so strong I could teleport to LA right this second.

"He wants me to come to LA instead," I say, already reaching for my backpack. I turn to Alex and Eva, scanning their faces like they might give me permission to feel whatever this is.

"I'd go," Alex says without hesitation, tossing a hand in the air like it's obvious.

"He sure would—wouldn't be married to me otherwise." Eva laughs, eyes sparkling. I glance between them, hoping one of them will say something that makes the decision easier.

"Eva was in Miami when I flew down to meet her. Dating site stuff." Alex shrugs. "Fuck it. You only live once. You'll always wonder what could've been if you don't go."

The ride home is cradled in the rhythms of "Bloodstream" by Stateless, another LimeWire find I've been playing on repeat.

Windows down, I speed along I-290. Chicago's summer air brushes my face. Heavy, humid, like the breath of change I already feel coming. I've never been bungee jumping, but this must be what it feels like. The heart-stopping pause before the leap. The wonder if the line will hold. Phoenix's message loops in my mind as I trace every possible future it opens.

Parked in Mom's driveway, my fingers hover over Anya's name—hesitating, uncertain. She's going to think I've completely lost my mind.

"Anya," I whisper, my voice a tightrope between hope and doubt. "Phoenix can't make it." My vision tilts, the familiar turning suddenly foreign.

"What happened?" Anya's voice slices through the spinning in my head. "Phoenix can't come," I repeat, tracing the grooves of the steering wheel. Calming comfort of repetition. But before I'm submerged in my own sea of thoughts, Anya cuts in: "I fucking knew it. I knew he was going to flake."

"But he asked me to come to LA," I blurt. I start flipping the air vent open and closed—one of those dumb soothing rituals. No one can see me do it, so I keep going. Anya's silence stretches on.

She exhales the kind of breath that makes space for truth.

"Lena, you're wild, you know that? Flying off to LA to meet someone you've never seen outside of a computer screen." There's a pause, and I brace for the blow of her skepticism. Then she surprises me.

"But maybe the real magic happens outside our comfort zones." Her words stir something in me—something Grandpa once said. A flicker of boldness sparks inside.

"I really feel I need to go. So I'll never wonder what could have been."

"Yeah, life's too short for what-ifs," she says.

Night falls. I'm perched on my bed in the compact sanctuary of my room. Mom's clay angels line the window ledge. The moon peers through the blinds, bathing the room in a soft, ghostly glow. Anya's words loop in my head like a stuck refrain, nudging me back to Phoenix's MySpace. Even though I know it by heart, I comb through his photos, captions, and comments—catching every subtle nuance, every hidden layer. In his deliberateness, I see a reflection of myself. Nothing is left to chance. "Bloodstream" by Stateless resonates through my headphones once more, streaming from my iPod shuffle. The piano's simplicity melts into the lyrics. So simple. Yet, it strikes with strange intensity. It's as though Phoenix himself is extending his presence through the melody, touching me from a distance. A shiver cascades from my ears down my spine. How is it possible to feel such a deep connection with someone you've never met? I set it as my profile song and change my bio to "following dots..." A nod to the journey I'm on. Unfinished. Always unfolding. With my eyes closed, the music spins my thoughts into vivid daydreams of Phoenix—making him feel realer than ever. As the final notes of the song fade, I open my eyes. Then, almost as if guided by an unseen force, my fingers glide across Expedia's website, securing a ticket to LA and a hotel room for Thursday.

I'm coming to LA Thursday :) I text. My heart hammers as I wait.

Then his reply flashes: !!! The three exclamation points pull a giggle from me, pure joy rising in my chest. Then another beep: **bloodstreams flowing in every direction.** He knows the song! It's ours now. His words glow on the screen. My heart feels like it could break out of my chest and run to him. What will he do when he sees me? A hug? A smile? Will he know me the way I already know him? I can already feel his heartbeat against mine. Maybe it already happened? Maybe we've already happened? Clutching my pillow, I rock gently, burying a silent scream in its softness.

MAGIC DAY

"Our restless hearts roam, like kites caught in the summer wind."

Thursday morning cracks open at O'Hare, pulsing with the rush of hurried souls weaving through its endless veins. I sit, shivering on a plastic bench that knows no warmth, my eyes pulled to the departures board like a magnet. Each blink of the screen bumps my flight to LAX a little closer to the top. The melodies and lyrics from my FIREneedsAIR playlist seep through my headphones. Each note nudges me deeper into this wild life leap I'm chasing. My heart doesn't race—it performs a ballet on the edge of something that feels like prophecy. It feels like I've tumbled into a movie—me, boarding a plane to LA to chase a connection I've only known through a screen. A man I met online. How fucking crazy. Is this real? Flying across the country to meet a man whose voice I've never even heard? My phone buzzes. Phoenix's message lights up on my phone:

i see you…but i haven't met you yet.

A warmth sparks low in my belly—slow, smoldering, like a charcoal fire. It sends a ripple through me so strong, even the freshly waxed hairs on my legs want to rise. **i feel you…but we haven't happened yet**, I type back, my fingers caressing the Motorola's keypad. A tactile contradiction to the flutter in my chest. Then his reply: **!!!**. I know exactly what it means. Our language. I laugh. It's a laughter that dances between thrill and fear—perched on the edge of the complete unknown.

Hypnotized by the unfolding poetry on my phone screen, I reach out to the only other voice that could possibly ground me in this whirlwind of emotion—other than Phoenix's.

"Hello?" His voice—soft, earthy—wraps around me like my Parisian sleeping bag once did. "Hi, Grandpa." I smile into the phone.

"My flower!" His voice beams back. As we slip into our usual rhythm—his gentle check-ins and the jokes that never fail to light me up—I tell him everything about Phoenix. Pour my whole heart out. Because if anyone could understand this kind of soul-deep connection, it's my artistic grandpa.

"So I'm here at the airport, about to fly to LA, and my heart…it feels like it might burst out of my chest before I even board," I confess, breath hitching. "That's good," Grandpa says. "That fluttering, that storm inside—it's the sign you're exactly where you need to be." His voice is a balm, softening the frantic edge of my heart.

"But what if I'm wrong again, Grandpa? What if this is another mistake?"

"You can't make a mistake if you follow your heart. It's the only compass that won't steer you wrong."

I pause, letting his words settle. His wisdom always hits hard. Lands right where I'll feel it most.

"You're right," I murmur. "Last time, I overthought everything to death. And it got me nowhere." The words float between us. More for me than for him. Reassurance, not a question.

"Let me tell you a story," he says. "Your grandma—she wasn't just smart, she was stunning. The most beautiful woman I have ever seen. Long blond hair. Eyes like summer sky. Heads turned when she walked into a room. And me? Just a village boy with big dreams and an artsy soul. She could've had doctors, lawyers, politicians—men with plans and money. But she chose me. A penniless, wild-hearted Mazowsze dancer with a sketchpad."

"You're one of a kind, Dziadziu. She knew it. Obviously."

"Well, we almost didn't make it to 'I do.' I rode my motorcycle thirty miles through a downpour. Showed up two hours late, soaked to the bone. She was still at the altar. People were whispering how awful I must be. I thought for sure she'd walk out."

"No way," I gasp, fully caught in the story now.

"Oh, yes. I'd ride through every storm to marry her again. She was my lover, my best friend—my everything." He pauses. I feel the ache in his voice. The space she left behind.

"That's the kind of love I want," I whisper.

"And you'll find it," he says softly. "Just keep following your heart—it knows the way." His voice settles over me like a spell.

"I love you so much, my wise old wizard," I whisper, my voice thick with emotion.

"Love you too, my little flower. Now go," he says. "Turn your reality into something better than your dreams."

As he hangs up, the airport PA crackles to life: "Good morning, ladies and gentlemen, we are now boarding American Airlines flight 7723 to LAX." I rise, clutching my backpack and a small carry-on—just enough for one night in LA. Despite my usual love of all things grungy, it holds a dress with a daring décolletage. Anya insisted I bring it. Said I should look sexy. I chuckle, stepping into the boarding line, a familiar mantra from Bjork's song looping in my mind. It becomes the beat beneath this leap I'm about to take—a dive from the skies into something vast and unknowable. As the line inches forward, a whisper surfaces: Will I fall...or will Phoenix be there to catch me?

Hours later, I rest my head against the cool acrylic window of seat 19A. Of course it had to be nineteen. I smile at the boarding pass in my hand—another artefact I'll have to save. Below, LA stretches wide beneath the sun, the coastline opening its arms as we begin our descent. The city unspools in a vast, glittering grid. Dreams stitched into its seams. I've heard artists come here to chase fame. A bit of magic also. And everything is bordered by the mountains. They remind me of the Bieszczady Mountains. I feel it here too—that same quiet magic. The same ancient hum I followed through the misty Polish peaks with my dad and Grandpa.

"You may now use your electronic devices." The announcement echoes through the cabin as we taxi to the gate. My phone immediately comes to life with the beeping of message notifications. Anya's message pops up first: **I hope he's not a serial killer.** I laugh under my breath.

Then Phoenix: **in my dream, we touch beyond flesh…a reality that hasn't happened yet.** His words bloom in my chest like Grandpa's pansies.

The terminal doors slide open to a wave of California heat. Palm trees line the road like sentinels, tall and welcoming. I've actually never seen one in real life. My destination is a charming boutique hotel called Le Petit. It's tucked-away in the heart of West Hollywood, at the corner of Larrabee and Cynthia, just steps away from the famous Viper room and Book Soup. Lush greenery greets me at the entrance. Bursts of fuchsia flowers. Its hidden charm reminds me of Kraków. Of winding alleyways and Grandpa's flowery balcony. And I hear the whispers of his wisdom. "The heart knows," I murmur, tugging my carry-on up the short staircase. My heart races, reminding me that it knows—without question.

"I'm so sorry, miss, but your room isn't ready yet. It'll be about an hour," the receptionist says, her smile wide and sunny. The classic California apology.

"Oh no, I need to shower—I have a meeting at one," I say, a hint of panic creeping in. My skin feels sticky from the flight, like it's wearing every hour of travel.

"That's in thirty minutes. You're welcome to use the gym showers if you'd like," she says, flashing that California smile again.

And so I end up in the gym shower—only to discover my hair gel has staged a full-blown mutiny, spilling all over the sexy dress Anya insisted I pack. Now a useless casualty of travel.

Laughter bubbles up. Looks like ripped jeans and a tee will be my armor today. With no gel to tame my pixie cut, I throw on a military green skull cap instead. Facing the mirror, I declare, "Fuck it. Love what you don't see." A message to Phoenix, sure—but mostly to myself. I seal it off with a cheeky wink to my reflection.

My pocket buzzes. Message from Phoenix: **almost there.**

I'm waiting outside, I type back, my fingertips lightly brushing the keyboard. Then I dash to drop my bag with the front desk. Phone, ID, credit card in my back pockets. That's it. I step outside, the CD—my Phoenix mix—spinning on my index finger. I wander a few steps from Le Petit and sink onto the curb. The concrete radiates warmth through my jeans, unexpectedly grounding. The CD catches beams of August sun, casting rainbows across my white sneakers. A disco-ball distraction from the nerves rising in my gut. From which direction will he come? The thought of him just driving up and motioning for me to hop in, like some budget action flick, makes panic skitter through me. Absolutely not. If that happens, I'm sprinting straight back to the hotel. No way any romance involving me starts like that.

Lost in a river of thoughts, I'm blinded by the holographic shimmer spinning off the CD. I close my eyes and inhale the summer breeze, rich with the musky scent of wax leaf privets. The breath of a new life. Sun on my skin. I open my eyes. Lift my gaze. Something turns me left—just as Phoenix rounds the corner.

Everything slows. Like a scene in a music video.

His tall, dancer-like frame pauses the moment our eyes lock. Then a wide smile breaks across his face as he strides toward me. He looks just like his MySpace photo—but in person, there's a heartbreaker charm glowing in that smile.

"Shit," I mutter, stunned. Time seems to stretch. I stand frozen, facing him. Excitement and nervousness pin me in place. But inside, there's no stillness. I'm bubbling with giggles. He's a mirror image of me: torn slouchy jeans, a skull baseball hat, and white sneakers. His airy white shirt flares open at the top, sheer enough to trace the edges of his tattoos—deliberately unbuttoned to reveal his sculpted chest. A black-and-red beaded necklace sways gently with each step he takes. A rhythm my heart echoes without permission. With no words—still strangers to each other's voices—he pulls me into a hug. My cheek finds the curve of his neck, and I melt into his soft, fragrant skin. He smells sweet and tangy. Like happiness itself. We're falling into each other. Fusing like pieces of molten lava. Hearts ignited with something I feel deeply but can't quite name. A twin flame, maybe. I close my eyes. His hands rest warm at my waist. Nothing feels awkward. He's not a stranger. My body and soul already know this touch. The world spins as we stand still. Two long-lost puzzle pieces finally snapping into place.

"I held you before," he whispers. His voice, smooth like velvet. I don't know if it's the words or how he says them, but a waterfall of goosebumps cascades across my skin. I look into his fiery walnut eyes. We speak without words. He cups my face. Gently. No words needed.

"Humans think time is linear," he says. "But past, present, and future—they're all happening at once. Most people are just stuck in one dimension. Never feeling…this." His breath warms my lips.

My answer is a soft smile and a silent prayer to the universe that this moment never ends. I get lost in his gaze—the only eye contact I've ever experienced that doesn't feel like an intrusion. He pulls me close again. I'm weightless. A helium-filled balloon. His lips graze my neck, accidental and electric. We fold into each other once more.

"Shit," he whispers—not a curse, but a revelation. After what feels like an eternity—our souls tumbling through time and dimensions on this quiet LA street—he gently pulls away, still cradling the small of my back. He raises an eyebrow, mischief blooming behind his eyes.

"So…I was thinking I could take you around LA. We could join my friends at a mansion party, or…" He pauses, narrowing his eyes. "…we could go have a magic day."

I laugh. "What kind of question is that? Of course a magic day."

His eyes shimmer, betraying exactly what he was hoping I'd say. Walnut eyes. His thoughts sparkle out of them like sunlight skipping across ocean waves.

He takes my hand, his fingers wrapping around mine as if they've always belonged there, and leads me around the corner to where his car is parked. "Magic day it is," he murmurs, opening the door and nodding for me to get in. Phoenix's beat-up Honda, which has probably seen more decades than I have, has a charming crack across its front window. I laugh to myself, thinking how much my grandpa would appreciate this free-spirited soul who is unbothered by impressing me with material things. Despite its rusty shell, the car smells like citrus and is spotless. As he turns the key, Phoenix glances at me.

"Your voice...it sounds like Björk's," he says.

"And yours is exactly how I imagined," I say, grinning as I hand him the CD. "This is for you."

He slips it into the CD player, his smile spreading. "Music is my favorite gift," he says, reaching into the backseat. As "The Kiss" from The Last of the Mohicans begins to play, he freezes, locking eyes with me.

"No way," he says, eyes wide as he hands me a CD of his own. "Guess the first track."

"Way." I laugh at the synchronicity.

We glide in comfortable silence along Pacific Coast Highway, ocean breeze threading between us through the open windows. My hand rests in his. His thumb draws gentle patterns on my skin. My gaze shifts between the line of his jaw, silhouetted against the ocean, and the mountains unfolding on the other side. He's as magical as California itself. And somehow, I feel like a traveler who's finally come home.

Every so often, as we twist through mountain roads, Phoenix's arm stretches protectively across my body—like he doesn't trust the seatbelt to do its job. Our first stop is Solvang—a whimsical, Dutch-inspired village to the north. Roaming its cobbled streets hand in hand with Phoenix, I feel untethered from reality. We search for the perfect pastry shop. His hand never leaves my waist. Every time we pass a bakery or cafe we say, "Next one," reluctant to break our connection for even a moment. Eventually, a street that seems to go nowhere delivers us straight to a bakery door. A delicious aroma of freshly baked pastries greets us as we step inside.

"We made it after all," Phoenix says.

I laugh. Somehow, it feels like he meant more than just directions. Outside, munching on a huge raspberry pastry and licking our fingers, we get lost in a moment, conversing about fate.

"So...last year I was trapped in a war in Lebanon. With my best friend, Danny," he says.

I remember the MySpace photo. Bombed building. Smoke. I hadn't understood the weight of it until now.

"I managed to get out in one piece, thankfully," he says. But the words land heavier than they sound.

I watch him—his eyes not quite on me, like he's still half-inhabiting that warzone.

Something in my chest twists. My heart spins, not wildly, but slow, measured. Like it's being cradled in the palm of his vulnerability.

"And now you're here," I say, tucking a flaky edge of raspberry pastry into my cheek. "Everything happens for a reason." My hand covers my mouth like the truth might be too naked without it.

"I was in an abusive marriage," I add quietly. "But I got out."

I look at him, throat tight. "We're all refugees, aren't we?"

"We sure are," he says. His voice dips low, rich with understanding. "You're right...everything does happen for a reason." His gaze doesn't flinch. It holds me. Like he's reading every word I haven't spoken.

"Yup." I nod repeatedly, chewing on the pastry. My mouth is dry.

"It's like...even our traumas wanted to meet," he says with a soft chuckle.

Our eyes lock. Emotional landscapes across timelines. Across wounds. Across the parts of ourselves we've kept tucked away. And in that silence, something settles.

"Maybe we're ready now," I whisper, gazing into his eyes. "To carry the lessons. Even the ones that nearly crushed us."

His arms wrap around me. And only then—in that moment—I realize I've been holding the pastry in my mouth this whole time. I finally swallow.

"We are ready," he murmurs. And I believe him.

We drive farther north to Pismo Beach, a coastal town nestled in the Pacific's embrace, and arrive just in time for sunset. We sit on a weathered bench as Phoenix lifts his Sony camera and captures not just me, but the whole moment. My green eyes are a fragment tucked into the corner, the rugged coastline stretching behind me, birds taking flight in the background. Countless people have photographed me before. But this feels like the first time someone captured my soul. No makeup. No posing. Just me. The Lena I am inside. Silhouetted by the setting sun, Phoenix leans in, our eyes swirling in the space between us. His lips brush against mine, and we drift into a kiss. Ocean birds cry overhead as our lips meet. Sparks shoot through every nerve ending, every place that's ever ached to be seen. Flashes of passion—and maybe the thirst for this kind of connection finally quenched—spread through my body.

"Wow...that was like fireworks I didn't see coming," he whispers, lips still brushing mine.

"Same," I manage. Someone pinch me. This can't be real. Our lips find each other again, hungry for a Dostoyevsky kind of love—mystical, desperate, sacred. Tongues weave. Souls dance. Goosebumps rise. The kind of kiss you only read about in the old books. Phoenix is the only witness to how real this feels. He gently removes my hat, his fingers brushing over my pixie cut.

"I love your short hair...it's so sexy," he murmurs, his gaze lighting more fires inside the one already burning.

"Am I in a dream?" I whisper against his lips, as the breeze sends a ripple over my skin.

"No, you're awake," he says. His forehead presses firmly against mine. "We're both awake."

Our gazes lock, charged with an energy that connects every electron between us. A chemical reaction that feels greater than life itself.

"I feel like you're filling the hole someone punched in my heart," I whisper. Lost in his eyes. Lost in the moment that one day will flash when I die.

"You're flowing in me," he murmurs. "You're my air." His lips curve into a smile against mine. He folds me in tighter. I feel like I'm expanding. Like the light is bursting from within us. Past, present, and future. Us happening all at once.

"Do you think it's luck, or God?" I ponder, marveling at how our paths have intertwined.

"Luck is God," Phoenix replies.

The horizon swallows the orange sun as we carry the scent of the Pacific back into Phoenix's citrusy Honda.

"Ready for more magic, my magician?" he asks as we speed north.

"Bring it on," I say, smiling as my hand weaves scoops of soft air through the open window. Night wraps around us as we turn into a woodsy grove, greeted by a sign that reads: Sycamore Mineral Springs.

"Wait here a second," Phoenix says, mischief dancing in the corner of his mouth.

He grabs his wallet and vanishes into the glow of a cream-colored building, across from what looks like a boutique hotel. While I wait, I check my phone—Anya's blown it up.

Girl, are you alive???

I laugh, typing back: **OMG! I can't wait to tell you everything. Feels like I'm living in a dream.**

Even just imagining her reaction—the wide eyes, the squeals—she will not believe any of this when we sit down for coffee tomorrow. Moments later, Phoenix reappears, holding the door open, with a grin and a nod.

That's when I see the white towels tucked under his arm. He retrieves a black leather backpack from the trunk, which clunks loudly as he closes it.

"You're gonna love this," he says, slipping his warm hand into mine.

He leads me up a mountain path lined with dark wood steps, tiny lamps casting soft pools of light into the pitch black. The sleeping forest around us is breathing so quietly. Occasional splashes of water and the thick scent of sulfur curling into the air add unexpected spice to the ambiance.

Phoenix's fingers tighten around mine as he pulls me aside, revealing a hidden entrance. A large hot tub, built into the wood, bubbles gently beneath ribbons of steam. The scent of sulfur rises, warm and earthy, clinging to the air like memory. Before I can catch up to the moment, Phoenix lays out towels on a wooden bench and pulls a small speaker from his bag.

"Bloodstream" begins to play from his iPod. I look over his shoulder and glimpse a playlist titled "Lena."

I freeze. My mind and heart light up like struck matches.

Then candles. He pulls them out one by one, lighting each until nineteen flicker surround us. Nineteen. Of course. My face burns, but the darkness does me a favor. I breathe deep, trying to ground myself. But then I look up. Phoenix is undressing. Completely. To the form in which God created him. The breath I've just taken lodges in my chest. He dives into the sulfurous water. The splash hides my loud gasp.

"Are you going to get in?" he teases, water dripping from his dark brows. He leans against the edge of the tub, looking up at me with a grin. Half invitation, half challenge. I stand motionless, like a mannequin.

A nervous giggle breaks out of me. I bite my lip and start unlacing my shoes. Phoenix leans in closer, hands stacked beneath his chin, eyes glinting with mischief. I peel off my socks and tuck them into my sneakers.

"You know," he says, "I thought to myself—there's gotta be something wrong with this girl. Maybe...ugly feet?"

His gaze lands on my red-polished toes. "But even your feet are gorgeous."

His humor slices through the tension, and I actually laugh. Genuine, no filter, laugh.

Then, like a child about to start a game of hide and seek, he covers his eyes with both hands and turns around. "I'm not looking."

Our laughter lingers around the steam as I peel off my jeans and tank top, stealing glances at his lean, strong back. Water trickles down the tattoo that runs his spine—I shiver just watching it.

The heat inside me rivals the tub. But I promise myself— he won't see all of me. Not tonight. I don't want him to think I'm "that" kind of girl. The bra and thong that don't match, stay on.

I'm hot and somehow still shivering as I lower myself into the water. He turns around and laughs.

"What?" I shrug, biting my lip again.

"You're adorable." He cups water in his palms and pours it over his shaved head. Candlelight dances off the ink on his biceps.

Before he even opens his eyes, my gaze traces the path of droplets on his skin—lips, neck, chest.

Then he looks at me. Flashlights and explosions. He floats toward me. Slow, smooth, like it takes no effort at all.

He licks a bead of sulfur water from his lips. And then— his hands find the small of my back.

He draws me closer. I'm a moon caught in the gravitational pull of his planet. And the water swirls around us, like it's reacting too.

His bare skin presses into mine—firmer, hotter than the steam. And in that moment, everything else stops existing. Only we exist now.

"So, your bio on MySpace says you're following dots," he whispers, his breath hot against my wet lips.

"Yes," I say. "Dots from the universe." A shiver runs through me, defiant against the heat.

He gently spins me around in the water, eyes locked on mine. Taking his time. Stretching the moment.

"Maybe this is one of your dots?" he says softly, gaze falling from my eyes to my lips. His fingers reach for a drop of water on my cheek, pausing there. Not just touching—feeling.

Tender. Present. Real. The candle flames flicker in the breeze. I close my eyes for a beat, breathing him in. Letting the moment etch itself into my memory, I whisper, "It is."

TAPESTRY OF LOVE

"Sometimes, you just have to leap and trust
the universe will catch you."

Our bodies intertwine like strands of silk.

Phoenix's hand grazes the lace edge of my thong, leaving a trail of goosebumps despite the heat rising from the sulfuric water.

My heart pounds as his lips brush mine—barely. The kind of almost-kiss that knows exactly what it's doing. He reaches for the faucet at the corner of the tub. The lone knob turns with a squeak. A sudden stream of cold water rushes in, slicing through the heat. A delicious chill sweeps across my thighs and stomach like ice on fevered skin. And I gasp.

"Do you prefer hot or cold?" Phoenix whispers, his mouth so close I can taste the words.

"Hot and cold," I reply, my fingers tracing the inked stories along his arms. His lips lock with mine. This time, the kiss isn't stolen. It's deliberate. Fire and ice. Like the water. A collision of senses.

When the cold creeps in too deep, Phoenix pulls back. But one hand stays firm at the small of my back while the other shuts off the flow. As he moves, the "carpe diem" tattoo on his inner arm comes into view.

"Seize the day, huh?" I trace the raised letters with my fingertip.

"Yes. Tomorrow is promised to no one," he says. Something flickers behind his eyes, dimming the usual spark. A war memory, maybe. Some wordless ghost. To soften the moment, I reach for his other arm and lift it gently into the candlelight.

"Can I see this one?"

Another fragment of him. Another story etched into his skin.

"Quod Me Nutrit, Me Destruit," I read aloud. "What nourishes me, destroys me," I translate, watching a flicker of surprise light up his eyes.

He squints, his thumb swiping gently across my lower lip as I say the last word.

"You know Latin?" he asks, the earlier shadow in his eyes lifting, replaced by curiosity. I glance at the swirls of steam rising from our bodies. The words of his tattoo echo inside me. I know what they mean. Being nourished by something that also breaks you. The thing you once thought was love. The past.

"I don't speak it," I say finally. "It's a dead language."

"Is it?"

"Well, no one speaks it anymore."

"You just did."

I side-eye him. A wet philosopher.

"You're right. There are no dead languages," I say, smirking. "Truth doesn't die. It speaks forever."

His fingers drift across my wing tattoo, dislodging drops of water that send a shiver in all directions.

"Yes. The truth lingers," he says. "Like ink. Like scars."

"Scars..." I echo. "Aren't we all just trying to cover them with tattoos?" I hold his gaze. He pulls me in.

"Scars," he whispers into my ear, "are just tattoos with even deeper stories."

For a moment, my mind slips. It drifts through all the old wounds—how they led me here, to his arms. I kiss the curve of his ear. He twirls me around, water splashing through the tunes from the speakers.

"The most beautiful stories come from the deepest pains," I say. The twirl pauses. Phoenix pulls back just enough to look at me. The candlelight catches in his eyes, turning his gaze molten.

"You're something else," he says, shaking his head with a grin that stretches ear to ear.

"That's what my best friend always says." I laugh as he plants kisses on my shoulder. The song ends.

"You hungry?" he asks.

"Starving," I say, realizing that raspberry pastry in Solvang was the only thing we've eaten all day.

He leans in, stealing a kiss from my lips. A kiss that's quick but suspended. Like a pressed flower caught in time. Then he leaps from the tub, playful and bare, steam rising off him into the night like smoke. He wraps a plush towel around his hips, and for a second, I wish he hadn't. For a second, I want to pull him right back in. He grabs another towel and drapes it over me, cocooning my shivering body in warmth. We dry off quickly, laughing at the chill, and pull our clothes back on.

Minutes later, we're in the hotel restaurant across the lot, the faint scent of sulfur still clinging to our skin.

At a quiet table in the corner, with a view of the mountain and the steaming springs, our stomachs growl in sync—loud, insistent. Like two starving wolves. And for the first time, I no longer feel that hunger. Not the kind that comes from the stomach, but the one that gnaws at the soul.

The contrast is almost cinematic. Around us, couples in designer clothes shimmer and sip wine like extras from *The Great Gatsby*. Meanwhile, Phoenix and I sit here—ripped jeans, skull caps, sulfur still clinging faintly to our skin. No makeup. No costume. I'm in damp clothes, sitting beside a man who hasn't let go of my hand since we walked in. And something about that—about all of this—feels like the truest freedom I've ever known. A kind of authentic me whom Tomek never touched. My soul feels like it's traveling and sitting still at the same time. I lock eyes with Phoenix. Am I the magician? Or is he?

"Hello, sir, miss," our waiter greets us—blond curls, tan skin, quintessential California surfer. He glances at me and adds, "You look beautiful, miss," and I flinch slightly, caught off guard.

A ghost memory from Paris flashes through me. But before I can sink, Phoenix's voice lifts me right out.

"Right? Isn't she just marvelous?" Phoenix says, proud and unbothered. "I'm the lucky one tonight." His voice doesn't have a trace of jealousy. Just joy. Ease. The kind of love that doesn't compete. Is this real life? A sigh I was holding turns into a giggle. It is real life. The waiter walks away with our order.

Phoenix's fiery walnut eyes lock with mine as his thumb drifts across the tattoo on my wrist.

"Your turn," he says. "What does this one mean?" His smile curves, a little crooked, like he's about to crack open a mystery just for the thrill of it.

"It's my lucky number. Nineteen."

He laughs—a sound so full and infectious it fills the air in our little corner. He leans closer, lowering his voice like he's sharing state secrets.

"You're fucking joking. Miss January second?" It hits me. My birthday. He's read my MySpace profile. And suddenly, I'm gasping.

"Stop it. When's your birthday?"

"July nineteenth."

"No. You're lying." I lean in. "Show me your ID." My pulse drums behind my eyes.

He lets go of my hand just long enough to pull out his wallet. Flips it open.

July 19, 1977. I stare at it, lips parted.

"You've got to be fucking kidding." I lean back, lip caught between my teeth, one hand rising instinctively to cover half my face—as if I need a shield from how unreal this feels. I'm grinning. Squinting. Half laughing. Half in shock.

We slip into his Honda just past midnight. Our stomachs are full of sea bass, mashed potatoes, and sautéed chard. The citrus scent still lingers—like he secretly swapped out the air freshener just before we got in.

As we drive back to LA, his hand clings to mine. He traces tiny hearts over my skin. Radiohead hums low through the speakers, the lyrics folding into the quiet like they were written for this exact stretch of highway. For this exact moment. For us.

"Shit," Phoenix says suddenly, a sheepish grin creeping in. "I spent all our gas money on the waiter's tip."

I glance at the dashboard—the fuel light is glowing red. We coast into a gas station, the car sighing into park.

"Don't worry." I flash my debit card from my back pocket. The absurdity of it makes us both laugh. And I remember Grandpa showing up to his own wedding two hours late, soaking wet. Phoenix is like that. Real. Immaculately honest.

Our lone headlights cut through the darkness, the road stretching ahead like ribbon. Radiohead plays on. A soundtrack narrating a story we haven't finished writing. Phoenix's hand finds mine again. His touch speaks a language I've never known but understand perfectly. And I want to know him. All of him.

Feeling braver—maybe because of the music, or the darkness—I let the silence open wider.

"Tell me about the war," I say softly. "I feel there's trauma in you...something that wants to break free."

For a moment, he glances at me. A quick sidelong look. Then he turns back to the road.

"I think our traumas might be trying to find each other," he says, gaze narrowing slightly.

I tighten my fingers around his. "Our traumas are the essence of who we become. I want to know yours."

My voice is quiet but certain. I trace circles on the back of his hand. Speaking his language. He looks at me and smiles. It's a sad smile. Then he takes a slow breath.

"Open the glove box," he says. "There's another gift...kind of."

The latch creaks open. I flick on my phone light. I find a small worn photo inside. A woman's face stares up at me. Distorted. Bruised. Wings have been drawn around her digitally. Like someone trying to sanctify what's broken. My fingers hover. My breath does too.

"Wow," I whisper, the breath catching in my throat.

"That's Rachel Corrie," Phoenix says, voice cracking a little. "She was trying to stop the demolition of a home in Palestine. No weapons—just a megaphone. Armed with nothing but a caring heart and words shouting for peace. A settler in a bulldozer drove over her. Crushed her until she couldn't scream anymore. She was trying to protect the home of a Palestinian doctor. And her killer walked free. No trial. No justice."

He pauses, his grip tightening on the wheel. "My friend Amina made this image. Gave her wings. Made her the angel she already was."

Tears well in my eyes.

"I know her story," I say, staring down at the photograph. "I remember just a blip on the news. They never cover these parts of the world."

And now it clicks. It's Rachel's last photo. The one her friends took after her death. A tear nearly lands on it before I catch it. Phoenix says nothing.

"Is this how the war felt?" I ask. The question slips out quiet, heavy. Knowing.

"Just like this," he says, eyes locked on the dark stretch of highway ahead. Maybe something darker still.

"Lost lives, lost love, everything lost," he adds.

"I'm sorry if I'm intruding," I say, uncertain if I've stepped too far into his shadows. "I hope the love you lost...will be found."

He turns toward me, and something in his face softens.

"Love lost just evolves," he says. The sorrow in his eyes softens into a small, quiet smile. He draws another heart on my thumb. There's no rush in his touch.

"I don't think true love can be lost," I whisper. It sounds more certain than I expected. I think of Tomek. And how what we had was never this. Never sacred. Never soft.

Phoenix doesn't answer. Not with words. He just wraps his hand around mine. A silent answer. A sign that our traumas aren't just overlapping. They're intertwining like strands of yarn. I lean in, the image of Rachel still glowing on my lap. Her wings. Her fearlessness.

Maybe one day, I'll be brave enough to change some corner of the world for the better.

"I just got my first med school interview yesterday," I say, my voice landing somewhere between excitement and nerves. It feels strange—raw—to say it out loud for the first time. Stranger still that Phoenix is the first to hear it.

"That's amazing!" he says, squeezing my hand.

"I dream of joining Doctors Without Borders one day." My hands move with my words, as if drawing my dreams into the space between us. "Imagine, going where healing is not just about medicine. Where humanity is needed." I pause. The weight of that word—humanity—lands heavy in my chest. "The world's gotten so cruel. Sometimes it feels like we've lost our humanity."

Phoenix doesn't speak. But his hand does—one warm, quiet squeeze. Then "Roads" by Portishead begins to play, winding through the citrus-scented cabin of the Honda. Sound smoke. Penetrating. A song for everything we don't have words for.

The LA skyline appears too soon. A fluorescent reminder that real life is still waiting. That my morning flight back to Chicago is only hours away. I don't want to go. I don't want this night to end. I don't want this to become a memory. At Le Petit, something bittersweet creeps in as we make our way to my room.

I already know: resisting Phoenix will take effort I don't have.

I see it all. A playboy smile. The way he carried me in the hot tub? That wasn't his first time.

He's a fucking Don Juan de Marco.

And me? I'm probably one of hundreds. Another spark he's lit.

"Ah, what a night." Phoenix says as he flops onto the king-sized bed like he's always belonged there. Easy and unbothered. Meanwhile, I escape to the bathroom. My what-ifs and maybe-nots trail behind me like ghosts. The warm shower cascades over me. My thoughts spin. Desire and doubt doing laps.

Yes, I want him. God, I want him. But I also know the signs. I stare into the mirror. Droplets race down my collarbones. They feel like his touch.

"I refuse," I whisper to my reflection, eyes locking with a girl who's come too far to just become a one-night stand. "I will not be another forgettable night."

I armor up in layers—navy sweatpants, the tank top spared by the hair gel catastrophe, and my favorite orange hoodie. One last glance.

"Not today, Satan," I mutter. The tiniest smirk tugs at my lips as I flip off the bathroom light.

After a deep, steadying breath in the steamy hush of the bathroom, I step back into the room.

Phoenix is sprawled across the bed, bare-chested, wrapped in a loose sarong like some tropical daydream. Notes of "Teardrop" by Massive Attack drift from his MacBook, casting a sultry spell across the space. His eyes meet mine, and for a split second, I see it—surprise. Real surprise. His gaze sweeps over my hooded form.

Orange hoodie. Sweatpants. Steam still trailing behind me. Then he laughs. Deep. Warm. Unfiltered. I blush. Hard. But it fades quickly. Because a hand finds mine and squeezes gently.

Then I hear it—a second laugh. Softer. Feminine. When I open my eyes, the steam is gone.

Dr. McKenna is smiling across her desk, shaking her head.

"You really can't make this stuff up," Phoenix says to her.

TWO DREAMS

"Manifestation is a form of delusion that makes dreams come true."

"The way our night was unfolding, I seriously thought she was going to step out of that steam-filled bathroom in some sexy, lacy lingerie," Phoenix says, grinning like he's telling the best skit. Instead, she came out looking like Kenny McCormick from South Park."

Dr. McKenna bursts into laughter. I shrug and offer her my best Mona Lisa smile.

"It was the wildest—but cutest—thing," Phoenix adds. "Forever etched in my memory."

Dr. McKenna leans forward, elbows resting on the desk, her tone shifting into something gently observational.

"This will be a straightforward diagnosis." She pushes her glasses up with her index finger. "What you've described is what

I like to call a 'malfunctioning social antenna.' It's actually very common in individuals with your profile, Dr. Hartley."

"Well, yay," I say, squeezing Phoenix's hand. "I feel slightly less like a weirdo now."

We share a glance. His eyes crinkle like he's saying, *See? Told you.*

"Would you say this happens often?" Dr. McKenna asks, pen poised midair.

"I guess so," I reply, realizing it as I speak. "But I usually don't notice unless someone else points it out. It all feels...normal in my head."

"Mmh." She scribbles something into my file, then sets the pen down with a soft click. Her gaze lifts. She's less clinician, more curious human. I look away and toy with my sweatpants drawstring.

"You've shared such an intriguing snapshot of your budding relationship with Phoenix," she says, voice warm but precise. "It makes me wonder about the moments that led to this. It's not just about where you are now—but how you got here."

Her comment pulls me back to the day that changed my trajectory.

"Actually, one of those turning points was the day of my med school interview," I say. The memory still crisp in my mind, as if it were yesterday.

I close my eyes. The present blurs with the past as my fingers twirl the drawstring of my hoodie.

Suddenly, I'm in my SLY—one hand gripping the steering wheel, the other twisting fabric like a talisman. I'm driving a winding road, speakers humming low. I zone out like always. Imagining. Dreaming. Driving calms the internal narrator. My mind loves motion.

The Smoky Mountains rise at the edges of the road. The horizon blushes with sunrise. I pull into a hotel in Middlesboro, Kentucky just as the first sunrays dance across the sky. The hotel is only a stone's throw from Lincoln Memorial University DeBusk College of Osteopathic Medicine—just across the Tennessee border, through a short tunnel.

The hotel I picked for proximity and price ends up serving one singular purpose: a fast shower to rinse off the chaos of the night. I had a minor accident on the way—just a blown tire, a scrape, a few new scars on SLY's bumper. Battle wounds. A little proof of our resilience, I guess.

Thankfully, the hotel held my room for me. I slip into my navy suit with minutes to spare. The lobby coffee is burnt, but I drink it like it holds divine power. It does. Somehow, I'm wide awake.

The drive to LMU-DCOM is uphill. Mist coils between lampposts like enchanted fog. And there, perched at the top, is a solitary building. It looks like something from a Tim Burton film. I laugh out loud. "Magicians would totally study here." I whisper to no one.

The moment feels suspended. Ache. Hope. A little exhaustion. I wonder if med school will feel like this. Some strange blend of wear and wonder.

That hill, that fog, that road—it all feels like a clear beginning. A whisper that life is about to change. Dramatically.

Once I've parked in front of the main entrance, my thoughts are sweetened by a text from Phoenix: **good luck today, my magician.**

I press the phone against my heart like his words might cast a spell—one that could make this dream real. A little charm from miles away. His belief in me sweeps away the last bits of old doubts Tomek plastered onto me. They had been annoying, hard to peel off. Like goose grass.

I take the stairs one at a time. Each step feels somehow light and heavy. It's familiar. Phoenix's voice echoes in my mind: Time isn't linear.

Maybe he's right. Past, present, future—they all meet me here, at the top of this hill. I can feel it. My future is close. Tethered to every step I take toward it.

"I'm here for the interview," I say at the reception desk, trying to sound more confident than I feel. The receptionist points to the bench in the hallway. There's a huddle of three other interviewees, all male, suited up and looking less nervous than me.

My guide is Steve, a first-year med student with electric blue eyes and a contagious bounce in his step. We'd crossed paths before—briefly, last year, on the Student Doctor Network forum. Now here he is, leading us through the winding halls like he helped build them.

"You guys are gonna love this," he says, practically vibrating as we near the anatomy lab.

He swipes his ID. The door beeps. A thick scent of formalin rushes out to meet us. My stomach lurches for a second, but I follow him in.

Inside, students lean over cadavers, so focused they barely notice us. The room murmurs with concentration. My eyes drift from the sleek dissection cameras dangling from the ceiling to something colorful—something unexpected in a clinical space like this.

A mural. It spans the far wall, bold and beautiful. "Painted by a fellow student," Steve says, proudly.

Art, in the hub of science. A pulse of beauty in a place built to take human bodies apart. While everyone else marvels at the tech, I stare at the mural like it's a fresco in the Sistine Chapel. Da Vinci. Michelangelo. Fioretti. Roman statues. All of the art history I have learned flashes through my mind.

Maybe art is science. Maybe it always was.

Steve's excited stride propels us down a long hallway toward the conference rooms set aside for interviews. "I'll find you after, Lena," he says with a grin, already peeling off toward another group.

I retreat to a quiet corner, skipping the nervous pre-interview chatter. My mind drifts to something softer—something far away from the cold chairs and clipped voices around me.

Phoenix. Our goodbye at the airport. That final embrace. The ghost of sulfur still clinging to his skin from our hot springs night, mingling with the sweet smell I'd memorized.

"I love you. Always have," he said. Madness. But the kind that made me feel more sane than anything else ever had. His words replay in my chest like a favorite song. They've rooted themselves there. Stubborn. Unforgettable.

This longing—this hunger for him—stretches out like an endless winter night. And I wonder:

How do I build a life that holds both things? This dream of medicine. The magic I've found with Phoenix. Where's the path that lets me have both? Is there one?

"Lena?" A voice at the doorway snaps me back. I blink, ground myself with a breath, and turn. The man standing there has kind eyes, soft lines at the edges, and silver is just beginning to touch his hair. "Good morning, I'm Dr. Hodge." His handshake is warm. Real. Not a formality.

The interview room is lit with too much morning light. It stings my eyes for a second. Inside, two other faculty members wait—Dr. Brown and Dr. Rosen. Dr. Brown is tall and lean, maybe mid-forties, sharp-eyed and analytical-seeming. Dr. Rosen—older, with a silver beard and calm presence—radiates quiet wisdom. Their presence at this recently established school, one still awaiting full accreditation, says everything. This place is serious. Scrappy. Ambitious. And it's drawing in giants. Everything that attracted me to apply here.

The interview goes smoothly. We move from the basics— why medicine, why osteopathy—into the story of how I got here.

Literally. The car accident. The tire. The bumper. How I almost didn't make it. The room goes still. Fuck, did I just overshare? Even Dr. Brown's sharp gaze softens. A hush falls. And I realize: they're not just listening. They're looking at me with a kind of admiration.

"Wow, and you still chose to drive all the way? Most people would've rescheduled," Dr. Hodge says, brow lifting slightly.

"I'm not most people," I say before I can stop myself. Unguarded honesty always gets me.

They glance at one another—astonishment passing between them like a silent ovation. Or is it more shock? Or both. I don't know. Shock and surprise sometimes look the same. But shock is usually sharper and can have negative context. A surprise is soft, gentle. Dr. Brown smiles, so I know it must be the surprise.

"As doctors," Dr. Rosen murmurs, fingers grazing his beard, "we are never like other people."

He doesn't say it for me. He says it like a truth he's lived. But still, I feel seen. Even though I'm not a doctor. Not yet.

There is a brief moment of silence that feels like too many breaths.

Dr. Brown breaks the silence with a question that slices through those breaths like a scalpel:

"With a background in art history, aren't you apprehensive about diving into the rigors of anatomy and physiology?"

For a second, I feel it—that old flicker of doubt trying to claw its way back in. Tomek telling me to stick to modeling. But I don't let it. I punch it down.

"Medicine, in its essence, is an art," I say, lifting my gaze to meet his. I won't shrink. Not now. "If I can unravel the visual complexities of hundreds of Caravaggio's and Da Vinci's masterpieces..." I pause for a dramatic effect. "Then the human anatomy is just another canvas to understand."

Dr. Rosen's light chuckle fills the room. It sounds almost like my Grandpa's. I smile.

"That's the most refreshingly unique perspective on medicine we've heard all day," he says.

Emboldened, I keep going. "Because at its core, being a doctor is about humanity. And if we strip the art from science... what are we? Just robots in white coats."

There's a pause. Their eyes are scanning me. An entertaining anomaly. Maybe I've gone too far?

Then Dr. Hodge raises a brow. "A fashion model," he says, almost to himself. "That's an unexpected detail for a med school application. How do you see that fitting into your future as a physician?"

I glance out the window, searching the trees for an answer. My fingers trace the seam of my suit. I try to take a breath without making it look like I need air.

"Modeling taught me to adapt. Quickly. To read a room. To stay composed when everything around me is chaotic or unfamiliar," I say. "Isn't that what doctors do every day?"

Dr. Rosen sets his pen down. Looks up. Dr. Brown tilts his head, a grin tugging at one side of his mouth.

"So," he says, "you're going to be our own Izzy Stevens?"

I laugh. I can't help it. The reference to Gray's Anatomy lands.

"I guess I am."

Steve catches up with me in the hallway, eyes searching mine for clues. "How'd it go?" he probes.

I let a wry smile slip. "Well...they'll definitely remember me."

There's a beat. Then he leans in, lowers his voice. "I've got a good feeling you're in," he whispers, like he's been eavesdropping on the admissions gods. It sounds like more than just a hunch.

We walk a few steps in silence before I finally ask what's been gnawing at me since the beginning. "Aren't you worried about the accreditation?"

"Not even a little," he says, waving it off like a mosquito. "Totally normal. Schools don't get accredited until after the first class graduates. We've got some of the best faculty members in the country. The AOA will have to grant it. And if for some freak reason they don't? They reimburse our tuition."

"That's comforting," I say, though my voice comes out flatter than I intend. "But I can't afford to gamble four years of my life. It's not about money."

My chest tightens. I think of Phoenix. Of what it might mean to spend four years here, far from him, and for what? Nothing?

Steve laughs. His blue eyes crinkle as he claps me on the shoulder.

"They'd have to fail us all spectacularly for that to happen," he grins. "And come on—we're med students. Overachieving is in our blood."

His optimism is relentless. And, for now, I let it win. I laugh. It's a tired laugh, but it's real.

Back in SLY, I peel off the navy suit jacket and slide into my orange hoodie—the one that still smells faintly like sulfur and Phoenix. I've refused to wash it. I don't want the scent to leave. Ever.

I start the car. LMU-DCOM fades in my rearview, swallowed by trees and fog and maybe a little fate. The wheels hum. The road stretches. But something inside me presses against the edge of my chest.

Tears pool. They don't fall, just hover, blurring out the world. My heart, like a compass needle without a north pole, spins in opposite directions, left to right. Even without an acceptance letter, I feel it. The future already knows.

Brushing away tears, I call Phoenix.

Two rings. Then his voice—soft, groggy, warm. "Hi, my magician. How was the interview?"

"It was great," I say, though the words catch on the edge of a sniffle. "The school...it's inspiring."

Tears well up in my eyes. There's a pause. "Aw, what's wrong?" His concern is gentle. Immediate. He always hears the things I don't say. Always reads between the lines.

"It's just..." I stammer, wrestling to articulate the whirlwind of emotions I'm feeling. "It's in Tennessee." The words feel like lead.

"Don't worry. We'll make it work," he says, easy as breath. "We'll visit each other. We'll find a way."

The hilly road curves beneath me. Leaves spinning like fire in the wind. Dancing in the zoom of my car.

A thought drifts out before I can stop it. "Maybe I could take a year off. Apply to California schools next year?"

There's silence. Then Phoenix says, "It's your dream, Lena. One you had long before me." His voice is supportive. And yet, the bittersweet edges are unmistakable. Like black coffee from the hotel.

I bury my nose into the hoodie's collar. Breathe him in.

"Why can't life just be easy?" I whisper to the trees flying past. "I know I'm strong. But sometimes I'm so tired of climbing every damn mountain."

I don't expect an answer. It was a rhetorical question.

"Life has a weird sense of humor," he says.

It makes me laugh. A shaky, bumpy sound like this road. The kind that wobbles on the edge of breaking.

"More like a sense of torment," I mutter.

Phoenix chuckles. "Nothing worth fighting for ever feels like a walk in the park, Lena."

There's truth in it. Truth I don't want but recognize. The essence of our journeys often lies in their challenge, not their ease.

"You're my heart," he says.

The words put me together. Fill the cracks. Hold all the scattered fragments of me. I release the accelerator just a little.

"And you're mine," I say.

Phoenix's voice still echoes through my mind hours after we hang up, just as Chicago's skyline—with the Sears Tower rising like a needle—appears on the horizon. He's right. The dream of being a doctor was born long before. Even before Tomek's damage. But now it unfolds with someone believing in me. What a contrast. Phoenix makes me feel loved in a way that's gentle. Selfless. A kind of support my heart never knew with Tomek. Still, I hesitate. What if this dream costs me the love that's just begun to bloom? Maybe I won't even get into med school this year. Maybe this tug-of-war between head and heart is for nothing—just unnecessary worrying in advance.

A couple of months whirl past—a blur of sleepless shadows and sharp-edged waiting. I step out of the dim maze of Advanced Renaissance Art History. My phone buzzes, and my heart skitters. I fish it from the back pocket of my jeans, half-hoping it's Phoenix. But it's an unknown number—maybe Polish?

"Hello?" I send the word into the crisp campus air, navigating down UIC's beige sidewalks toward the parking lot.

"Hi, Lena, this is Dr. Rosen from LMU-DCOM," comes the gentle, familiar voice on the other end. I stop. Frozen in place. A mooring post in the river of passing students.

"Hi, Dr. Rosen," I manage, though words barely register over the thunder in my chest.

"I have some great news for you. We'd like to offer you admission to LMU-DCOM, class of twenty-twelve," he says. Just like that, goosebumps scatter across my arms. Something tight catches in my throat—like I've swallowed a golf ball. A grin takes over my face. Before I know it, my fist punches the gray Chicago sky. Then—beep. Phoenix's name flashes. The call waiting chimes in, and suddenly Dr. Rosen's voice dissolves into static. I go on autopilot, responses automatic and hollow, as I stand unmoving in a stream of passing faces. Joy tangles with conflict. The realization that one dream might eclipse another drapes itself over the moment—like a velvet veil pulled over a gallery painting you're not supposed to see yet.

Still standing on the sidewalk, I call Phoenix back. "I got in!"

"That's incredible! Congratulations, my magician." His enthusiasm vibrates through the phone. Yet, beneath it, there's a whisper of sadness, subtle, but I can tell. A nudge from the tide of students sends me stumbling. I slip away from the current of bodies, looking for stillness to keep talking to him. I settle onto the cold curb. My backpack presses against my spine like an anchor. It suddenly feels heavy.

"Thank you," I manage, voice thin.

"How do you feel?" he asks, always reading the undercurrents to my words.

"Honestly...I don't know." I stare at a nearby tree, at the few stubborn leaves still clinging to bare branches. Silence. He's waiting. Fishing for the rest of what I wanted to say.

"I thought I'd be overjoyed. And part of me is...it's just—"

My voice falters. Thoughts scatter like birds startled off a wire, refusing to line up again.

"I miss you so much, my heart," Phoenix says softly. Then, firmer: "I'm so proud of you. My girl's going to be a doctor. We'll figure it out. Don't worry." His words wrap around me like a sun-warmed blanket. Like California heat on bare shoulders. They tilt the scale inside me—toward hope. We will make it work.

"Lena!" A familiar voice slices through the campus noise.

Anya. Finding me on my little island, parked on the curb. "I'll call you back, my fire," I whisper, then hang up. Anya, in her bright red coat, weaves through the crowd. A burst of color cutting through all the grayness, even the one in my mind. "I just got the call—I got into LMU-DCOM," I say, the words out before

I can measure them. My smile stretches but feels like someone stitched it at the corners.

"Oh my God!" Anya's voice twirls with excitement, her eyes blooming wide. "I knew it!" She pulls me into a hug, and just like that, the news sinks in. Her pride brushes lightly across my emotional canvas. We walk toward the parking lot. Our steps sync unconsciously.

"It just sucks we won't be staying in Chicago together," I say, breath catching between sharp gusts of wind.

"I'll miss you. Every single day," she says, her voice soft. Her smile dims to match mine—barely there now. "I'm so proud of us. You'll be a doctor, and I'll be a dentist," she says, nudging me with her shoulder. I'm silent.

"UIC Dental School, baby!" She wiggles her hips in a victory dance, still riding the high from yesterday's news.

"I'm proud of us too," I say. An inhale. Maybe a beat too long. It betrays me. Anya stops. Looks at me hard. Deeper than eyes should be able to look.

"But how do you really feel, Lena?"

Her words land right where it hurts. She knows. This dream doesn't just pull me from Phoenix. It pulls me from her too. My eyes start to mist.

"Lonely," I say. The word echoes like it traveled from another world. I wonder if that word is naming my future.

"Oh, my sweetheart. We'll be drowning in books—we won't even have time to feel lonely. And Tennessee's not that far. We'll see each other on holidays. I'll call you every day." Her words keep my tears from falling. Just barely.

I exhale slowly, like it might hold everything in place.

Anya studies my face. "It's Phoenix too, isn't it?"

Her aim is perfect. A sad, "Yeah," escapes me. A tiny word that carries so much weight.

The loneliness gets louder on the drive home. I turn off the music and let the sound of SLY's tires rolling over the road fill the silence. Every song reminds me of him. His touch. His kiss. I can't take it. The tumbling tires are the soundtrack now. How strange. You fight so hard for a dream, and when you finally hold it, you wonder if the price was too steep. But isn't love always expensive? Always asking for more than you thought you could give?

Later, getting ready for work, I press brown shadow onto my tired lids. Eyelids sore from holding back an avalanche of tears. At least Mom's overjoyed. She's already calling everyone in her contacts.

"Lena got into med school!" echoes from the kitchen, cutting through the fog of her cigarette smoke.

The security at Visage waves me through. "What's up, beautiful?" He's always smiling, a smile that doesn't match a scary 6'7" guy. I say nothing. Just tap his shoulder with a smile and glance at the line outside, stretching like a ribbon down the block. The pulse of the DJ spinning, the heartbeat of Visage I usually adore, feels off tonight. Almost irritating. The lights, sharp as lasers, cut through the dark and sting my eyes. Luc, all Energizer Bunny charm, greets me with his usual smile and kiss on the cheek. I model. Like usual. Masking what I feel. It's fake, but necessary.

Later in the night, he clocks me. "What's wrong, Lena?"

"I got into med school," I say, my smile tugging weirdly at the corners.

"That's fantastic! Congrats!" he beams, pulling me into a quick half-hug.

I force a smile. Luc catches it. His brows lift.

"But?" he asks, hands open, waiting.

"It's in Tennessee," I say with a shrug, my gaze drifting over the dance floor pulsing under the lights.

"Shit. Phoenix is in LA," Luc says, connecting the dots.

"Exactly," I say, my head bobbing to the beat. I let it carry me for a moment. The music thumps in my bones. Solace in repetition.

"When does med school start?" he asks, right as someone leans over to shout an order.

"August," I yell back. "Next year."

He holds up a finger. "Wait a sec!" and turns to make a Cosmo. He's been doing it forever—a shake, a flick of the wrist, bam—martini glass down, foam floating on the pink liquid. Then he's back fast, like he's got something important to unload. He leans in close, hand cupped around my ear like he's about to spill the secret of the universe.

"Listen—move to LA for the eight months after you graduate. Give it a real shot with the guy. Problem solved." I blink. Step back. A real smile sneaks up before I can stop it.

"That feels impossible," I say. The idea is so clean, it's almost absurd.

Luc shrugs, confidence undimmed. "You make shit happen. You just have to want it hard enough."

I roll my eyes. Playful. But his words carry more weight than I want to admit. Luc moves to the rhythm of the music, his smile as wide as if he's just stumbled upon a newfound continent. In Poland, when I was a kid, we used to say, "Why are you smiling? Did you discover America?" It's contagious, though. I let the rhythm take over my body too.

My phone vibrates with a message from Phoenix: **i love you, my magician…can't wait until you're in my arms again.**

I stop. The fire his words ignite paralyzes me. I stand frozen in the middle of the club, remembering every second of his touch. His lips. The way he looks at me like he sees ME. I feel like I'm not here. Like a ghost. And the tears I've been holding since this morning have nowhere left to go. They spill over, racing down my cheeks like a spring mountain river. I dab them away with a black napkin.

ALL I NEED

"Sometimes the only way, is right through."

My cheeks are drowning in tears when I feel a box of tissues slip into my hand, pulling me back to the present. As I blink through the blur, Phoenix's face comes into focus.

"I'm here, my love," he whispers, his warm eyes shimmering with empathy. He settles beside me on Dr. McKenna's couch. I blow my nose and dab at the tears. The office feels heavy with my emotions.

"We can take a break if you need one, Dr. Hartley," Dr. McKenna says. Her voice is quiet, almost a whisper. I lock eyes with her for a moment. How does she do it? All this heaviness of other people's lives. So much empathy. It beams through her eyes.

"No, it's okay. I'd rather keep going. In a couple of hours, we have to pick up our daughter." I chuckle through sniffles. She straightens slightly, measuring her words. We lock eyes.

"Med school is very hard and often a lonely journey," she says. "Before we delve into that, how did you end up with Phoenix? Did you move to LA?"

"After Luc planted that idea, I had to find a way," I say. "When I want something, I don't quit until I make it happen."

"Yup, that's my wife," Phoenix says, all pride—no trace of sadness left in his eyes. The comment makes me smile.

"I didn't want to just move in with Phoenix. I wanted us to have a real shot, so figuring out our living situation was a challenge. But then one thing led to another, and I met Monique online."

"Monique?" Dr. McKenna leans in.

"Yes, she's a famous Polish tapestry artist living in Pasadena. During one of our chats, she invited me to stay with her," I say, the memory bubbling up with excitement. "She said I could help on a piece she was making for a synagogue in La Jolla." My thoughts drift to Monique's beautiful home and the profound conversations we shared while laboring for months over that thirteen-foot tapestry.

"Had you ever woven a tapestry before?" Dr. McKenna asks, lifting an eyebrow.

"Never, but she was willing to teach me," I say with a shrug, drawing a chesty laugh from Phoenix. "My wife is something else," he says, nodding with a proud smile. A hand squeeze. I chuckle and shrug again. Dr. McKenna's laughter fills the room. It bounces off her diplomas. At least that's how I envision the sound wave.

"This is so typical. I absolutely love it," she says.

"She came prepared—she even locked down a spot with a modeling agency in LA before leaving Chicago," Phoenix says. Our hands meet again. Instinctively. We are always tethered by an invisible string.

"Well, yeah...I needed to be sure I could stand on my own two feet in California," I say.

"And how did you get yourself to LA?" she asks, leaning back in her chair. I glance at Phoenix's eyes—the same eyes whose gravity pulled me across a continent, the same fire fluttering in my stomach like a thousand butterfly wings. The rush of my solo drive to California pulses in my chest. Goosebumps ripple across my skin. Dr. McKenna's office dissolves. It's dawn, and I'm on Mom's driveway.

SLY is packed to the roof. My life condensed into the backseat and trunk. The front passenger seat is a makeshift pantry—snacks and water bottles, a parting gift from Mom. Mom's embrace is a fortress, her voice quivering with swallowed sadness.

"I love you so much...you're my favorite daughter," she manages to joke through the tears. As she steps back, her misty eyes lock onto mine. Mine are wet too. Her arm stays around me as she presses a white envelope into my hand. The weight of the cash bulges against my palm, pushing the tears closer to the surface.

"Mom!" I protest, trying to shove it back into her robe pocket. She bats my hand away.

"Didn't I teach you? When the universe gives you something, you take it." She shoves the envelope into my back pocket, gives my butt a light knee kick. "For good luck!" she declares.

We both laugh at the strange Polish custom. A good luck butt kick. So Mom.

Pulling onto the snowy street, I catch one last glimpse of Mom waving—tears streaking down her cheeks. "Drive safe!" she calls, her warm words turning to plumes in the freezing air. Even when she doesn't smoke, she's still my dragon. The pink hues of winter rise on the horizon, casting a farewell glow as Chicago's skyline fades in my rearview. Phoenix's music sets the mood through the speakers. The road stretches out. Almost empty. A quiet tunnel carved through the remnants of a snowstorm that delayed me three days. But there's no frustration. Just a poetic kind of acceptance. January 19th (of course, 19) now feels like the day the universe ordained me to leave it all behind. To drive toward love, toward the uncharted and the yet-to-happen. The new life. Yesterday's goodbye with Anya replays in my thoughts. Her sweet, knowing smile. Arms wrapping around me. Her tease: "Is this the last stage of insanity?"

We laughed so hard I thought we might fall over. Then my face softened into something more serious as I said: "I don't think so. Sometimes our heart goes somewhere before we do— mine is in California, my body is just following it there." I will miss my best friend. I wonder—how steep is the price we pay for love? For dreams? Life is funny that way, it never lets us have it all. Wanting to share the road with someone, and knowing Phoenix is probably still asleep, I dial Grandpa.

"Hi, my little flower." Grandpa's soft, crinkly voice weaves through the speaker, tugging a smile from me. "How's the road?"

"Good. I'm cruising through Iowa. It's nice and flat, roads mostly clear," I say, watching SLY glide down the empty highway, dusted with winter's fingerprints. "So, this walnut-eyed guy must be truly special, huh?" Grandpa's curiosity twinkles through the phone.

"My intuition tells me so," I say. I let the endless road conjure a memory of Phoenix at Pismo Beach. His eyes mirroring the sunset right before we kissed. The thought warms me as Grandpa sighs softly.

"Intuition, my dear, is just your heart speaking out loud."

Grandpa, like Phoenix, speaks in quotes-of-the-day. His words echo inside me long after the call ends. I'm in Nebraska now. The road unfolds like a perfect arrow, stretching into the vastness where the sky kisses the earth. A miniature sun, like a suspended ping-pong ball, dips at the edge of the horizon. SLY charges toward its last fading gleam. The flatness of Nebraska casts a surreal spell. Colorado's mountains feel like a distant promise. My phone rings, cutting through the ambient hum of Telefon Tel Aviv. Phoenix's name lights up the screen, sending a shiver through me.

"Hi, my air," he greets, his voice a soft whisper over the line.

"Hi, my fire," I respond, feeling the space between us diminish as my foot presses on the accelerator. "I wish you could see this," I say, mesmerized by the orange glow painting the sky. "The sunset clouds over Nebraska look like God's hand reaching west."

"He's guiding you," Phoenix responds with a light chuckle.

"Seems that God and my heart both know what's up," I quip.

"At this rate, I'll be taking you out for some sushi tomorrow," Phoenix says. "I can't wait to feel your lips on mine. Drive safe." His words send a hot wave through me. SLY climbs to 100 mph on the meter.

"Same," I whisper, as the last rays of sun stretch and vanish down the endless road.

After we hang up, I lower the window. My orange hoodie catches the cooling air. I stretch my hand into the rushing wind. The air slides over my skin. It's cold like the rush of water was in the tub with Phoenix. Why do I feel everything so intensely? Like it dives straight into my soul? Since I was a kid, my senses have always been sharp. Overwhelming.

But Phoenix makes me want to seek the world's touch. He makes every feeling beautiful. No matter how many times I've asked him, I still catch myself wondering—am I dreaming? Will I wake up any second and just say, "What the fuck?"

Hours melt into the rhythm of the road. SLY swipes snow from his window as we pass a sign: "Welcome to Colorful Colorado." By the time I reach Denver, night has already swallowed Colorado's landscapes. I keep driving. The road climbs fast and turns sharply. SLY's tires flirt with the icy edge, slipping like a sled. My heart jumps into my throat. My foot is almost pushing the brake pedal through the floor. "Looks like it's time to call it a day," I whisper to SLY, my hand patting the steering wheel as if to steady both our nerves. After one of the sketchiest U-turns of my life, teetering way too close to the edge, I steer us back toward the heart of the city. Finally, SLY and I find refuge at a Motel 6. Inside the dingy motel room, I collapse onto the bed after a quick shower. A thousand miles weigh down my bones. Even texting feels monumental. My fingers manage to type a quick update to Mom and Phoenix: **Made it to Denver. Stopping for some sleep.** Phoenix's reply comes instantly. A beep of light in my fogged-up world. **you're almost here, my love.** I stare at the heart emoji that follows. So small. Holding so many unsaid words. My lids are too heavy to dream up his face from my memory.

I twitch awake. 4:44 a.m. glows from the nightstand, mocking the alarm I set for 5:00. My hand is still wrapped around my phone. Even in sleep, I couldn't let go of my lifeline to Phoenix. The future I'm racing toward.

The gas station coffee finally kicks in just as SLY begins his climb up a monster of a mountain. The incline is so steep, I'm not even sure the gas pedal is doing anything. Eventually the snow-covered summit bursts into a glittering spectacle as the first rays break over Colorado. I grew up in the mountains of Poland. But these? These mountains dwarf those memories. They make me feel like an ant. This time, I don't call anyone. Just me, the music, and the road. I let my soul drink in all this vastness. Something stirs inside me. Something too big for words. A drugged feeling. A sense of euphoria. Is it God?

The question lingers as the hours melt. I pull into a gas station just shy of the Utah border. Another Red Bull buzzes through my veins, battling the fatigue. Sliding back into SLY, I hear the beep—message waiting. It's a photo of Phoenix's hand—his wrist now inked with a black and red heart. The caption reads: "fire needs air...where are you?" His words clear the haze faster than any Red Bull ever could. I drive a few miles from the station. The mountains rise ahead. Majestic waypoints for whatever comes next. I pull over. I stretch my hand toward the sky and snap a photo. Trying to hold something that can't be held. **Remembering our future...I'm in Utah**, I type, and send it off into the ether. On an empty road, veils of powdery snow shimmer across SLY. "All I Need" by Radiohead shuffles on, syncing perfectly with the view. Goosebumps erupt, not just from the music frisson, but a visual one as well. Above, the sun dips. The sky explodes. Orange, pink, purple. Clouds light up from the inside like molten lava. "This is God," I whisper. "This road is a temple."

Los Angeles unfolds in sprawling veins of light, pulsing with life even at this late hour. The city's mesmerizing energy hums in my own pulse. A stark contrast to the hush I left behind. Traffic on the 405 moves in a rhythmic dance—taillights, headlights. LA's endless heartbeat. My phone rings, slicing through the freeway noise.

"Where are you?" Phoenix's voice carries a sweet note of anticipation.

"Might've taken a scenic detour. I keep missing this damn exit," I confess, head swiveling. LA's exits are a labyrinth, and its drivers move like a stampede. Navigation here feels like survival.

"Just head toward the mountains," he says.

"I've been driving toward the mountains since Colorado."

We laugh. Who gives directions like this? He always makes me laugh. Even when I fight for my life on this freeway, in the chaos blinking outside my windows. Dodging cars moving like torpedos, I weave my way through the glittering streets toward the Beverly Hills Hotel. Phoenix is waiting there. The sight of him—and the adrenaline of my marathon drive—makes the moment feel weightless. Like I'm floating the last few feet into a new life. I pull up SLY into the valet. The stop feels like it will never happen as we lock eyes.

Still in my travel-worn orange hoodie, I must look wildly out of place amid all this elegance. The hotel's opulence hits me. I hadn't realized how grand the place Phoenix booked would be. But caught in the whirlwind of my own excitement, the curious glances from well-heeled guests barely register. The second Phoenix sees me, the rest of the world fades out. He sweeps me up in a twirl right there, on the red carpet. And just like that, any feeling of being out of place evaporates. With Phoenix, somehow my awkwardness turns into acceptance, and I can be myself. Smiling without a word, he hoists my bulky bag like it's no more than a feather.

"Come." He pulls me. We walk through the hallways of a hotel that screams old money. Over-glitzed everything. He stops by our door. My luggage drops with a thud. Passion erupts on my lips. Then his tongue trails down my neck. I slide my hand up his T-shirt. Fingers tracing the hills and valleys of his abs. A door slams down the hallway, startling us. A chatty couple spills into the hall.

"Shit. You're just so irresistible." Phoenix laughs, digging for the room key in his back pocket.

"Let's not get kicked out," I say. He chuckles as the door beeps open.

Inside, the room whispers old wealth: desert-sand walls, a king-sized bed wrapped in nude leather, heavy vanilla silk drapes framing the windows.

My heart flutters like a moth caught in the light when his lips graze mine. "The restaurant might be closed, but the bar serves some exquisite snacks," he whispers, his breath a melody of the want rising between us. With the heat still humming between us, Phoenix's gaze lifts. "Or...we could get room service instead?"

"Considering this hoodie already collected enough stink-eyes downstairs," I say, "room service sounds like a safer choice."

Phoenix smiles.

"Doesn't matter what you're wearing—you're always beautiful." He tilts my chin up and kisses me again. Tender but claiming. Completely disarming. "Room service it is, then." His lips find my neck again. I must taste like sweat.

"Let me wash off the road grime," I say, laughing into the warm space between us. Pulling away from him feels like trying to separate magnets—a tug against the natural order.

The lavish granite bathroom embraces me. Just like the shower water splashing in unruly gushes, I'm a hot mess. The water drums against my skin, peeling away the miles, the exhaustion sunk deep into my bones. And the fear of fucking this up. I linger. Wrapped in the gravity of what's about to happen. Our sexual pull is so strong. I won't be able to resist him this time. How strange. Wanting something and being scared of it in the same breath. I let the solitude soak into me for one more minute.

I forget the robe. Just yank the orange hoodie back over my damp skin. My heart punches, about to burst out of my chest.

Music curls into the air as I step into the room. Candles everywhere. Phoenix sits on the bed—wearing nothing but a black and red sarong, swallowed by a sea of rose petals.

The sight knocks the breath out of me. The air is heavy—steak, truffles, berries—all mixing into a dizzying sweetness. And I just stand there. Frozen. Every nerve pulled so tight it might snap.

Phoenix rises. Steps towards me. His sarong cascades to the floor. Walnut eyes. Hot. Hungry. So sure. So penetrating. I try to take a breath, but it turns into a gasp as I feel his hands on my skin.

They find my waist, sliding under the hoodie like he's memorizing my shape. Me.

"What would you like to eat?" he asks, voice rough at the edges. My hoodie's zipper gives up in his hands.

"You," I whisper. The word falls out before I can reclaim it. Bloodstream tunes spill through the room. The soundtrack of our souls colliding. I feel everything. Phoenix's hands move slow between my breasts, down to my stomach, leaving traces of fire that doesn't burn.

"Aren't you hungry for actual food?" he teases between kisses.

"No" I say. Our dancing tongues say the rest. A breath needed. A confluence of everything unspoken. Every mile I drove. Every wall I tore down. Every damn fear I left bleeding behind me. In this moment, there's no hunger food could touch. Just this. Us. Fully not hungry. His lips, my hot skin. And I don't know where he ends and I begin.

The first crack of sun slips through the heavy curtains. A sign that the night we wished could last forever gave birth to a new day. I blink against the light, cheek pressed to Phoenix's chest. He twists a piece of my short hair around his fingers. His other hand gently brushing the dip at my waist.

"You're my new beginning," he whispers. "I thought I'd lost all hope. That the fates took it." I look up at him. Beneath the euphoria, darkness flickers in his eyes. I don't know what words could reach that place. So I just tighten my arm around him and press a kiss to his chest. Right over his heart.

His phone buzzes against the nightstand, breaking the hush.

Phoenix glances at it, thumbs a quick reply. Lips curve into a smile.

"Let's get ready," he says, running his hand through my pixie. "There's someone I really want you to meet."

I throw on simple makeup. Just a dab of concealer to hide almost two thousand miles still stubbornly clinging under my eyes. I tame my dark brows with my toothbrush. A dab of lip gloss. Blush is pointless—Phoenix is doing a better job than any blush ever could. I tug the violet dress from the top of my suitcase, thankful I packed it in such easy reach. Phoenix pulls on a pair of vintage blue jeans and a white button-down, sleeves shoved up to his elbows. My eyes trail the sculpted lines of his forearms. The simplicity only makes him sexier. I almost drag him back to bed. He could undo me without even trying.

We retrieve his car from the valet. Outside, the city is already sweating under the early sun as the winding road cuts up into the Hollywood Hills. We pull up to a mansion that from the outside looks half-forgotten—vines curling up the walls, the paint kissed by too many summers.

But the street outside buzzes. Crowds are clinging to their phones, trying to talk or text their way in. Phoenix laces his fingers through mine. He walks us straight to the door.

"What's up, Phoenix, brother," the tall security guy says, tapping his shoulder and flashing me a grin.

"Good, good," Phoenix answers, clasping his hand for a second. A typical dude handshake.

"Have fun, gorgeous." He glances at me and waves us in, past a sea of restless, hungry eyes. I'm sure they all hate us for getting in so fast, while they still wait outside.

"Wow, you really know some people," I say as we step inside.

"I do," he winks. Of course he does. He probably runs this city.

Inside, the mansion thrums with life. DJ beats crash off the walls. We can barely move. Every few steps, someone pulls Phoenix into a hug, a handshake, a shout of his name.

"This is Lena," he says each time, grinning. "My girl."

The words make my cheeks flush hotter. I knew blush wouldn't be necessary.

My eyes dart everywhere. A dizzying swirl of humans, bold paintings, messy neon splashes of Mr. Brainwash. The whole place is buzzing with color and sound. I smell spilled champagne.

In the middle of it all, a man with a huge, contagious smile spots us.

"Phoenix, habibi!" he shouts, laughing as he barrels into Phoenix with a hug that looks like it could knock them both over.

The way they light up—arms slapping backs, heads thrown back in real laughter—makes me miss Anya's company.

"Lena, meet Danny—my best friend," Phoenix says, pulling me into the sunspot.

Danny kisses my cheek. His Middle Eastern accent is warm. The words, "Hi gorgeous," land in my ear like a welcome gift. He moves like the beat is part of him. So alive. A person that could resurrect an entire cemetery with his contagious energy. Before I can react, he yanks both Phoenix and me into a half-hug, one of us tucked under each of his arms.

"You must be the famous war-Danny," I say, laughing as he steers us towards the terrace.

"Yup. Phoenix, Michelle, and I survived that damn war," he says, squeezing me tighter. His hug is weirdly comforting—more earnest than intrusive.

Before I can even catch my breath, Danny's eyes flick past me. His whole face lights up.

"Michelle!" he shouts, his voice cutting clean through the thumping music.

The redhead turns. She's stunning, like she wandered out of a Renaissance painting. She almost looks like she doesn't belong in the hot, debouched crush of this party.

Green eyes lock onto us. She approaches with the poise of a model. She's definitely walked a runway before. Seamless. She ignores the boys and walks straight over to me.

"Hi! You must be Lena," she says. I feel she's a girls' girl. And her eyes have a strong twinkle of intelligence.

"Yes, I'm Lena," I say, feeling my body start to mirror hers, caught in the contagious beat. She moves with the music, hips swaying, her rhythm pulling me into it without even trying. Her slender fingers close around mine.

"Phoenix has told us so much about you," she says, that same electric smile lighting up her whole face, "and I can already see what he meant."

Phoenix and Danny are already deep in their own laughter somewhere behind us.

"What exactly did he mean?" I ask. Curiosity momentarily tugs me off the beat.

Michelle's hands lift, sketching shapes in the air, like she's plucking thoughts from above. Almost like Josionne.

"I think you're the healing love he's been searching for," she says.

Her words hit me. I try to hide the stumble and the sudden sting at the back of my throat. The fear of not being enough to heal his bruised heart. She reads me instantly.

"We lived through some heavy shit in Lebanon," she says, voice lowering.

"I'm not sure how much he's told you." Her eyes search mine.

I shake my head. She hesitates, then says it straight:

"He was close to proposing to someone there. Aleyna. A Lebanese heiress. Danny was engaged too."

I must look like I just got slapped, because Michelle immediately grabs my hand and steers me toward a quieter spot by the pool. We sink onto cream cushions. The blue flames behind a glass fireplace paint soft light over her face. She inches closer, giving me space but not letting me float away.

I stare at the fire for a second, hypnotized by the slow sway of it.

"I had no idea," I say finally.

"After Aleyna...he built walls around his heart," she says.

And it feels like a punch to the stomach. My throat pinches tight, but somehow, I find her eyes. "Why?" I say. "What happened?"

SUMMER OF LOVE

"Even rocks can't stop a mountain tree from growing."

Michelle takes a moment before she speaks.

Her eyes slowly close like a doll. Like she's rewinding something she isn't ready to look at head-on.

"Last year," she says quietly, "Danny—he's from Beirut—invited us to Lebanon."

A shadow crosses her face. I lean in.

"He was putting together a 50 Cent concert there."

Her eyes intensify. I try to absorb her words, but my gaze slips from the sharp green of her eyes to the slow, steady sway of the blue flames.

She leans in, face inches from mine. I catch the soft trace of her floral perfume.

"That summer was something else," she says.

"The concert went off without a hitch. There were talks of new projects, maybe even staying in Lebanon forever. But then... overnight..."

She glances over her shoulder. Phoenix and Danny are just a few feet away, lost in their own world, laughing like the weight of the war she's talking about never touched them. Phoenix catches my eyes and winks. I blink, forcing my gaze back to Michelle as she drags in a long breath.

"Everything changed. We woke up in the middle of a war zone."

Her voice trails off—heavy and fast at the same time, like the words are tripping over themselves to get out. A sharp pang cuts through my chest.

I reach out without thinking, fingers brushing hers.

"That sounds horrible," I whisper.

"The situation was dire," she says. Her eyes gloss over.

"Phoenix was pulling injured...and dead children...out of the rubble."

She swallows, blinking fast. Same thing I do when I'm trying to shove the tears back in.

"I'm—I'm so sorry." The words catch halfway up my throat, so instead, I squeeze her hand.

"The image of him—covered in dust and blood—is burned into my mind," she says, dabbing under her eyes. "Did my mascara smear?"

I blot a tiny black tear from the corner of her eye.

"There. You're good," I say, and pull her into a hug. Holding my breath. Afraid even breathing too loud might break her.

We sit like that for a few breaths, then she pulls away. I look at her. The listening kind of look.

"I managed to get out. To Syria. In a taxi." Her voice cracks on the word 'taxi,' almost disappearing. I barely catch it.

"But Phoenix and Danny stayed behind. Love kept them there."

She stops, her whole body tightening like she's holding herself together with the last thread. I catch movement out of the corner of my eye—Phoenix and Danny heading toward us. Phoenix sees me, and his face shifts. His smile breaks through whatever storm Michelle just left hanging over us. Before they reach us, Michelle leans in, her voice barely above a whisper.

"Aleyna and her father got airlifted out on a helicopter by the German government. Phoenix could've gone too. But he wouldn't leave Danny behind." She rushes everything in one breath. I imagine the helicopter, Michelle leaving in a taxi, through a damn warzone. The emotional chaos that must have been.

"You're so strong," I say. "Our pain really does shape us, doesn't it?"

Michelle glances at me, her vibrant eyes glistening. "I'm starting to really like you," she says. She squeezes my hand, and I squeeze back.

Danny and Phoenix reach us, their laughter spilling over into our small, somber bubble. Michelle leans in, a mischievous glint erasing the sadness from her face.

"But that's a story for another time," she says.

We leave the house hand in hand, laughter still echoing behind us.

But a heaviness trails after us too, like a scent you can't shake. As we drive back to the hotel in the delicate glimmer of the afternoon sun, I steal glances at Phoenix. Our hands are tangled. The joy of last night still flowing between us. Yet, even when he laughs, it can't fully mask the shadow in his eyes. Or maybe I just see it more clearly now.

"I want to ask you something," I say, heart pounding, "but I'm afraid to."

"I sense what you're going to ask me," he says, locking eyes with mine.

"Really? You think you can read my mind?"

"Yes," he says, pulling the car to a gentle stop in a residential area not far from the hotel. He shuts off the engine and turns toward me. His eyes penetrate deeply, as if he's trying to touch my soul. His gaze is completely disarming. I bite my lip. My fingers skim the seam of the seat upholstery.

"You want to ask about why I've chosen not to go back to Lebanon. To be with Aleyna." He leans his head back against the window, but his hand never lets go of mine.

Without a word, I lean back into the seat, swallowing the lump in my throat, giving him space to open up. He takes a long breath, his eyes tracing the invisible lines of the palm trees outside, their arms stretching up into the sky.

"There are parts of this world where love never wins," he says, his voice breaking a little. "Where parents bury their children. Where there's no justice for the innocent. Where peace feels like nothing but a mirage." Tears pool in his eyes, threatening to spill over. I lean in and cup his hand between mine. He looks at me. A single tear rolls down his cheek. I catch it with my fingers. He kisses it off and smiles.

"I heard my calling as an artist here," he says, voice quivering. "In the West. Our media lies. Most artists are afraid to tell the truth. You know how you want to heal people? I want to heal them too—their souls. That's always been my dream."

His thumb rubs over my knuckles. Another kiss. A touch of butterfly's wings. I smile, even though my eyes mist.

"I hate that you had to go through that," I say, squeezing his hand. "No one deserves that."

He closes his eyes for a second, like he's feeling the weight all over again.

"War changed me. Emptied my vessel," he says quietly. "After everything...I couldn't go back."

He looks at me again, and even though his hand is still in mine, a piece of him feels far away.

"If I ever went back," he says, "I would've lost the best parts of myself. My dream would've rotted into anger." I sit with that. With him. With the heavy silence between us. I wonder—how much of ourselves can we sacrifice for love? And does it make it more real? And then, before I can stop myself—

"Do you still love her?"

His gaze lifts to the palm trees, then finds mine again.

"Part of me always will," he says. "She was a chapter of my life I can't erase. Taught me lessons I needed. But my heart..." He squeezes my hand. "My heart is yours now." He pulls me into a kiss. And I feel it from my earlobes to my ankles.

On the way back to the Beverly Hills Hotel, my thoughts race like the palm trees blurring past the windows. Am I the new love—the healing love—who has appeared in his life to brush away the shadows of his traumatic past? He makes me feel like I am, even before I can fully believe it myself. Maybe we all heal ourselves by healing someone else.

When we pull up to the hotel and SLY is handed back to us by the valet, Phoenix wraps his arms around me. Tight. A ring of safety that makes the whole world disappear.

"Do you really have to go?" he asks.

"Yes. I'll be living with the tapestry lady, remember?"

"Why can't you just stay with me?"

"Maybe I will...one day." I laugh. He hates my answer. I hate it too. But I don't want to depend on a man. Not again.

"My arms don't want to let you go," he murmurs, his cheek resting against mine, the words carrying both longing and something heavier, like a goodbye he refuses to say.

"Same," I whisper, the word tickling his ear as I add, "See you tomorrow, my fire." His arms barely loosen. His fingers cling to mine, stretching the final touch into an endless moment as I slip into the driver's seat.

The drive to Monique's house in Pasadena is a blur. My thoughts spiral back, lost in everything I've just learned about my new lover. The California winter air slips through the open window, but all I can feel is his absence. His sweet musky scent still clings to my skin. His touch lingers in the spaces between my fingers. Despite everything he's endured, the flame in his eyes hasn't faded. It's incredible, how some people turn their pain into fuel for life.

Perhaps I am the air for his fire? Can I be the healing love Michelle spoke of? A healer. A magician who replaces his pain with joy? Was the babushka fortune-teller right? It's a hopeful thought. A prayer. Because in so many ways, he's already healing me. I never knew love could feel like this—complex yet strangely simple. Maybe love is only complicated when we fight it. Maybe when you finally surrender, it's simple.

The waning sun casts golden rays through the lush greenery around Monique's home, bathing everything in an enchanted kind of glow. It looks like a fairy lives here. Monique waves me in from the driveway, her petite figure wrapped in a handmade collage of colorful fabrics. She probably made the clothes herself. Her long blond hair dances with the evening breeze. She looks completely ephemeral. A living Tinker Bell, with an enormous Old English Sheepdog trotting around her, barking at the stranger pulling into their driveway.

As I step out of SLY, the grassy, woodsy smell of her plants encircles me.

"Hi, Lena," she says, her Polish accent curling softly around the words.

Her beautiful, wisdom-lined face beams with an energy that feels almost mystical. She pulls me into a warm hug.

"Hi, Monique," I say, taking in her vibrant garden. "It's like walking into a fairyland here."

At my side, her dog nudges my hand, insistent, until I cave and scratch behind his floppy ears.

"Pelusio, behave yourself around a lady," she says with a laugh, her voice as light and ethereal as the rest of her.

She leads me inside.

The corridor is a gallery of her textile masterpieces, each one bursting with colorful yarn. I stop, caught off guard by the sight of an antique Polish Hussar armor—its distinctive wings rising behind it, poised as if ready for battle.

The wings, I remember from Polish history class, were meant to terrify enemies on the battlefield. When the wind caught them, the haunting sound could spook even war horses.

"You like my Hussar?" Monique grins, clearly delighted by my reaction. "I almost caused an international incident bringing it here from Poland."

I blink, still a little stunned.

"Customs didn't believe it was a replica," she says, mischief dancing in her eyes. "They thought I was smuggling art."

She laughs again, and the sound fills her hallway like wind chimes as we move into her vast living room—a treasure trove of paintings, sculptures, and wild beautiful things. Each piece hums with its own story.

"David!" she calls, her voice lifting toward the staircase that curves up to the second floor.

A moment later, a tall man with a broad smile and white hair descends the staircase. His simple, monochromatic attire and thick glasses are a sharp contrast to Monique's artistic flamboyance, bringing a quiet balance to the colorful energy swirling around them.

They seem made for each other—plaques and honors from NASA. He works at JPL. A true man of service and science.

"Welcome! You must be the new addition to our family," David says, offering a handshake so warm it makes me feel instantly at home. After Monique shows me to a cozy room upstairs, and David kindly helps with my luggage, I follow her down a narrow hallway to her studio.

It's tucked at the far end of the house, bathed in soft natural light—her creative sanctuary. Dominating the room is a giant loom cradling her current project, a tapestry destined for the grand opening of a synagogue in La Jolla. The threads shimmer in bold reds, blues, and yellows, woven in a way that almost seems to make the colors radiate their own light.

"Sit here next to me. I'll show you the basics," she says, sliding a wooden stool closer. Her fingers dance across the threads with the grace of a concert harpist, weaving the yarn into intricate patterns spun from her imagination. "You grip these vertical threads this way," she says, slowing her movements so I can follow. My eyes track every small motion, desperate to catch and memorize each step. "And then the yarn weaves through them— over two, under one."

Mimicking her movements feels like my first wobbly steps as a kid.

Clumsy. Eyes locked on the crimson yarn, threading it, trying not to lose it.

"Over two, under one," I whisper, trying to hold the rhythm in my hands before they stumble. Monique leans closer, watching.

"Yes. Like that," she says. I let out a breath I didn't even know I was holding. She notices.

"Borders are easier." She smiles. "Let's start there." And somehow, my fingers loosen.

The next few months unfold with a comforting predictability. Wake up. Weave. Laugh. Tell stories. Repeat. Phoenix's music fills the studio. The CDs he gave me, still carrying his fingerprints, make him feel closer, even when he's not here. I tell Monique stories about him. About his paintings and photographs. About the way he calls me "my air." About how it still feels impossible, even now, that he's real. The way my heart jumps when I know I'll see him at the end of the day. We spend every evening together.

Our evenings together feel like the reward after a long day.

We make love. Then sit tangled together, flipping through progress photos of the tapestry. I tell Phoenix about Monique's life.

"She's just incredible."

The daughter of a famed comic book author in Poland, she was raised in a home brimming with art. While studying art conservation and painting, she stood in front of a giant Renaissance tapestry at a museum one day...and that changed everything. She fell in love with tapestry art.

She taught herself how to weave by looking at tapestries, figuring it out thread by thread. A master of a medium most people thought was dying.

Now her tapestries hang in museums, libraries, and the homes of celebrities all over the world.

Monique and I stand looking up at the thirteen-foot tapestry draped elegantly from the second-floor railing of her home. The finished tapestry looks marvelous.

"Are you excited for the unveiling tomorrow?" I ask, throwing my backpack over my shoulder.

"Absolutely. It's going to radiate in the Beth El Temple with all that natural light," she says, her eyes sparkling with pride. Then she turns to me, a playful glint in her gaze.

"Now, Lena, with those new weaving skills, you're practically ready to be a surgeon."

My laughter bursts out.

"Guess I'll have suturing down to an art."

But even as the words leave my mouth, a little shadow flickers through me.

Medical school. It's coming faster than I want to admit.

I shake it off. I still have a few months before that chapter starts.

I grip my backpack tighter.

"Is Phoenix coming with you tomorrow?"

"Yeah. We'll head over together from his place," I say, giving her a hug before heading out to him.

The next day, as we step into Beth El Temple, sunlight filters through the big windows, wrapping Monique's tapestry in gold. It looks alive. The colors catch every beam of light, glowing against the quiet solemnity of the synagogue.

Around us, a crowd buzzes with admiration. Nine months of Monique's work, now stretched above us. Phoenix stands by my side, contemplative. His mouth tugs into occasional smiles as people gush over her masterpiece.

I lean closer, sensing emotions rippling under his stillness.

"Are you okay?" I whisper.

He glances at the tapestry, then back at me. Layers of dark unspoken thoughts.

"God is love," he says quietly. "And yet, humans spend everything—money, time, their own lives—figuring out new ways to kill each other."

The faces fade for a second. What a brutal definition of humanity.

Why can't love alone ever be the answer?

Later, when we buckle up in SLY, he's still somewhere deep in his thoughts.

He strokes the steering wheel absently, his forearm flexing with the motion. I let him be in this silence. When his eyes meet mine, something wild flashes there.

"Ready?" His smile is mischievous.

"For what?" I squeeze my thumb, bracing for the answer.

With a soft chuckle, he leans in, pulling me into a kiss that's way too bold for the temple parking lot—and still feels perfectly right.

"For a magical weekend." His breath dissolves on my lips, fingers slipping up to the top button of my shirt. He loosens it with a daring little flick. Goosebumps race across my chest.

"I'm ready for all the magic," I whisper. "A whole life of it." The words trail off into a sound that's almost a moan.

"Let's go, my magician," he says, winking as he slides a CD into the player.

"xoxo" is scrawled across it in black marker. SLY carries us away, merging onto the freeway. Radiohead's new album spills into the car. A few hours pass.

The early April evening unfurls with wide open stretches of road. The world outside is painted in splashes of wild desert blooms against the far-off snow-capped mountains. Phoenix holds my hand. Our energies fuse effortlessly like atoms.

"Do you think love is a chemical reaction?" I think out loud. My gaze flits between Phoenix—every beat of the music pulsing through him—and the wild beauty outside. He squeezes my hand.

"I think it's more like alchemy," he says. I look at him. My mystic dancer. His silhouette against the backdrop of the Eastern Sierra Nevadas. The way his body moves. The way the flowers on the fields look like he sprinkled them there while talking. His smile. I memorize this moment. I memorize him.

"You're right," I whisper. I trace the ink on his forearm, my fingers slow, half-daring. A shiver moves through him—and widens until it pulls me under too. "It has to be alchemy. Because chemistry? That's just science stripped of any magic."

He looks at me—those walnut eyes burning without a single word. Hand squeezing mine, always. Radiohead's "Videotape" fills SLY, haunting and beautiful, as the night folds around us. We wind our way toward Mammoth Lakes, the road silvered by moonlight. When we finally pull into the parking lot of a small motel, even the stars seem tired. The heat of the shower feels like a luxury.

Later, in the soft glow of the bedside lamp, Phoenix wraps himself around me. His breath is slow and rhythmic against my neck. The most beautiful lullaby.

I dream we're soaring over the mountains, our bodies tangled like strands of hair caught in the wind. But then something yanks us downward—hard. The air vanishes. We're falling. My eyes flutter open. Phoenix is thrashing beside me, trapped in some nightmare, a scream caught behind his clenched teeth. Before I can move, he bolts upright, tears streaking down from closed eyes.

"Shh, it's just a bad dream," I whisper, throwing my arms around him. But he jerks violently, arms cutting the air. Almost hits me.

"I'm right here, Phoenix," I say, catching his flailing arms, wrapping myself around him. "Shh. Just a bad dream. I love you. I love you. I love you."

It spills out like a mantra. I rock us back and forth, holding him tighter, until finally—finally—his eyelids lift. The dream lets go of him.

A lonely tear escapes down his cheek, and I catch it with a kiss.

"You're safe," I murmur.

"I love you, Lena," he breathes. His voice trembles like his body. "So much."

"I love you too, Phoenix," I say, my voice choked with emotion. We finally said what we have been saying without words. The first light of dawn leaks into the motel room. We just sit there, breathing together. Our bodies tangled. Our hearts hammering the same beat. I think of my favorite Beksiński painting—lovers embraced so tightly you can't tell where one body ends and the other begins. Phoenix presses a kiss to my shoulder, his day-old beard rough against my skin. His hand traces soft, endless circles on my back.

"Since we're up..." he murmurs, voice almost a joke, almost not, "want to catch the sunrise over Mono Lake?"

The early morning light tussles with the last whispers of night as we head toward the lake. The sun teases the horizon, a shy glimmer just barely touching the sky. Standing by the mirror-like stillness of Mono Lake, Phoenix unpacks his Nikon, already lost in the moment. The cold nips at my fingers, turning them stiff as I snap photos of him. The artist in his element.

He bows, arms outstretched, like he's pulling the light straight out of the sky.

Letting it radiate through him.

"Was it about the war?" The question slips out. Before I have a chance to clarify, he simply nods yes. I knew it. But still, I search his face, hoping for more than just that silent answer. Phoenix settles on a rock, pulling in a deep breath, his gaze drifting out over the water, catching its first gold.

"It's hard to go through something like war and not come out changed by it. Not come out seeing everything...differently," he says finally. I sit down next to him. The stone underneath feels cool, rugged. He turns, a soft smile playing at his mouth. Something deeper flickers in his eyes.

"Being in the synagogue yesterday...I felt it," he says. "God isn't just one thing. Or one place." His fingers brush against mine like feathers.

"I always felt that spirituality in your photos," I say, thinking back.

"The way you stretch your arms out...it's like you're trying to embrace something bigger than yourself."

He laughs, sunlight catching in his eyes, making them look even more intense.

"That gesture—arms wide open against the backdrop of the world—is inspired by the purest acts of faith I ever saw. People praying in the middle of chaos. God's not stuck in some building." He gestures to the quiet lake. "He's everywhere. He's here, in this moment, by this lake. He was there, in those candlelit rooms, where hope flickered in children's eyes amid the darkness of war."

Tears sting my eyes. I finally see the pain he usually keeps tucked away.

"Yes," I say. "God is here. But you have to open yourself to feel him. Some people never do."

Our fingers interlock. The squeeze says everything words don't. A real smile breaks across his face.

"Maybe we're just vessels," he says, pulling me closer. "Made to be filled."

His breath is warm against my cheek. I can't answer; he left me speechless. I just breathe him in.

"We can hold so much love, so much light. Yet, we're so fragile that life cracks us open." His eyes drift to the rising sun, the lake flashing molten gold in its reflection.

"But it's through those cracks," I whisper, my voice barely reaching Phoenix, though the words feel more meant for myself—or perhaps even for God. "That's where the light seeps in. And sometimes, we have to empty our vessel to make room for something even more beautiful."

A breeze stirs the water, scattering shimmers across its surface. Hypnotizing shimmers. And for a moment, my past flickers through me like scenes from a movie. Images and feelings. Flashes of everything I've survived.

Phoenix's laughter breaks the solemnity.

"You're right, my magician. Sometimes you have to empty your vessel."

He leans in, and when our lips meet, it feels like a conversation with the divine. The water whispers ancient stories around us as we walk back toward SLY, hands linked. Halfway there, he pauses, tipping his head at me.

"Do you like mountains?"

The question stops me in my tracks. A rush of adrenaline sparks under my skin.

"Mountains were my first love," I say. Memories flood in. Southeastern Poland's rugged hills. The smell of wet moss. The redness of poppies. "They're home."

A spark lights in his eyes. "In that case," he teases, winking, "you're really going to love where we're headed next."

The towering Sierras reach for the clouds as we weave along the winding roads into Yosemite National Park. Old sequoias line the path. Oldest giants still living on Earth. Their colossal limbs are stretching skywards. Like they are challenging the mountains themselves.

Phoenix squeezes my hand tighter. Hans Zimmer spills through the speakers, and it feels like the whole landscape is breathing with us. My heart pounds against my ribs. The air sticks in my throat. Tears blur the giant trees into halos of green and gold.

God is here. I think to myself.

"Are you cold?" Phoenix asks, noticing the shiver that has my forearm hairs standing.

"No, just feeling," I mumble, neck stretched out the window, my gaze lost in the emotional landscape. The Half Dome rises ahead—impossibly vast, impossibly real—igniting a silent scream inside my chest. "I wish my eyes could take photos."

The misty forest air kisses my face. I'm feeling everything everywhere. My senses are wide open, catching every detail. Sharp. Wild. Intoxicating. I don't know if it's the landscape, Phoenix, or God that makes me feel like I could explode. Maybe it's all of it.

We hike, or maybe float, to Glacier Point. The mist from the waterfall clings to our skin. Phoenix stands on the rocky edge in his signature pose: arms flung wide, shaved head bowed toward the summit like a monk in prayer. I lift the Nikon, capture him. This perfect moment. My tears blur the viewfinder, blending with the mist. I lower the camera. Breathe. My gaze catches on a solitary Jeffrey pine. It clings to the edge of the cliff with nothing but sheer stubborn grace.

"What's wrong?" Phoenix asks, closing the distance between us. He wraps me in his arms. His sleeve catches my tears.

"This tree...it's like me," I manage to whisper, nodding to the pine clinging to the vertical ridge. Tears threaten to spill.

"This pain," he says softly, rocking me like a baby, "does it come from your ex?"

The sky and mountains blur.

"Yes," I sob. It rips out of me. Sharp. Ugly. Real. All the pent-up energy spilling free.

"You're right. You are that tree." His voice is so sure. "So let me be your roots."

He whispers into my neck, hug tightening, trying to break my sob. Absorb it.

"You are my roots," I echo. The words dissolve into the vastness around us. The vanilla scent of the pine's bark anchors me. To this moment. To Phoenix. My lifeline. My magic. And somewhere inside, I ask God the question I'm too scared to speak out loud: How could you possibly make me choose between this connection and my calling to be a doctor?

Phoenix rocks us gently, like he can feel the storm gathering behind my ribs.

The Yosemite Valley stretches out in front of us. Wild, holy, and heartbreakingly beautiful. I close my eyes, trying to hold onto this moment.

Even as the future tugs at the edges of my heart, whispering of the loneliness to come.

CALIFORNIA DREAMING

"Live today, no one is guaranteed a tomorrow."

I became the 8 of swords. Like the tarot card, jailed in my own mind. Bound only by my own self-sabotage. He kisses my shoulder. His lips tender, warm. A fire from which goosebumps spread in all directions. Yet, between my soft moans and the white silky sheets ruffling beneath me, my mind can't stop. I'm trapped in the future. In the little studio room in med school. Loneliness pointing its swords at me. Cold against my ribs. Nicking my skin even as he kisses it. Why is my mind like this? Stuck between the present and what-ifs. A blessing and a curse. Phoenix's hand traces my inner thigh, leaving a shimmering shiver behind it. His lips brush against my breath, heavy. Like he's trying to kiss away all the worry so I can step into this moment. But my mind is a cage. Numbing his touch. A touch that holds a key to the present.

"Let her go. We're here," he whispers. Always reading me like a book.

"It's so hard." I breathe. "My brain is stuck"

Phoenix cups my face between his hands. Leans his forehead on mine. His eyes find me—reaching deep, piercing through all the dark thoughts.

"Tomorrow is promised to no one, my magician. Now is all we have."

We roll over the bed, fusing together like drops of rain on the glass. His lips fall on mine. Hands hot, tracing my neck, my breasts, my hips. Memorizing every inch. And I float free. Free in our dance. Free above the blindfold of my own mind. Phoenix's love liberates me. The 8 of Swords flips into reverse.

"I don't ever want to let you go," he whispers against my neck. "Move in with me until you have to leave for med school." His arms tighten around me.

I rest my cheek against Phoenix's chest, tracing the shape of his collarbone, the slope of his chest muscles. I inhale him. Coconut and clean cotton. My ear on the calming drum of his heart.

For a moment, everything feels weightless.

But then it creeps in. 8 of swords.

Three more months. That's the expiration date stamped on our happiness. The idea of staying forever starts digging its claws into me.

It's tempting. Terrifying.

Imagining a life here, with him, makes something warm bloom in my chest, spreading all the way to my fingertips. But the ambition to become a doctor still burns at the edges of my mind. A flame I can't put out.

"Maybe..." I say, my voice catching. "Maybe I could take a year off. Reapply. Here. In California."

Phoenix shifts, making sure he's looking straight into my eyes. His hand brushes my pixie hair back from my forehead.

"Absolutely not," he says, voice fierce and soft at the same time. "You've worked too hard for this. We'll find a way."

The way he says it—we—cuts right through me.

Not you. We.

"I just wish you could come with me," I whisper.

The words slip out by accident.

His dreams—screenwriting, acting, everything he's been building—are here. And I can't ask him to give it up.

"I wish that too," he says. "I keep playing the lotto. They just won't let me win."

He laughs against my skin, trying to lighten the weight crushing us both.

"Damn lotto," I say, the words breaking into a half-laugh, half-sigh.

He kisses my forehead. "Seems I used all my luck winning you."

I close my eyes. Fall into him. Into the place where everything is still okay.

Living with Phoenix feels like swinging between worlds. My heart is a pendulum—caught between the ecstasy of his closeness and the shadow of loneliness creeping closer every day. Every touch, every kiss, every stupid little smile is bittersweet now.

It's already slipping in my mind, even as I try to hold the present.

Phoenix keeps teaching me how to cherish each day. How to live in the now.

His words hum in my mind like a repeated spell: Each fleeting moment is a fragment of our destiny. Gone forever once it passes.

Through him, I'm not just healing. I'm learning the art of now. Of feeling alive.

"Looks gorgeous," Phoenix says, coming up behind me by the window.

I'm hunched over my little mini loom (a parting gift from Monique), threading a strand of blue yarn through a small tapestry.

"You like it?" I pause, the yarn still suspended between my fingers.

He wraps his arms around me. His lips feather a kiss onto my shoulder, and a ripple of goosebumps races across my skin.

"Is this us?" he asks, studying the image. Two lovers tangled together against a burning sky. A bright blue butterfly covers its eyes with its wings.

"Yes," slips out as he turns me around. Our lips collide. My heart flutters like the butterfly trying to fly off my tapestry. For a second, everything else fades away.

It's just us. Threaded into each other like strands of yarn.

"Your hands..." he whispers against my mouth, tracing his fingers over mine, "they manifest beauty into life."

He plucks a tiny loose strand of blue yarn from the loom, tucks it into his pocket like it's the most precious thing in the world.

"I'm so thankful for our moments. I collect them all in my mind," I say, my lips grazing his neck. His hand whispers down my spine, from my neck to my butt. I shiver—not from cold. From the heat.

"How about a magic day?" he murmurs into my ear.

"Another magic day?" My smile breaks wide across my face.

Without a word, he grins like a kid about to spill a secret and darts into the bedroom. When he reappears, he's holding his LV carry-on in one hand.

"We're all set," he says. "I already packed for us."

I laugh, shaking my head, giving him a mock-serious side-eye. Phoenix and his thoughtfulness. Always one step ahead, attuned to needs I don't even realize I have. He just keeps deepening what I feel for him. This mystical, impossible, beautiful love.

Driving through LA is normally a torture—the traffic, the chaos—but somehow, with Phoenix, it feels different. The insane congestion seems less oppressive. Almost inconsequential. His thumb sketches little hearts into my palm, and every doodle sends a bloom of warmth straight to my face. How can he exist? What the fuck.

Eventually we pull into the Marina del Rey docks where the sun slaps off the white boats. The salty, sunscreen-soaked air wraps around us the second we step out of SLY. House music pounds from a nearby yacht. The bass thuds in my chest. I can smell grilled fish in the air. And then I see him. Danny spots us on the boardwalk, grinning like he's been waiting all year. He waves us aboard one-handed, somehow still managing to DJ with his other.

Phoenix smiles. "Habibi!"

Danny's energy is so contagious, and I can't help but grin too.

We weave through the crowd on the two-story yacht, the blur of faces and hugs and laughter spinning around us. Michelle waves from across the deck.

Someone hands me a drink I didn't even ask for. It's dripping with tiny lime chunks and wet fingerprints. I immediately put it down on the table and wipe my hand on my dress.

"Danny! It's such a nice surprise to see you today!" I shout over the music.

He slides one of the headphones off and pulls me into a big bear hug.

"Hey, gorgeous! Hey, handsome!" he says, slapping Phoenix on the back.

"We've been waiting for you two—let's head out!"

But mid-sentence, typical Danny, he gets distracted by someone else. Still DJing, he resumes the conversation he had paused when we arrived.

As the yacht lurches away from the harbor, Danny, with chunky headphones sliding off one ear, is already the heartbeat of the whole thing.

House music pulses through the air, syncing with people dancing, laughing, shouting over each other on the deck.

The marina glides past. Neat rows of homes. White boats bobbing lazily. A weirdly calm backdrop to the chaos we're carrying on board.

We pass a ridge of boulders—and the air punches me. A whole wall of pelican shit. But it seems like I'm the only one who notices. I lean into Phoenix, trying to mask the stench with a whiff of cologne off his neck. He pulls me closer, his arm looping tighter around my waist. The boat veers right, away from the stink, cutting into the open ocean. We rise and fall with the current. Waves crash against the hull, washing the stinky moment clean.

For a second, between the bursts of laughter and the shimmer of the sun, a tight knot twists in my chest. A shadow. The ache of knowing—I'm about to leave a part of myself on these California shores. Phoenix's arms encircle me. All of his affection. So warm, like sunbeams caressing my face. I shake off the future. I let the now never end.

"Where are we headed?" I whisper into his ear, swaying with the boat's slow dance over the current.

"To Catalina Island, mi amor," he murmurs against the back of my neck.

Mi amor. It's the first time he's said it. Every nerve ending sparks. I'm a wildfire.

The Pacific sun scatters diamonds across the water. Friends sway around us, their hands slicing the air, moving like they're dancing with the wind. It reminds me—of Europe, of sailing trips on Solina Lake with my dad and Grandpa, the air thick with smoke and the sharp scent of kielbasa roasting over open fire. Somehow, California has become my new Poland. My home. And Phoenix is the heart of it. Funny, isn't it? We leave what we love to chase dreams across oceans...only to realize what we were chasing was never a place. It was a feeling.

We reach Catalina faster than I expect. Danny steers the yacht into Avalon Bay, bobbing between the other boats like he's done it a thousand times. The island rises around us. Green. Raw. Mesmerizing. I lean over the rail, watching forests of kelp sway beneath the surface, their long fingers stretching up like they're trying to touch the sun.

The water isn't the clear blue I imagined. It's darker. Mysterious. A deep, moody blue that hides its secrets well.

"We're here!" Danny calls out from the captain's seat, cranking down the house music at the DJ table he ingeniously installed next to the wheel. Only Danny would need a built-in DJ setup to survive steering a yacht. I laugh under my breath. It suits his need for multitasking perfectly.

Phoenix takes my hand. "I have something special for you," he says, tugging me toward the stairs. "But you'll need your swimsuit."

I don't even ask. I trust him. We stumble into the little downstairs bedroom, giggling, tripping over each other as we wrestle with our swimwear. Hard-to-tame desire flickers between us. We have to peel ourselves from each other.

"Save it for later." I giggle as he unties the bikini top I just tied.

Eventually we make our way back on the top deck. I don't know how.

Ocean air plays with the heat on our skin. Despite a hot summer sun, the ocean breeze tingles my bare legs with its cold fingers. I hesitate at the rail, staring down at the water. Fucking cold.

Phoenix reads it immediately. "Don't think. Just jump, Lena."

And before I can argue, he cannonballs into the ocean. The splash slaps me. He surfaces, grinning, arms outstretched.

"Come!" he shouts.

I close my eyes and jump.

The ocean sucker-punches me. Ice-cold. Breath ripped from my lungs. For a moment, it's pure panic—like falling into the snow hole. But Phoenix pulls me against him. His chest, his arms, everything about him blazes compared to the icy water.

"Hot and cold," he says, grinning, water dripping down his lashes. "Just how you like it."

A laugh bursts out of me, messy and gasping, my teeth chattering so hard I can barely breathe.

Phoenix strokes through the water with that effortless strength he has, heading toward the island. "Come on," he calls over the slap of waves. "Keep moving. It'll help you warm up."

I push through the water after him, my arms burning, my skin freezing. With each stroke, the chill begins to fade. I don't know how he does it. He doesn't just pull me through the ocean. He pulls me back to life.

As we get closer to shore, my toes brush the sandy bottom. I stand, water lapping at my neck. Phoenix surfaces beside me, his hand slipping into mine under the waves. Our fingers intertwine. His mouth finds mine, a salty kiss. Ocean's heartbeat.

"Hot and cold," he teases again, forehead pressed to mine. "Just the way my baby likes it."

I laugh—messy and free. The sound of crashing waves carries it away. As we wade toward the beach, the shivers start to ease. Phoenix squeezes my hand, leading me up the pebble shore, the smooth stones shifting under our bare, wet feet. He pauses, looking inland toward the small cove.

"What is this place?" I ask, following his gaze.

There's a white ranch-style building tucked into the hill, overlooking the dock. Rainbow-colored canoes are stacked up like giant pieces of Lego.

"This is the Catalina Island Marine Institute," he says, voice softer now. "It's a special place for me."

I wait. Feel the pause stretch. His gaze sweeps the glittering water.

"I almost died here once," he adds, like it's nothing. A casual shrug.

"Stop it," I gasp, half laughing, half serious.

"I'm dead serious," he says, grinning at his own terrible pun.

He nods toward the building, framed by tall, skinny palms. "Seventh grade. I was here for marine camp. We stayed in those bunks. Snorkeled around this cove. I remember the fish—how colorful they were. How it felt like being part of their world."

I picture him. A teenage Phoenix in a wetsuit too big, all energy and wonder, diving after flashes of neon fish, desperate to memorize every part of the ocean. I smile. Of course he's a science nerd under all that artist fire. Just like me.

His eyes flicker with something I can't quite name. Nostalgia, maybe. Or a ghost of some heavy past.

"One morning, while snorkeling around that rock"—he points to a jagged boulder jutting from the water, not far from where we stand—"I spotted an abalone shell on the ocean floor.

It shimmered like a fallen star. Like it was calling me. I couldn't resist."

His hand tightens around mine. I can feel the pulse in his fingers.

"Everyone else moved on, but I dove down alone," he says. "I grabbed the shell...but it slipped through my fingers. Floated back down."

I watch his muscles tense up over his body. I can almost feel it—the cold water, the fading light, the wild panic.

"In that moment," he says, "with the sunlight dimming and the water turning murky...I had to decide. Fast."

"You went back for it?" I whisper.

He smiles. "Didn't even hesitate. My want reached for it before my fingers did."

His gaze shifts out to the ocean, somewhere far beyond the rock.

"When I grabbed it again," he says, "I held on tighter. But I misjudged the depth. I looked up—and for a second—I wasn't sure if I had enough air to make it back. And I thought this was my last chance to ever hold something so desired."

I cover my mouth with my hand, shaking my head. Terrified. Even though he's standing right here in front of me.

"Every kick felt like a desperate struggle, and I started inhaling water—a real 'this is it' moment," he continues, his voice strained.

"How did you get out?" I whisper.

"I didn't. The instructor had to pull me to shore and start CPR."

I gasp. "You almost died for a shell?"

"Almost," he says. His mouth quirks, but there's no humor in it. "But what truly died was my naive passion to chase dreams recklessly. That kid I was...he drowned down there. Became a ghost."

"That's so crazy," I say, squinting, trying to pull on the rest of the story. He runs his thumb over the back of my hand. A deep inhale.

"It wasn't until the war that I finally understood," he says, voice even softer. "Every day's a gift. You can't take it for granted. You can't be afraid to risk everything...even if it's just to touch your dreams." His words hang in the air as I gently caress his shaved head, feeling the softness beneath my fingertips. Trying to memorize this version of him. Real. Raw. Unarmored.

"Tomorrow is promised to no one, Lena," he whispers, his lips brushing my ear.

I pull back just enough to meet his gaze. His eyes. God, his hypnotic eyes. They hold nothing back.

"Well," I say, my voice shaking with everything I can't put into words, "I'm really fucking glad you didn't die."

His mouth quivers, like he's fighting for the right words. One arm stays tight around me. With the other, he fumbles into the pocket of his swim trunks. He doesn't break eye contact. Not for a second.

"I'm a broken man with many flaws," he says. "But when I'm with you, I feel whole again. I'm no longer afraid to love." His words bring tears to my eyes, my heart pounding with a surreal intensity, like waking from a vivid dream.

I'm speechless. Just standing there, soaked in saltwater and sunlight, as Phoenix drops to one knee. He opens his hand. A piece of blue yarn from my tapestry.

"Will you walk through life with me and let me fill your days with more magic, my magician?"

His stare is so intense. Yet, there's peace in it. The sunlight dances in his walnut eyes as he waits, searching my face.

Tears mix with the ocean drops still clinging to my cheeks.

"In The Count of Monte Cristo," he says, "Edmond couldn't afford an engagement ring. So Mercedes tied a piece of string around her finger to symbolize their love."

I'm frozen. Processing what is happening. He smiles a little. Takes a nervous breath. Doesn't rush the moment.

"This blue thread from our tapestry...it's my love for you," he says.

"It's not expensive or glamorous, nothing for others to envy, and it can't be bought or sold. It's a promise that my heart is yours."

I nod. Overwhelmed. Too stunned to speak as he wraps the soft blue string around my ring finger. Its fibers are soft and ticklish. Like our love.

Voice caught in my chest, I finally manage to whisper, "Yes."

He lifts me off the ground in one swooping, spinning motion, kissing me so fiercely I'm spiraling through time and space.

"Yes," I breathe against his mouth, "Yes, to a lifetime of magic days with you."

We're so tangled up in each other that we don't notice the man in the beige uniform until he's practically sprinting at us.

"Excuse me!" he shouts, waving his arms.

"Fuck," Phoenix mutters, eyes wide. He sets me down fast, grabs my hand, and we take off—splashing straight back into the ocean like two kids.

We dive under just as the man's angry face looms at the edge of the beach.

"Are we trespassing?" I gasp, kicking hard, aiming for Danny's yacht still thumping with music in the distance.

"Most definitely," Phoenix says, laughing, biting his lip. "But it was worth it," he adds, winking at me.

I glance down at my blue yarn engagement ring, glistening with seawater, and say, "It sure was."

As we dry off on Danny's yacht, the world explodes into cheers and hugs. Chocolate-strawberry cake appears from nowhere. Champagne pops. Laughter ripples through the boat, mixing with the delicious smell of fish and chips someone has whipped up on board.

Michelle and Danny are clapping like maniacs, faces lit up. Turns out Phoenix had planned everything, and I was the only one left in the dark.

"I'm so happy you're now one of the homies, my best friend's fiancée!" Danny shouts, pulling Phoenix and me into a messy huddle. Michelle dives in too. Her long red hair whips in the ocean breeze, its strands tickling my arms.

"I love you guys!" she beams.

Later, back in dry clothes, full from fish and chips and too much cake, we sail back toward Marina del Rey. I sit on a bench at the top deck, leaning into Phoenix. He wraps himself around me, chin hooked over my shoulder.

As his fingers gently twirl the yarn ring on my finger, he whispers, "I love you."

"I love you more," I say, turning to kiss him. His lips taste like sun and salt and champagne.

The sun hangs heavy and orange over the water as Danny's boat makes its final turn toward the dock.

"There's too much champagne in my bladder," Phoenix says, grinning as he excuses himself and heads below deck. The second he disappears, my heart caves in.

"Only one month left," I murmur to myself. The absence of his touch already tying knots in my stomach.

Danny, catching the shift in my face, pauses mid-conversation and walks over.

"Are you okay?" Danny asks, his big expressive eyes scanning mine for an answer.

I let out a long sigh. "No. Not really. I have to leave in a month. For med school."

"How long is med school?" he asks, like he's thinking maybe it's not that big of a deal.

"Four years," I say. Saying it out loud makes it real. Makes it terrifying. But Danny doesn't seem to catch the full weight of it.

"You know," he says, tipping his head back, looking at the sky, "I always thought Phoenix would stay single forever."

I let out a small laugh. "Yeah. I can see that. He does have that playboy streak."

Danny grins, like all the girls Phoenix ever had just flashed before his eyes. Then he squints. "He really must love you."

"I love him too." I try to force the words out over a wave of nausea. "But he's here. And I'll be in Tennessee." The last rays of sun scatter across the water, painting the docked boats in soft, pearly light. It's too beautiful for this sad feeling. Danny leans in, dropping his voice to near-whisper.

"Let me tell you a story," he says. "When we were in Lebanon, I was engaged too. Her name was Sana."

I blink. The way he says her name. There's an ache there. Soul-deep.

"After the war," he says, "I spent thousands trying to bring her here. Lawyers, paperwork, everything. But nothing worked." He shrugs. A sad little shrug that doesn't match the animated Danny I know. "They wouldn't let her in. Because her father was a Hezbollah militant."

My eyes widen. "What happened to her?"

"She got tired of waiting," he says, tipping his hat lower to shield his eyes from the past. "She married some sheikh from Dubai."

"I'm sorry," I whisper.

Danny just shrugs again. But even the shrug can't hide the scar.

Before he can say more, Phoenix appears, climbing the stairs from the cockpit below. His eyes search for me immediately.

"Look, at least you and Phoenix are in the same country. You'll figure it out," Danny says, patting my back with a grin that almost covers the sadness from before. "If there's true love, everything will fall into place." He winks at me, and a soft chuckle bubbles out of him.

"Habibi!" he shouts, grabbing Phoenix into a bear hug like they haven't seen each other in years. Despite the heaviness of my conversation with Danny, their ridiculous friendship pulls a smile out of me. It's impossible not to smile around them.

Danny bounces back to the DJ table. The air vibrates with his favorite remixes. I feel the bass all over my skin. People are drunk, laughing, and the wet evening air bites sharply. Wind and sounds—all now skewering through me. Phoenix notices the discomfort before I even realize it.

"You want to go inside?" he asks, already tugging me gently toward the stairs.

Before I can fully nod, he's guiding me below deck. The roar of the party softens into a cozy hum. Phoenix pulls me into him. I tuck my face into his neck, hiding from everything but him. He smells like a sweet mountain wind from my childhood.

We sink into the little leather couch. He takes my hand, brushing his thumb over the blue yarn on my finger, like it's the most precious jewel in the world.

"My fiancée." His voice. A warm lullaby.

As Phoenix's finger traces the blue yarn, my vision blurs. I blink—and the yarn dissolves. In its place is a red initial. "P" tattooed on the web of my finger.

The crisp ocean air fades into the soothing lavender scent of Dr. McKenna's office.

"Wow, what a story," she says, adjusting her glasses with one finger. "Kudos to Phoenix for recognizing your sensory overload."

"He's got a talent for reading between the lines." I nudge him gently.

"Does it with our daughter too."

"Do you often get overwhelmed like this?" she asks, her pen hovering over my file, waiting.

"Yes," I admit. "Especially when I'm stressed. Though... sometimes I crave it. All the sensations. As much as I can handle." I glance at Phoenix. He nods. We know that hunger. That burn.

"Mmm, that's quite common," she says, jotting something down. She shifts her attention to Phoenix.

"So, Phoenix—say you two go to a party. What does Lena do? Does she mingle with everyone? Or keep to herself?" Dr. McKenna leans in, studying him from behind her glasses.

Phoenix chuckles, gives me that look like we're sharing an inside joke.

"First, she does everything humanly possible to not go," he says.

I laugh under my breath. It's not even the slightest exaggeration.

"If she can't avoid it," he adds, "she sticks to people she already knows. Or finds someone who actually wants to talk about one of her interests."

"I just prefer living inside my head or talking about something concrete," I add, shrugging.

"Would you say your social battery drains quickly?" Dr. McKenna says, locking eyes with me.

I nod. What social battery? I think. In social situations, it feels like I'm always running on borrowed energy. Drained before I even start.

She rests her chin on her palm, eyes both sharp and warm.

"It must have been really challenging for you," she says, "moving to med school. New place. New people. New routine. How did you manage?"

I inhale so deep it stings. My eyes fixed to her mahogany desk. I stare till memories rewind like a film. And suddenly, I'm back there—stepping into my tiny studio dorm in Harrogate, Tennessee.

FIND YOUR STRENGTH

"Some wounds deepen with time."

The next few weeks feel like I'm moving through fog. Class. Anatomy lab. Study till collapse. I go through the motions, but my mind is somewhere else. The only thing tethering me to who I was is my new iPhone—a parting gift from my mom. Late-night calls with Phoenix are the only time I feel anything close to real.

He's started working at Danny's new hotspot in LA. I tell myself not to look, but I still end up scrolling through the nightclub's Facebook page. The photos with girls clinging to him. Girls draped over him like accessories. Sticky with their dazzling confidence. I hate how much it messes with me.

I'm back on ramen. My favorite jeans hang off me, but I keep pushing. Med school life.

After bombing my first anatomy exam—along with seventy percent of the class—I start to wonder if it's all a setup. Like they fail us on purpose. A slap-in-the-face reminder: you're training to be a doctor now, get your shit together.

It's past 2 a.m., and I'm alone in the anatomy lab. Netter Atlas of Human Anatomy is cracked open across one of the cadavers. I'm tracing nerves, vasculature, muscles of the upper extremity. Gotta be able to identify the structures on all eight bodies, one after the other. Humans vary.

The ID swipe at the door beeps.

Then it swings open—fast, like someone caught it on a gust of wind.

A tall, muscular Filipino guy strides in. He halts when he sees me—clearly didn't expect anyone else here. His brown eyes scan me fast. I hold his gaze just long enough not to flinch.

"I guess we're the two crazy ones studying at this hour," he says. His smile flashes—perfect pearly teeth against warm brown skin. "I'm Allan." He drops his backpack onto the nearest stainless-steel table.

I shrug without a word. My iPod blasts through the little portable speaker. The loud music helps. Makes this eerie place—eight cadavers marinating in formaldehyde—slightly more bearable.

God bless their sacrifice for science, I think, glancing at the open bag with a body halfway zipped out.

"I like your music," Allan says as he sets up beside me.

I instinctively stiffen. A big man. In the cadaver lab. In the middle of the night. And I'm alone. What the fuck?

He catches my unease. Grins. "Promise I'm harmless. You can ask my boyfriend—he calls me The Rock, but teddy bear edition." His voice is warm. Confident in that way that feels earned, not performative. Something in me unclenches.

"You really like my music?" I ask, eyeing his khakis and plain gray T-shirt. Still a bit suspicious. "Or are you just saying that to break the ice?"

He laughs. "No, really. It's a cool Radiohead remix." He pulls out his notes, arranging them methodically. When he taps his iPhone awake, I catch the lock screen—him and a smiling redheaded man, cheek to cheek. Phew. He really does have a boyfriend. Thank God.

"Thanks," I say, letting my shoulders drop. "It's just something to drown out the...atmosphere." I nod toward the dissected arm hanging limp outside the bag.

"You're hilarious," Allan chuckles.

"Want to study together?" I ask before he can. He was already inching closer, polite about it.

"Sure, if it's okay."

"Of course." I offer a real smile this time.

"I've already pinned all the structures in this one," I say, gesturing to the cadaver in front of me. The upper limb is marked with tiny flags: nerves, arteries, muscles, all labeled.

"We've got all night to get the upper extremity down before the daytime crowd invades every inch of this place," I add.

Allan's eyes are kind. There's this aura of softness around him, and his openness about being gay is refreshing. There's something beautifully unfiltered about him that makes me feel instantly connected.

"I'm Lena," I say, extending my hand.

"So nice to meet you." He shakes it. His grip is gentle and warm. "Let's get to work. I failed my anatomy exam."

"So did I." I chuckle along. "Most of us did. I guess hitting the brick wall is our wakeup call to get our shit together." Our laughter fills the stale formaldehyde air.

Engrossed in our study, we lose track of time, moving from one cadaver to another, identifying every muscle, bone, vessel, and nerve. Confidence builds with each memorized structure. We're leaning over one body that looks like he died young, tracing the branches of the brachial plexus, when the door beeps. A man in a security uniform walks in—mid-fifties, clearly surprised to see us. He scans my hooded form, head to toe, then quickly glances at Allan.

"I'm sorry, miss," he says stiffly, "this area is designated only for students."

I blink, caught off guard. "I know," I say, arching a brow.

His expression tightens. "May I see your ID?"

Allan locks eyes with me, clearly annoyed on my behalf.

"Here you go." I hand it over, matching his irritation with my own.

He studies it for a second. "So sorry, miss. You just don't look like a med student."

And there it is. Classic mansplaining.

I don't respond. Just let my eyes say everything my mouth doesn't. All the fuck-you energy I can summon.

"Just make sure you clean up before you leave," he adds as he turns. The door slams shut behind him a second later.

Allan shakes his head. "I guess you're too pretty to be a med student." We burst out laughing.

"I guess he's never watched Grey's Anatomy," I say.

Allan squints. "You sure do look like a brunette Izzy Stevens."

I roll my eyes. "I hate this shit. Not the Izzy part—but that people judge me by my looks. They call it 'pretty privilege,' but most days it feels like a curse."

"How dare you be both gorgeous and smart. The travesty," he teases.

My laugh echoes his. The loneliness I've been drowning in since med school started cracks open. A little light gets in.

"I like you." I smile, nudging him playfully.

"It's mutual," he says, locking eyes with me.

And just like that, I know: I've found my brother from another mother.

The next month is a blur. Allan and I become inseparable. Instead of going to anatomy lectures, we pull all-nighters in the lab—a risky strategy that pays off. We both ace the second practical exam with a 98%.

We miss the same question: a pin placed ambiguously right between the medial brachial cutaneous nerve and the radial nerve. It was hard to discern which structure Dr. Hodge is asking us to identify. We both pick the wrong answer, even though we can identify both structures on every cadaver in the lab.

On weekends, we escape to Allan's loft in Knoxville. It's a breath of fresh air from the middle-of-nowhere vibe of Harrogate. His boyfriend Jimmy—just as sweet as Allan—is always there, arms open and jokes at the ready. His jokes make me laugh just like Grandpa's.

As night falls, the loft fills with the smells of Allan's cooking: garlic, soy sauce, something spicy always simmering. "This is absolutely delicious," I say, biting into a homemade dumpling.

"Aww, I'm so glad you like it." Allan grins, reaching across the table to pile more onto my plate. He winks, his whole face lighting up. His love language is food. Just like my grandpa.

They've set up a whole room for me here—my own little space, complete with an en suite bathroom stocked with hand-picked soaps, candles, and lotions. They call it the "princess suite." It makes me laugh every time they say it. I always sleep best here, wrapped in the warmth of something I didn't know I needed: a found family. Allan and Jimmy are the brothers I always wanted.

Late at night, I lie in the dark, staring out at the train tracks behind their sliding glass doors. I'm not sure why these tracks are even here. I've never seen a train go by, but I like imagining one might.

My phone buzzes. "Hi, my love." I answer it instantly.

"Hi, my magician," Phoenix whispers. I hear the rustle of sheets on his end. "I miss you so much. Wish I was holding you instead of this pillow."

His scent invades my thoughts. It's been two months, but my memory clings to him fiercely.

"I miss you too. I feel so empty without you." I close my eyes, imagining his hands gliding over my thighs, his lips pressing against mine.

"Why don't I get you a ticket to come for Thanksgiving?" Phoenix asks, a hint of desperation in his tone. "I'm going crazy here without my future wife."

I roll over on the mattress, giggling at the thought. I close my eyes, letting his words wash over me. Hearing Phoenix's voice—so full of love—makes my heart feel suspended in the distance between us. The idea of seeing him again, being in his arms, feeling his heartbeat against mine, making love...it fills me with a fierce yearning that threatens to overflow.

"I would absolutely love that," I whisper-yell, careful not to wake Allan and J, asleep in the next room.

"Let's get you a ticket tomorrow. You should sleep now," he says, his voice a gentle caress.

"Will you stay on the line until I fall asleep?" I ask, rolling onto my side. The phone pressed beneath my ear becomes a stand-in for his chest. I miss the way his heartbeat used to lull me to sleep. His breath.

"Of course, my air," he whispers. "I'm picturing you here in my arms."

His voice softens even more, and the gentle music playing in the background filters through. My breath slows. My eyelids grow heavy. My hand traces the edge of the pillow, imaging it's his collarbone. His voice becomes a distant murmur. I count the breaths. The heartbeats. The miles between us. I'm lost in a swirl of memories. His smile, his touch, his eyes.

"Lena?" Phoenix's voice nudges me back.

My eyes flutter open, landing again on Dr. McKenna's desk—exactly where they'd been before the memory pulled me under.

"I was saying," she leans in, smiling, "it sounds like med school was a particularly lonely time for you, Dr. Hartley. Especially with the long-distance relationship. I'm glad you found a friend like Allan."

"I honestly don't think I would've survived that time without him," I say. The weight of those days still presses on my chest. "Med school was brutal. And with the long distance...some days, I was just drowning in tears. Wanting to quit."

Dr. McKenna nods. "Med school is indeed brutal. But you and Phoenix are now married and have a daughter. I'm curious—how did you manage the long distance?"

"We didn't," I say, then burst out laughing. But the laugh is hollow, laced with bitterness. "It was overwhelming. Phoenix's life and dreams were unfolding in California. He was thriving—acting, screenwriting, VIP hosting at Hollywood's hottest nightclub. Traveling to Ibiza, Burning Man, Vegas. Girls clinging to him every step. It drove me insane."

"But I always invited you," Phoenix says, his voice edged with old hurt. "I always wanted you there with me."

His words hang in the air. Echoes of our over-the-phone arguments. I roll my eyes, the loneliness of those med school years still coiled tight around my throat. Dr. McKenna says nothing, just lets us unravel like some kind of emotional autopsy.

"Yeah, I was scared of getting hurt. Stuck in med school. Trapped in this dream of becoming a doctor—a dream that was slowly swallowing me. I kept asking myself if it was even worth it. All the sacrifices, all my young years spent buried in textbooks, life slipping through my fingers. Then, when I didn't match in California and had to go to Chicago for residency...that moment shattered me. Four years of long distance, only to face three more? I couldn't do it. I had to let go."

Phoenix rubs soft circles on my back. He knows how much that time still guts me.

Dr. McKenna leans forward slightly. "You broke up?"

I breathe in deep. My shoulders sag. My fingers tug at the drawstring of my sweatpants. I can't find the right words.

"Lena broke up with me when she started her residency," Phoenix says quietly.

Dr. McKenna's eyebrows lift.

"You broke my heart when you sent back the yarn ring in the mail," he adds, glancing at me.

"At the time, I didn't feel like I fit in your world anymore," I whisper. His arms tighten around me. I blink fast, willing the tears to stay where they are.

Dr. McKenna's eyes are gentle yet probing. Like she's trying to see the whole knot of us and figure out where it first tangled.

"This kind of avoidance is very common, Lena," she says, scribbling something down. Then she sets her pen aside and looks up—first at me, then at Phoenix.

"How did you find your way back to each other?"

I glance at Phoenix, managing a smile through the tears as he nudges me gently.

"Yeah, tell that story," he says, one eyebrow raised with that familiar, playful push.

Dr. McKenna tilts her head, arms folding in quiet anticipation. I chuckle softly. My fingers trace the red L tattooed on his ring finger. The initial blurs into a vivid memory, swelling until I'm back there. A cold Chicago winter.

I'm holding a letter from Grandpa. It's my birthday—a day I've always hated—but this one feels especially bleak. The gray slush of Chicago mirrors the emptiness in my chest. It's been months since I last spoke to Phoenix, yet the wound of our separation seems only to deepen with time. His presence haunts me—in every new song, every film, every piece of art, and now, even in this letter. Their handwriting is eerily similar. For a moment, I trick myself into thinking the letter is from Phoenix. But holding my grandpa's words still brings a different kind of comfort. One I hadn't realized I needed.

As I sit on a bed in the sparse hospital call-room, the taste of stale black coffee lingers in my mouth. I've been running back and forth to the ER all night for admissions.

In a rare quiet moment—though we never dare call it that in medicine—I pull the letter from the pocket of my white coat. The envelope is soft and slightly bent, the card decorated with fuchsia pansies. I start to open it, fingers jittery with caffeine. I'm praying my pager stays silent just a couple more minutes.

But before I can even unfold the paper, the hospital overhead snaps through the stillness:

"Rapid response, three north, adult. Room 3204."

My heart kicks. I shove the card back into my pocket and bolt from the call room. As I pound the elevator button, another announcement erupts—"Code blue, three north, adult. Room 3204."

They're not breathing. Screw the elevator. I sprint for the stairs, my coat flying behind me like wings. The hallway on 3 North flashes past in a blur until I reach room 3204.

Inside, a young man—barely an adult—is gasping for air, his skin dusky, lips the color of overripe blueberries. Three nurses flank the bedside, eyes snapping to me. Waiting for orders.

"Eighteen-year-old Hispanic male," one says quickly. "Admitted earlier today by Team A for pneumonia. He suddenly became tachypneic. Still low on the nasal cannula."

Shit. My senior isn't here yet. I force myself to breathe calmly. My eyes flick to the name tag of the nurse nearest me.

"Angela, put him on a non-rebreather. Fifteen liters," I say, trying to keep my voice from shaking. Inside, I'm freaking out.

I glance at another nurse, her badge hidden by her stethoscope. "Get a crash cart!" She bolts before I even finish the last syllable. In a code situation, we read each other's minds. An autopilot we trained for.

The patient is thin, gasping for air, unable to utter a word. His terrified brown eyes lock onto mine, pleading for help. It's the worst kind of look. You never want to see it. It haunts you forever.

"Don't worry. We've got you," I whisper, placing my stethoscope to his chest.

Rales. Bilateral.

"Any chest pain?"

He nods weakly, trying to form words through the oxygen mask now strapped to his face. His O2 sats are tanking, now barely at 78%, despite all the oxygen.

The squeal of crash cart wheels shrieks through the hallway. Getting louder. More staff rush in. I spot a young blond nurse. Horror in her eyes. She sees the ghost already.

"Get an EKG, start an IV. Call for a chest X-ray. Page the ICU hospitalist. Stat!" I yell. The words shoot out, sharp, like rounds from an automatic weapon. Angela wheels the crash cart into the room, barely missing the chipped wall.

The patient jerks forward suddenly, clutching his chest. A strangled moan escapes before he collapses back onto the bed. Limp. Lifeless. I lunge for his neck. No carotid pulse.

"Start compressions!" I shout, yanking open the drawer for the intubation kit.

The thump of chest compressions begins. Sharp. Rhythmic. The faint sound of cracking ribs punctuates the air.

"Hold compressions!" I slide the laryngoscope blade past his epiglottis. Guide the tube in. "I'm in. Resume compressions."

A sweet, musky scent rises up. The unmistakable smell of death.

The room spins into controlled chaos.

Just then, Dr. Wong—an ICU hospitalist renowned for her formidable intellect—bursts into the room, with my senior resident following closely behind. She immediately takes command of the code, and the chaotic energy shifts. Like a conductor leading an orchestra, she deftly coordinates our frantic efforts into a symphony of life-saving actions. How does she stay so calm?

"His veins have collapsed. I can't get a line in," a nurse reports, her voice urgent.

"Lena, start a femoral," Dr. Wong instructs, then moves to auscultate the patient's lungs, confirming my tube placement is correct. "Good job on intubation," she affirms, nodding to me.

Angela hands me the central line kit. I palpate the femoral artery and go medial. The needle slides in smoothly, dark blood splashing onto the pristine hospital sheets.

"I'm in!" I announce. Blood from my gloves smearing on his thigh as I secure the line.

We try to resuscitate the patient for forty minutes, administering countless rounds of IV epinephrine. His chest crunches under our hands as we switch, taking turns with the chest compressions every two minutes. Suddenly, his mother, who had only just stepped out before he decompensated, enters the room. The bowl of chicken noodle soup she carries spills everywhere, like her scream. Someone ushers her out as we continue the code.

Another sixteen minutes pass before Dr. Wong calls it: "Time of death, 4:44 a.m." She acknowledges the grim reality—that even if we could restore a spontaneous pulse, his brain would never recover from the lack of oxygen. A collective sigh of defeat seems to lower every shoulder in the room. The heavy hand of death. Tonight, she wins. Even the brightest doctors aren't God.

"Would you mind debriefing his mother?" Dr. Wong asks me gently.

I nod, feeling the knots in my stomach tighten. My sneakers squeak against the floor as I walk to the family room, where his mother is pacing back and forth, her sweet face etched with every emotion. When she sees me, it turns to mostly fear. The words I have to deliver pierce her heart as she collapses into my arms, sobbing.

"No, no. Miguel, no!" It's the way she says his name that slices deep into me. And in this moment, I wish I were truly a magician. Someone who could reverse her pain. Take it away. She slumps into my shoulder, and just then, as I embrace her, I notice a drop of blood on my shoe. His blood.

The rest of the night feels like I'm a fish in an aquarium. Everything muffled. Movement slow. Sorrow clinging to the glass. A reminder of how fragile life really is. Katie, my senior resident, and I sign out and walk to the parking lot, still shaken.

"We couldn't save him," I say quietly.

Katie looks at me, her big blue eyes glassy. "We did everything we could," she replies, her breath turning to vapor in the icy Chicago air.

I look up at the sky, maybe speaking to God more than to her. "Sometimes I wonder if what we do makes any difference."

"Life is fucked up," she says. Her voice is flat. That soul-guarded tone I've come to recognize in second- and third-years. The kind trained into us like armor. A wall of indifference to stay sane doing what we do.

"Yup," I murmur, already walking toward SLY.

"Are you okay, Lena?" she calls after me.

I wave a hand behind me, not turning around. "I'll be fine."

Inside the car, I sit still for a second. Rocking a little, without meaning to. My fingers slide into my pocket and wrap around the rippled edges of Grandpa's letter.

I know why Katie asked. Last week, we lost a second-year resident to suicide. The silence around it still hasn't broken. They always brush these things under the carpet. I keep wondering what medicine does to us. How we start with such idealism—wanting to help, to heal—and end up drowning in this grind. Depressed. Too deep in it to quit.

Medicine is like going to war. And by the time we finish, we're all just a bunch of broken soldiers, released into the wild to save others—while we bleed quietly ourselves.

Back at my tiny studio, I peel off my scrubs and step into a hot shower, letting it scald the grief off me. As the early morning sun sneaks through the blinds, I sit on my bed and open Grandpa's letter again.

His handwriting still carries the scratch of his voice. I swear I can smell his delicious żurek as I read:

"Dear Lena,

Live in such a way that each day surpasses the last, becoming more incredible and special. Chase every moment, so that later, your memories will brim with joy. Let the sun, raindrops, and the smiles of others infuse you with life's vibrant energy.

Live as beautifully as you can, in your own unique way.

Find your strength.

Sending you a big hug and a kiss, fired from my soul gun.

Love,

Dziadziu Stach."

My fingers tremble. Tears drip onto the letter. A sob rises, thick and loud, breaking from my throat—just as the doorbell rings.

I flinch, startled. My heart skips. Probably my mom. Or Anya. I swipe my sleeve across my face, trying to erase the tears.

"Find your strength," echoes in my mind as I walk to the door. A glimmer of hope I sure needed today. I open the door and freeze.

The world drops out from under me. Grandpa's letter slips from my hand and flutters down like a feather...landing on a pair of familiar red and black sneakers.

The hallway light catches his face. I can't breathe. Can't think.

I bend to pick up the letter, and before I can stand, his arms are around me. Pulling me in like gravity. Emotions cascade down my spine.

"I just can't live without you, my magician," Phoenix whispers. His warm lips graze my ear, sending shivers that unravel everything knotted inside me.

I melt into him like a marshmallow over summer fire. My heartbeat slows. My whole body exhales.

"I love you," I whisper, my tears soaking into his cheek.

"I love you more. I never want to be without you." His arms tighten around me. "Will you let me in?"

I grab his hand and pull him inside.

And when our lips meet, it feels like God cracked open the sky and stitched our souls back together.

ANGEL'S EYES

"Collecting the rainbow as the rain fades away."

"**W**ow." Dr. McKenna's voice pulls me back from the depths of a memory that spans over a decade.

Phoenix's thumb traces little hearts on the back of my hand. I exhale. A soft smile curls at the edges of my lips—touched by the ghost of his kiss, the memory of Grandpa's letter pulling me out of that dark place.

"Did Phoenix move to Chicago to be with you?" Dr. McKenna asks.

"No. I moved to California a few months later," I say, warmth blooming in my chest. "A second-year residency spot opened up in Ventura. I interviewed, got it, and by July, I was navigating the chaos of California hospital."

Phoenix nods, pride gleaming in his eyes. "Like I said—if there's no door, my wife will carve one out. I love her persistence." He laughs, and Dr. McKenna smiles back.

"That's fantastic. Must've been such a relief—to finally be together," she says. There's a genuine happiness for us in her eyes. Something you'd see in a friend.

"It was incredible," Phoenix says. "Like the morning fog clearing to reveal the sun." He lifts his hands, miming it as if clearing clouds from the sky.

Dr. McKenna glances at the clock and folds her hands. "We've got one more hour. Thank goodness these assessments are long."

Phoenix and I exchange a look—half amused, half amazed. Time has disappeared in this room. My memories, stretching back through years of chaos, ache, and grace, have wrapped around us like a web. A hopeful kind of web. One made of clarity and self-awareness.

"So, tell me why you're really here."

Dr. McKenna's voice tugs me back. Her expression shifts— soft lines turning sharp. "Tell me about your daughter."

A heat rises in my chest. Not embarrassment. Not fear. That sacred kind of warmth only a mother knows.

"I'm here more for her than for myself," I say, digging my phone from the pocket of my oversized gray sweatpants. I tap the screen.

Ruby's eyes fill the frame—amber and ancient, like the sun caught fire and chose her to carry it. A perfect blend of Phoenix and me.

Sunlight spills through her curls like it's blessing her. She looks like a little forest fairy.

I close my eyes. One breath in. A pulse of determination beats in my chest.

"She's the real reason I'm here."

Dr. McKenna leans back, silent now. Waiting. Like a reader who knows the next chapter is about to unravel.

I glance back at my phone again. Ruby still glowing on the screen. My finger hovers near her cheek, tracing the light dancing across it. My heart kicks up.

That morning rises up in me like a wave—quiet but unstoppable.

Sunrise creeps through the cream blinds of our La Playa hotel suite in Carmel-by-the-Sea. A golden glow spills across Ruby's sleeping face. Sixteen months old, and already a mirror of her father—those dark baby eyebrows, dramatic as if painted by Da Vinci. Her lips, soft and parted from nursing, hold the calm of dreams. I lean in. Press a kiss to her tiny fist. She tightens her fingers around mine, even in sleep. Won't let me go. Something breaks open inside me. The profound weight of motherhood. The realization: I have to find strength to speak up. For her. Tears slip down my cheeks before I can stop them. My sniffling stirs Phoenix. His arm stretches across the sheets, sleepily searching for his girls.

When his eyes flutter open, they land on me. Then on her. And soften.

"Lena, what's wrong?" he whispers, careful not to wake Ruby.

I exhale. The breath is shallow, unsatisfying. My chest aches for more air, but anxiety clamps down. Tight. Relentless. Phoenix's fingers thread gently through Ruby's curls—each stroke a lullaby.

He watches me, eyes full of quiet questions.

I slowly release myself from her grasp. Her fingers twitch in protest, then relax.

Dark curls spill across the pillow, pooling beside Phoenix like swirls of dark melted chocolate.

She smiles in her sleep, untouched by the storm rising inside me.

The sight of her—so safe, so unaware—squeezes fresh tears from my eyes.

"Let's sit by the window and talk," Phoenix says softly.

He rises, goosebumps forming on his bare chest from the morning chill. I feel his warm hand on the small of my back as the chilly air wafts in from the slightly open window.

I grab my laptop and follow him into the parlor.

We settle into two bamboo chairs facing the Pacific, the window blurring the horizon where green cliffs dissolve into endless blue. You can smell the ocean. I set the laptop on the glass table. The screen lights up my face as a dozen tabs blink open. Each one a breadcrumb from another sleepless night.

Each one a piece of the mosaic in my mind, still missing vital fragments. "Phoenix," I whisper. Words lodge in my throat. "Ruby... I think Ruby might be autistic." I swallow. The words drop into the space between us like stones in a deep well. There's an echo.

Phoenix goes still. His shoulders tense. Eyes darken—not with fear, but gravity.

"Come on, Lena. This again?" He shakes his head, already slipping behind the wall. "You've got to let this go."

My heart slams against my ribs. "But..." I manage. The rest of the words crumble in my mouth. There's too much. Too much to say, and no way to say it.

"She's fine," he says softly. The gentleness of his denial almost hurts more. "You're overthinking it. Just...try to relax." His words press like a lid on a boiling pot. And I'm already bubbling over.

His hand cups mine. Feels the tremble. His eyes search mine. I say nothing. Just look at him. But inside, I'm burning.

The ocean breathes softly. I glance at Ruby. She sleeps curled like a comma. So peaceful. None of this tranquility touches the volcano inside me. This fucking anxiety has been choking me for weeks. I pull out my phone. My fingers shake.

Tap. The video plays. Ruby at the playground, rushing up to a little girl, babbling inches away from her face. Invading her personal space. The girl backs away, frowning.

"Can't you see it?" I ask, voice cracking. "She has no social antenna. This isn't normal."

He says nothing. Just stares. Silence extends painfully in his eyes. His face caught somewhere between disbelief and frustration. I swipe to another clip. Him and Ruby with the red balloon.

"Look, she uses your hand like a tool. Doesn't even look at you."

I'm pleading now. Please see it. Please. Something flickers in his eyes. Doubt.

He leans back, recoiling like the screen just slapped him.

His gaze escapes out the window, into the blur of ocean and sky. The sky that is waking up like he should.

"She barely makes eye contact. She doesn't point. She doesn't even respond to her name!" The fear leaks into every word. I'm unraveling.

"She is fine." He snaps, rising from his chair so fast it scrapes against the floor.

His shoulders knot up, a storm rolling just beneath the skin.

"No, Phoenix." I rise too. My voice shakes as I reach for him, fingers brushing his shoulder.

"You need to see what I'm seeing. Something isn't right."

He turns but won't meet my eyes.

I turn the laptop toward him. Tap play on a video titled Early Signs of Autism.

Clips begin to roll. Children avoiding eye contact. Not responding. Spinning. Flapping.

Phoenix's jaw tightens. His eyes stay fixed. Distant. Like he's watching it through fog. Not seeing.

I pause the video. The silence that follows feels thick. Oppressive.

"Can't you see? Our daughter does all of that!" I say, pointing at the screen, heart pounding in my ears.

"She's stopped saying any words—not even Mama or Dada."

I shut my eyes for a second and clench my fists.

"She flaps her hands. She runs in circles around the kitchen island. Yesterday, we watched her climb on and off the couch for fifteen minutes straight. Repeatedly. I had to distract her just to get her to stop." I gesture toward the beige-striped loveseat, its presence now a trigger. "These are all signs," I whisper-yell.

Phoenix exhales sharply. His hand slices the air in dismissal.

"Jesus, Lena. She's a toddler. Toddlers do weird shit!"

His voice cuts through the morning stillness—no longer a whisper, but a hiss.

I flinch. I'm sensitive to this kind of tone. It reminds me of Tomek. The anger in Phoenix's voice isn't aimed at me. It's rooted in fear of what an autism diagnosis might mean for our family. Still, his denial lands heavy on my chest.

"I know you don't want to hear this," I say, my voice soft again, "but autism isn't the end of the world. She needs to be evaluated, though. She needs help. Services."

My fingers find the drawstring of my pajamas. I twist it, trying to ground myself.

"She's fine, Lena! Didn't you make me ask her music teacher last week? And the speech therapist? They both said she's not autistic." He squints, veins bulging in his neck. "Just drop it already! You're driving yourself crazy."

I look into the distance. Watch the waves crash against the rocks. Heat floods my face.

"They're not autism experts," I murmur. "And autistic people can mask."

"Mask?" he asks. I feel his eyes on me but keep mine on the horizon.

"Yes. Like pretending you're not autistic. Hiding. Acting 'normal.' It's what girls often do. Makes it harder to diagnose in females."

Phoenix starts pacing near the window, his expression tightening, skin flushed.

"She's been in speech therapy for two months," I say. "No progress."

I meet his eyes this time. "I think she needs an autism evaluation."

He stops. Turns. Stalks over to the table—and slams the laptop shut.

His wedding ring hits the metal with a sharp clang. The sound echoes through the room. Through my mind.

"My daughter does not have autism," he spits. Then he storms out to the bedroom to hold Ruby. She's asleep. Unaware of the storm of worry around her.

His words echo in my head like a bad refrain. My heart pounds in my throat.

I slump into the chair and bury my face in my hands. Tears slip between my fingers.

And just when the feeling of invisibility threatens to erase me—through the blur of sobs—I feel Phoenix's hands wrap around me.

He kneels in front of me, eyes wet.

"I'm sorry," he whispers. "I don't want to be the reason you cry." His lips brush my forehead. He lifts my chin gently, fingers catching my tears.

"I just have this feeling," I murmur, sniffling. "All I want is to help her. What if ten years from now she can't talk? Can't tell us what she needs? Can't manage basic tasks—because we missed the window? When therapy could've changed her whole life?"

"I would never forgive myself," he says, instantly. He pulls me into a full hug, his warmth chasing away the cold creeping onto my skin through the window.

I wipe my nose with my sleeve and look up at him. "I've done all the research. Early therapy is everything. The longer we wait, the harder it gets for her."

Phoenix sighs. His embrace feels a bit deflated.

"Do you really think she's autistic?" His voice is quiet, but I can hear the tremble beneath it. I meet his eyes. So much love there. So much fear.

"Yes," I say. Then add, "But autism is a spectrum. Every autistic person is different.

A diagnosis doesn't change who Ruby is—it just helps us help her."

He nods slowly. Then smiles. It's a forced smile. Like I do sometimes with strangers.

His arms tighten around me again. And for a moment, we stand there. Not broken. Just holding each other. A new kind of unity beginning to form between us.

The weeks blur into a collage of sleepless nights and relentless research.

My laptop brims with open tabs—medical journals, TED Talks, parenting articles on autism. As we begin to accept the possibility of Ruby's diagnosis, more signs start to crystallize. She's lost all her words—even "ball," her favorite. Her eye contact drifts more each day. Her repetitive behaviors grow sharper, harder to ignore.

Now we're navigating new terrain—texture issues with food. Thank God I'm still breastfeeding. It takes the edge off the worry, since tofu and seaweed are the only solids she'll eat without protest.

"Trust me, she'll grow out of it. You were just like this," my mom says, brushing it off. She reminds me of my own fussy eating and the endless nasty iron supplements I had to take as a kid. And the cod oil. The thought still makes me nauseous. I nod. But inside, I'm terrified.

A coworker at the hospital pulls some strings—calls in a colleague favor. We skip some of the months-long waitlist. Only six weeks. And suddenly, the assessment is real. Booked.

It's a beautiful day when we arrive. Ruby is fast asleep, cheek pressed to my chest in the Boba carrier. Oblivious to the gravity of the day.

I rock her gently, trying to match the rhythm of her breath. I can't stop hoping—quietly, fiercely—that today will bring clarity. A path. A way to help her.

Phoenix scans the waiting room. Nervous. His eyes land on an older boy across from us—screaming. Nothing sounds like recognizable words. His parents try to soothe him, visibly exhausted. I watch Phoenix tense.

"Ruby Hartley!" The nurse calls out, her voice echoing down the sterile hallway.

She leads us into a room that feels more like an interrogation chamber than a pediatric office—mirrored windows, too-bright lighting, a silence that feels watched.

Dr. Lim waits inside, along with her assistant. A tall stack of questionnaires rests on the table. Phoenix and I sit. And something in me tightens. We are here.

The assessment stretches for hours. Each moment slower than the last.

Having already devoured the research, I recognize every test as it unfolds—speech, motor skills, cognitive tasks, social cues. I watch them unfold like scenes from a movie I've watched a hundred times. Only now, it features my daughter.

At one point, Ruby plays quietly with a doll. The shoe slips off. She picks it up and, without looking at me, hands it over— her gaze locked on the shoe, never reaching my face. Not even for a second. I fix it. Slide the shoe back onto the doll's foot. Out of the corner of my eye, I catch Dr. Lim jotting a note into the file. She already knows.

The weight in the room grows denser with every scribble of the pen. Every silent exchange between clinician and clipboard. By the time Dr. Lim finally speaks, I already know. The answer has been circling us for hours.

"Mrs. and Mr. Hartley," she begins, her voice gentle, but steady, "based on today's assessment, I am fairly certain Ruby is on the autism spectrum. We'll review all the data and schedule a full debriefing next week to walk through our findings and recommendations. But from my initial observations, it seems quite clear."

Relief and fear flood through me at once. A strange alchemy of vindication and grief. My instincts were right. And now everything changes.

Beside me, Phoenix shifts. His face goes pale. Like the floor beneath him just gave way. A physical echo of the earthquake rippling through his world.

The following week, we receive the official diagnosis: Moderate to severe autism spectrum disorder.

"Ruby's lowest scores were in speech," Dr. Lim says, peering over her glasses at us. "Her expressive abilities are at the level of a five-month-old, and her receptive abilities are closer to eight months."

Phoenix stares blankly, still trying to take it in. I nod. Urging her to keep going.

"However," she continues, her tone softening, "her cognitive skills are above average for her age. At eighteen months, she's performing at the level of a two-year-old. That typically means she'll respond well to therapy." She offers a small smile. A sliver of hope.

"I've already arranged the referrals," she adds.

"You're lucky—you live near one of the top autism programs in the country. Blooming Steps. They'll contact you for an initial assessment. But please be prepared...there may be a wait."

Relief and determination fuse together as we step out of Dr. Lim's office.

No more guessing. No more circling.

"Time to turn into mama bear," I mutter, already dialing Blooming Steps. I pace outside the car, phone pressed to my ear. Phoenix buckles Ruby into her car seat, gently brushing her curls from her eyes. She's sleepy. Peaceful. Unaware of the battle we've just entered.

I hang up and slide into the passenger seat, slamming the door harder than I mean to.

"What did they say?" Phoenix asks.

"She's on the waitlist." I grip the phone. "They said October."

"Are you serious?" His voice sharpens. "That's five months from now."

"And we have insurance," I say, gripping my phone, barely resisting the urge to throw it. "Imagine the families who don't."

He looks out the windshield, jaw clenched.

"I'll keep calling," I add.

Then sink back into the seat. For a moment, I feel deflated. But under it, a fire is already burning. I'll fight for her. Every single day if I have to.

Phoenix pulls out of the hospital parking lot, his face flushed with anger.

His forearm muscles tense on the steering wheel, but he says nothing. Ruby drifts into deeper sleep, lulled by the hum of the car. As we merge onto I-5, I can almost hear his thoughts churning.

"These are kids, for God's sake. Kids. Inmates get better care in this country," he finally mutters. Every word spilling out with agitation.

He glances at Ruby in the rearview mirror, her face soft in sleep, and lowers his voice further. His head shakes. Slow, bitter.

"We pour billions of tax money into wars," he says. "Yet, our own children—the future of humanity—can't get the support they desperately need. It's completely fucked up!"

At home, after dinner, we settle into routine: Rapunzel on repeat. Ruby's deep in her Disney princess obsession. There's one scene she loves—Rapunzel dancing in town, her hair braided with flowers. Every time this scene comes on, I scoop Ruby up and twirl her. She giggles wildly. But she never looks at me while we dance.

The only time I catch her amber eyes is during nursing. Those moments are sacred.

"Don't worry, my baby," I whisper, brushing her curls aside as her eyelids flutter close. Heavy with dreams. "Mama hates eye contact too."

She breathes slow, her face nestled against my chest. So peaceful. And I wish I could freeze this moment. How do I keep her safe from what's coming? From a world that might not understand her? Judge her?

My mind races—through every blog post, every thread, every horror story.

The bullying. The abuse. The cruelty people unleash on kids who are different.

How do I protect her from that?

"Is she asleep?" Phoenix whispers, sneaking into the bedroom, careful not to let the hallway light spill too far.

"Mhm," I murmur, gently laying our little angel on her rainbow pillow.

He pulls me into an embrace. Our foreheads rest together. Breaths sync.

"Remember that quote you had on your MySpace bio?" I whisper. "That no prayer ever goes unanswered?"

His smile brightens. His hands squeeze mine. He's not religious. Neither am I.

But he's the most spiritual person I know. We stand there in silence, sending up our hopes.

"God will guide her," Phoenix says softly.

"I know."

And for a moment, it feels like something greater than us is holding all three of us. A strength we can't name, but feel... nonetheless.

MORE

"Love is the best therapy."

"Hello, Mr. Smith, I'm Dr. Hartley. How can I help you today?" I greet my sixty-two-year-old patient as I enter the exam room the next day.

His eyes widen, like he's seen a ghost. He gives me a suspicious once-over.

"Are you the doctor?"

If my brain could sigh, it would.

"Yes, I'm Dr. Hartley," I repeat, extending my hand. He shakes it—hesitantly.

I sit beside the exam table, logging into his chart.

"You're so young to be a doctor," he says, stone-faced. "You look like a model. I thought you'd be a man."

I laugh it off, resisting the urge to quip and say, "Been there, done that. But now I'm a doctor."

His eyes go wider. I didn't know that was even anatomically possible.

It's nothing new. Patients often second-guess me until I win them over. But that doesn't make it any less exhausting. To not be taken seriously.

I think of the time a colleague introduced me to a resident interviewing with our group for a position as just "Lena," while all my male coworkers got "Doctor." It's hilarious. I still wonder how my grandmother navigated this kind of sexism in medicine decades ago—when it was worse, and even less subtle.

Mr. Smith glances up at a poster on the wall—my headshot under the caption: Congratulations to the Female Doctor of the Year.

His expression softens. He scoots forward, finally warming.

"Ah, okay. Hello, Doctor." He lifts his hand, showing me a mess of gauze and duct tape around his index finger. "I sliced it open with a box cutter. My wife tried to wrap it, but it just wouldn't stop bleeding."

I begin carefully unwrapping the makeshift dressing when my phone rings. Blooming Steps, the screen reads. My heart leaps.

"Mr. Smith, would you excuse me for a moment? I'll be right back." I strip off my gloves and rush into the hallway.

"Hi, Mrs. Hartley, this is Susan from Blooming Steps," comes a kind voice on the other end. "I have great news. A spot just opened up for Ruby. Can you come in tomorrow for her initial therapy evaluation?"

"Absolutely!" I nearly shout, tears prickling my eyes. I run through my mental calendar. I'm off tomorrow. Thank God.

Taking a deep breath, I text Phoenix the good news, then pocket my phone and return to Mr. Smith. After carefully suturing his lacerated finger, he beams.

"You're the best doctor! Thank you so much."

"You're very welcome. We'll see you in seven days for suture removal—unless there's any issues with healing, then come back right away."

"Thanks again!" He waves, smiling. I return a smile, imagining him telling his wife about the model-doctor who stitched him up. That'll make a story. I move on to the next urgent care patient. And a next...and a next. The rest of my day whirls by in a blur of charts, procedures, lab results, EKGs, and consults.

The next morning, Phoenix and I sit on a dark brown couch in Susan's office while Ruby is evaluated in another room. Susan outlines their Building Bridges program—speech, occupational, and ABA therapy. Everything I've been researching for months. Phoenix, though, looks overwhelmed. His eyes flick around the room, occasionally landing on the Star Wars memorabilia decorating her desk.

"I know this is a lot to take in," Susan says, her gaze shifting back and forth between both of us. "Do you have any questions?"

I shake my head—not yet. But Phoenix speaks up, his voice tight.

"I'm really concerned about ABA therapy," he says in a rush. "I've read some really troubling things. That it was developed by the same person who created conversion therapy. That it's like training a dog. And that it's traumatized a lot of people."

His leg bounces with nervous energy. But I know he's just trying to protect Ruby.

Susan leans forward, smoothing her short bob behind one ear.

"But ABA has evolved a lot in the last few decades. Here at Blooming Steps, we use a play-based, neurodiverse-affirming approach. We don't believe in suppressing who a child is—we support who they are." She pauses. Her eyes move between us. She's trying to read the room.

Acknowledging Susan's explanation, I add, "Our main concern isn't the therapy itself—it's the idea of trying to cure or fundamentally change who our daughter is. We don't believe autism needs curing. Ruby will always be autistic, and that's not something we want to erase. We just want to help her thrive in a world that isn't always built to include her. To teach her how to express her needs safely. To support her through daily life challenges."

I glance at Phoenix, hoping my words help to smooth a ripple of worry forming between his brows.

Susan nods slowly. Admiration flickers across her face.

"My wife's a doctor," Phoenix adds with a small, proud laugh, easing the tension. I chuckle too. And the worry between his brows dissolves.

After our meeting with Susan, we're introduced to Carolyn, Ruby's occupational therapist—a bubbly blond with a calm, magnetic energy.

When we walk into the therapy room, Ruby is breathless with giggles under Carolyn's gentle guidance. Seeing her like that—free, laughing—I can't help but smile. Hope pours into me like early spring rain. Phoenix was right. No prayer goes unanswered.

"Have you noticed any issues with feeding or texture avoidance at home?" Carolyn asks, arranging an array of sensory toys on the mat—slime buckets, playdough, spiky balls, a bowl of dried beans. Ruby immediately flinches at the sight of slime.

"Yes," I say, watching her explore a spiky ball with laser focus. "She's refusing more foods lately. But I've also noticed some sensory-seeking behaviors."

"No worries," Carolyn says. "We'll work on that. It's important that she doesn't lose weight, but as long as her sensory-seeking behaviors are safe, it's okay for her to engage in them. She might start masking once she gets to school—many autistic kids do, unfortunately." Her tone softens on that last word.

There's empathy in it. And regret. I read somewhere that girls learn to mask early on, and it can be exhausting. I totally relate. I am always so drained after a day full of people. After smiling and modulating my tone to make sure I sound professional. And I'm not even autistic.

The last specialist we meet is Liz, Ruby's speech therapist. Young, nerdy, bright-eyed—she radiates curiosity and commitment. The kind of person who will chase every tool, every technique, every emerging study just to help a child find their voice.

"So Ruby's lost all her words?" she asks, gently encouraging her to blow bubbles—an exercise to check muscle control.

"Yes," I say. "She just mumbles now."

The weight of words hits me. I glance at Phoenix. It hits him too. Liz nods, jotting a note in Ruby's chart.

"How do you usually figure out what she needs?"

"By reading her mind, quite literally," Phoenix jokes. His laugh echoes heavily in the room, but my mind drifts. To all the times he's done exactly that—not just with Ruby, but with me. He just always knows. His intuition, so quietly potent, feels like the invisible threads knitting our family together.

Liz nods. "I've noticed some muscle weakness around her mouth. We'll work on strengthening that, but I also want to introduce some basic sign language.

It'll help Ruby communicate more directly—so you don't only have to rely on intuition." She winks at Phoenix. Her confidence injects a fresh dose of hope into our hearts. A small, vital spark of hope. Leaving Blooming Steps, I feel like we've hit the jackpot.

The depth of care and expertise here is staggering. We're both stunned. And so, so thankful. Ruby clings to her new therapists, hugging Liz's leg tightly before we leave. I feel it. That rare lightness of optimism. Phoenix smiles the whole drive home, holding my hand like always, but now there's even more warmth radiating through it.

Over the next few months, life settles into a new rhythm shaped by the Building Bridges program—twice-weekly occupational and speech therapy, plus twenty hours a week of in-home ABA.

Our ABA therapist, Mina, is nothing short of a miracle worker.

Every day, the doorbell rings at 3:55 p.m., and Ruby dashes to the door—squealing, hands flapping with joy.

"Hi, Mina," I say, opening the door. Ruby throws her arms around her like they're old friends. Joy pouring out of her in waves.

Ruby is making progress. So much progress. But she still doesn't speak.

"What if she never says a word?" Phoenix wonders one night, his voice soft but aching.

"She will," I say. "Let me show you something." I pull up a TED Talk on autism by Jacob Barnett. Non-speaking until five. Astrophysicist by sixteen. We watch together, the glow of the screen lighting Phoenix's face. I see the tears before he wipes them away.

"One day she won't shut up. You'll see," I whisper, grinning through the lump in my throat. He squeezes my hand. Like the future I believe in is already here—just waiting for our daughter to catch up to it.

Sometimes, clinging to what seems like a delusion is the only way to make things real. Because without hope, everything falls apart. And I refuse to lose that hope. I cradle Phoenix's face in my hands.

Our eyes lock. I share something I once read—a piece of wisdom from The Spark, the memoir by Jacob Barnett's mother.

"She described autism as like living in a treehouse. You're happy there. Content. You don't feel the need to climb down, even when everyone's calling for you to come. But when someone climbs up—really climbs up all the way to your treehouse—and sees the world through your eyes, then maybe you'll trust them enough to visit their world too. To come down every now and then."

I pause. Let the image sit between us. "We just have to keep climbing into her treehouse."

Phoenix's eyes mist over.

"I love you so much," he whispers. "You're not just mine. You're Ruby's magician too." Then he kisses me. And I light up like some distant galaxy being born.

We've lived in a blur of routines for months now. Therapies. Appointments. Insurance appeals. Lost in the logistics of survival. We had forgotten to nurture our own connection. But here he is. Bringing it back. Touch by touch. Kiss by kiss.

"I didn't know I could love you more," I whisper. "But watching you with our daughter—your gentleness, your patience...I just do."

He doesn't answer. Just lets his kisses chase away my tears.

A few weeks later, we're running on fumes. Therapies, diets, never-ending insurance calls, milestone logs, parent meetings— it's a second full-time job. Maybe two. So we decide to carve out a day for magic. Disneyland. Ruby's second birthday. She insists on wearing her new Sleeping Beauty dress, and when we step into the park's dreamlike glow, she's spellbound. She may be non-speaking, but her face says it all.

Despite our ongoing efforts to teach her sign language, nothing has quite clicked yet. But today, we let go of the checklist.

We sing "Happy Birthday," and she blows out her two candles with wild delight, flapping her hands, babbling something in her sweet treehouse language. For a few hours, we forget the "autism parents" label. We're just...a family in Disneyland.

The park is a sensory storm—the cacophony of sounds and the whirl of colors are dizzying. Ruby is wide-eyed, captivated. But I start to short-circuit.

"I'm going to run to the bathroom real quick," I say to Phoenix, excusing myself to a quiet spot. The hum of the crowd softens to a murmur. I close my eyes. Breathe. It feels like a film beat. A moment to recenter after the action sequence.

As the sun dips lower in the California sky, marking the end of a magical day, we head home. Pulling out of the parking lot, Phoenix glances in the rearview mirror. "What is it, Ruby baby?" he asks, eyes wide. I turn to look—and my heart kicks. There, in the backseat, our little princess is signing "more." Over and over. Her tiny index fingers touching together as if drawn by a magnet, her eyes locked on the fading lights of Disneyland.

"Oh my God! She is signing 'more'!" I shout, unable to contain it. I twist around, face to face with her soft, sad expression. "Baby," I whisper. "You want more Disney?" She meets my gaze. Just for a moment.

Then her fingers press together again—harder this time. Her version of screaming yes. Hell yes! Without a second thought, Phoenix makes a swift U-turn heading straight back to the park. We spend the rest of the evening indulging in Ruby's newfound ability to communicate, riding each attraction again and again as she keeps signing "more," right up until the park closes.

On the drive home, I whisper, "I think she came down from her treehouse tonight." Tears pool in my eyes. His thumb traces little hearts into my palm—his secret language. In the backseat, Ruby's curls bounce gently as she drifts into sleep.

Cradled by the hum of the engine, rocked by the soft vibration of the road.

"I can't believe it," Phoenix says, voice trembling. "She communicated with us. All evening. On her own." His eyes shine with emotion, catching glints of freeway light.

I smile. My heart races like a child discovering a hidden gift beneath the Christmas tree.

"It's a nugget," I whisper. "A little gift from God—reminding us to never stop believing in her."

Phoenix squeezes my hand tighter. "You're both magical," he says softly. "Her. And you." And I think of Grandpa. Of all the times he believed in me—even when I didn't believe in myself. And I whisper, "Love is the best therapy."

Months pass like clouds in a fall sky. Ruby keeps making progress—steady, beautiful progress. But she still doesn't speak. She signs now, her hands telling stories her mouth can't yet hold. And we're facing a new challenge: sensory issues around food.

Today, my mom and I watch a feeding therapy session at Blooming Steps. She is visiting for a few days from Chicago. We're both cracking up at Ruby dressed as Maleficent. Horns and all. We are deeply stuck in the Disney character phase. She refuses to wear any normal clothes. Carolyn sits across from her, beaming positivity as always.

"Mmm, it's so fluffy!" Carolyn says brightly, spraying more whipped cream onto the plate. My little villainess eyes it suspiciously, spoon in hand. She pokes the whipped cream. Again. Still unwilling to touch it with her fingers, she just keeps stabbing at it. A frown curls her lips—then comes the gag. I stifle a laugh. How fitting, I think. Mistress of Evil, disgusted with a light, cloudy dessert.

"You were exactly the same," my mom whispers.

"I was?" Not a real question. I remember it vividly—screaming and gagging when she tried to feed me grits or oatmeal. To this day, I can't even smell them without flinching. As Carolyn allows Ruby to explore food at her own pace, memories of my Grandpa flood in. Żurek, now my favorite soup, was once a nauseating concoction.

"You wouldn't eat it for weeks," he'd told me on the phone once.

"But every day, I put it in front of you. With little sprinkles of fried pig skin on top."

He'd chuckle. "By the end of the summer, you licked the plate clean."

I smile, remembering the glint in his eye.

The way he'd lick his own plate. So dramatically. And he would smack his lips like it was the most delicious thing in the world (because it is) until I couldn't help but laugh. And try a spoonful. And then another. "How in the world..." My parents couldn't believe it. I was eating.

By the time I turn thirty-six, our home has transformed into a full-blown sensory play therapy center. Kinetic sand. Slime. Spiky balls. Beads. Puzzles. Bubble makers. Yarn. And Disney plushies. Dozens of them—treasures Phoenix keeps bringing home for Ruby. In speech therapy sessions, Liz continues to work on strengthening Ruby's muscle control. Now Ruby can blow into a whistle and produce a sound. And every time it works, she giggles. She also laughs every time she lifts Phoenix's hat—bald head, exposed. Girl has a sense of humor.

But the loneliness is what gets to me—not my own, but Ruby's. Every day off work, I take her to the playground, hoping for a breakthrough. Hoping today will be the day another child will see her. But we leave in tears. Every time. Watching my sweet angel being shunned by other children is heart-wrenching. Kids always seem to sense it. That she's different. They don't mean to be cruel, but they push her away. It stirs painful memories of my own childhood. Of wandering alone through mountainous fields with my rescue dog, Misiek. Playing in a lonely corner because I was the weird one. I didn't have a human friend until the fourth grade.

As I sit on a bench, I watch Ruby approach a group of kids playing near a slide. She approaches—bubbling with joy, flapping her hands, trying for the briefest eye contact. One boy shoves her. Hard. She stumbles backward, arms flaring like a startled baby bird.

My heart wrings itself dry. I shoot up from the bench and scoop her into my arms. "Come, my love," I whisper into her curls, kissing her cheeks. Taking away all the loneliness. "Mommy knows the funnest place."

Minutes later, we walk into Billy Beez, a new indoor playground in Santa Clarita. The place is massive—jungle gyms, slides, padded towers—echoing with the happy shrieks of kids running wild. Ruby's eyes go wide. For a second, she meets my gaze—face lit up with joy. As we navigate through the attractions, her giggles and squeals make me momentarily forget our struggles. Her diagnosis. All the stupid labels.

I'm sweaty. Out of breath. I reach into my backpack for water.

And when I look up—Ruby is hugging another child. A little blond girl about her age. They're holding each other like old friends. Nearby, a woman with a friendly, girl-next-door vibe waves at me. Her blond hair is neatly tied in a ponytail, and she wears almost no makeup—just a swipe of lip gloss she probably hastily threw on in the car, like every mom of a toddler. She moves with a grace of a ballet dancer. I rush over, breathless.

"Oh my God, I'm so sorry," I blurt. "My daughter's autistic—she loves hugs," I add quickly, trying to disguise my flustered panic with a sheepish smile.

"Oh, that's totally fine," the woman replies with a warm, genuine smile. "My daughter loves hugs—so we're all good."

My hand, reaching for Ruby, freezes midair.

"Hi, I'm Lindsey," the blonde woman adds, extending her hand.

I shake it, feeling almost as if I'm dreaming. "I'm Lena."

"And this is my daughter, Olivia. How old is your little one?"

"She's two and a half. Her name is Ruby," I say, as we settle on the mat and lean against the wall. Our daughters are running wild like they've known each other from some past lives.

"Yay, Olivia is the same age! Your daughter is an absolute sweetheart," Lindsey says, pointing at the girls as they take turns kicking a ball. Every now and then, Ruby grabs Olivia's hand and leads her toward something new.

I just smile. The words don't come. I'm too stunned by the sheer beauty of the moment.

"We've been coming here since they opened, but she's never connected so much with anyone. We should exchange numbers," Lindsey says, leaning in so close I can nearly feel her smile on my skin.

I nod, still slightly in shock, and hand her my phone. I watch her fingers dance across the screen, saving her name into our lives. The girls twirl in circles, giggling. This. This is all I ever wanted for my daughter. A friend. My heart swells. Lindsey calls the next day. And the day after that. And before we know it, several months have passed. Ruby and Olivia become inseparable, their hands often clasped together as if magnetically connected. We enroll them in ballet and swimming classes together, nurturing their little friendship. They share everything—snacks, toys, hugs. But nothing glues them together more than their mutual love for Disney princesses. That shared obsession becomes their language, their world. And just like that, Ruby begins spending more and more time down here with us—away from her treehouse.

Olivia's birthday comes just a few days before Ruby's, so we decide to celebrate together at Disneyland. The moment Ruby spots her in the crowd, her whole face lights up. She breaks into a run. "Livia!" she calls—one of the few words she's mastered. Another is "yeahyes," which, thanks to Olivia's patient decoding, we now know means "princess."

Their bond keeps growing, transforming not only their lives but ours. Watching them together—seeing the genuine affection and understanding they share—brings a kind of joy that feels almost holy, magical. The power of friendship. The soft, stubborn magic of being truly seen. A reminder that in the world of parenting a neurodiverse child, small victories can feel like miracles. And as their friendship blossoms, so does Ruby. She's spending less and less time in her treehouse now. She still goes up there, but she doesn't stay as long. More and more, she brings her magic down to meet us. She even makes eye contact.

One night, as I'm brushing my teeth, I feel a gentle tug at my pajamas. I turn to find her there, eyes locked on mine. "Mama, yeahyes," she says, tugging me toward the living room.

The town dance scene from Rapunzel plays on the screen. I lift her into my arms and spin. She giggles. I laugh. We rewind and spin again. And again. Dizzy from joy. And when the music fades, she places her hand on my cheek, looks straight into my soul, and says, "Aya-woo."

My eyes blur with tears. She catches one with her tiny hand.

"I love you too," I whisper.

LITTLE FLOWER

"When the world aches, an angel is born."

"Hello?" I answer the phone, watching the early morning light sneak through the blinds. It touches the walls with its rainbowy fingers. I sip my matcha—warm, grassy, invigorating—and breathe in the newness of the day. Set my intentions. Mornings are sacred to me.

"Hi, happy birthday, my little flower!" Grandpa's scratchy voice cuts through, warm and vibrant like my matcha. He's always the first to call.

I smile. "Hi, Grandpa! Thank you! How are you?" I send him a hug across the miles.

"I'm fine, my love. Just a little dizzy. You know, young spirit in an old body," he says with a chuckle that tickles my ear.

"Dizzy? Are you okay?" My doctor brain flickers on, concern threading through my voice.

"I'm okay. It's just age, I'm sure. How's my great-granddaughter?" he says, dodging the question like he always does.

"She's doing great. Making progress every day—she's even started saying short sentences," I say, pride blooming in my chest. "They think she'll be able to join an inclusion preschool this fall."

"That's fantastic!"

"It is. But I'm just...so tired," I whisper, not really meaning to say it out loud. I think of the last time I did something for myself. A hike. A spa day. A date night with Phoenix that feels like it happened in another lifetime. "Sometimes, it feels like I'm running out of strength."

He breathes in deep, wheezy. A soft cough breaks it. Then he clears his throat. "My little flower, you're not running out of strength. Strength is who you are. It freed you from an abusive relationship. It got you into med school. It took you across the country for love. And it's that same strength helping your daughter bloom—like one of our rare Polish flowers."

"I love you, Dziadziu," I whisper, eyes burning, wet. I picture his twinkling blue gaze and the way light dances on the walls of his cozy Kraków apartment. His books, his pansies, his art. The birds flocking to his balcony feeder. I see us at Wawel Castle, feeding swans, listening to his stories—the nightingale's nest in his mother's rosebush, the Polish legends, poetry, and lullabies.

He's always been my anchor. My best friend. Maybe the only person who's ever truly understood me.

So I ask the question that's been building inside me for months:

"Grandpa, do you think I might be autistic too?"

He chuckles softly, then spills more of his wisdom.

"You were just like your daughter once. A lonely, friendless child, scared of loud noises and new tastes, playing with Grandma's balls of yarn instead of all the dolls she would get for you."

He coughs again. A sharp inhale follows.

"I'm sorry, my little flower. Back then, we didn't know what autism was. I just knew you were different...special. Like that single purple pansy you once brought me." He pauses. I close my eyes. All the colorful pansies from his balcony rain into my memories. I smile.

He continues. "You just needed someone to believe in you. And the only therapy I knew was love. Because love is all the strength you need. Love makes everything bloom."

My eyes sting. His words pool in my chest. And I realize it's never been just his green thumb that made all his flowers blossom—including me. It was his delicate love—the kind that doesn't force a flower to be like the rest but celebrates its uniqueness.

Just then, I hear soft footsteps. Phoenix and Ruby.

She climbs into my lap and plants a big, juicy kiss on my cheek. A tear escapes before I can catch it. Phoenix wraps his arm around me. Warmth spreads through me. All the people I love. My cocoon. I place my phone on the glass coffee table. Birds chirp outside the window. I grin and press the speakerphone button.

"Dziadziu, Ruby just woke up," I say. "She's here."

Her arms are already around me. I whisper in her ear. "Do you want to say hi to your great-grandpa?"

She flaps her hands, giggling.

"Say 'Hi, Dziadziu,'" I coax gently.

"Hi, Dadu," she says, bubbling with joy.

Silence. For a second, I think the call dropped.

Then I hear him sniffle.

"Hi, Ruby," his voice breaks softly through the line. A melody from the heart.

"Dadu, dadu, dadu," she repeats, delighted.

"Ruby," he says, voice trembling, "your voice just brought out the sun over these Polish gray skies. The whole apartment is glowing now. Even my plants are smiling. Grandpa loves you so much.

And I will always be here—for my girls."

Phoenix's embrace tightens, and tears blur my vision. Ruby rests her head against my chest, her ear tuned to the rhythm of my heartbeat. I wipe my eyes. "Grandpa, I can't describe how much I miss you. Out of all the flowers you so gracefully cared for, I think I am the one you helped to bloom the most."

His laughter fills our quiet home. Then he starts to sing—an old song from my childhood about flames in the forest. Sitting here with my family, listening to his voice, I realize the steep mountains I've climbed have only made my legs stronger. My path was never flat or easy. But the turbulence in my sky allowed my wings to soar higher. And it was his flame that guided my way through the darkest moments of my journey.

"I have to go now," he says gently. "But remember, our goodbyes are never forever." His words still echo in my mind as Phoenix, Ruby, and I drive north along Pacific Coast

Highway—Phoenix's birthday surprise. Back to Santa Barbara. Back to where we got married.

The windows are down. Music fills the car. The breeze rolls in, cool and salty, tinged with seaweed. I close my eyes and reach into the wind, my hand weaving through air like I used to—feeling its plush, invisible force between my fingers. Ruby, dressed in her Mulan costume, is sleeping, her head gently bobbing against her pink car seat in rhythm with the road.

Phoenix traces hearts on my hand. His wink catches me like sunlight through the windshield.

The mountains rise to the right—their peaks passing us slowly like cherished memories. I stare at them. Hypnotizing landscape. I can feel Phoenix's glance on me.

"I heard you asking your grandpa if he thought you were autistic," he says. His voice is blending with the music and hum of the road. "And I wanted to share something."

He lets go of my hand briefly to turn down the music, then takes it back. Locking it in like a puzzle piece. Like always. And squeezes it for emphasis.

"Yeah," I sigh, still lost in the repetitive peekaboo of the mountains, the question too tangled to answer out loud. I squeeze his hand back.

"Last week, Susan mentioned something. She said autism is genetic. I told her I don't have it—it doesn't run in my family. She laughed and said, 'I wasn't talking about you.'"

My gaze lets go of the mountains. I turn to him, a smile spreading slowly across my face. Not forced. Just...peaceful.

"Do you think I'm autistic?" I ask, my eyes drifting behind him to the glittering ocean that frames his profile.

He shrugs, glancing at me with a softness. The kind that makes every dark thought melt like hot chocolate.

"I'm not a doctor. I just love you the way you are."

I giggle, leaning my head against his shoulder. He kisses my head. And I am like a flower. Heart and mind opening. Thoughts clearing the way for the revelation that, like Ruby, I am different. Our petals in the first rays of light, expanding, touched by the morning dew. Love makes everything bloom—like Grandpa says.

The rest of the drive melts into sunlight. By late afternoon, we're strolling the breezy pier in Santa Barbara. The salty air mingles with the grilled smells coming from The Harbor Restaurant.

We settle at a little ocean-view table at this local favorite that's renowned for its clam chowder. Triggered by Carolyn's effective feeding therapy, Ruby's curiosity gets the better of her, and she insists on trying a spoonful. But before we can even get excited she tried something new, she's already moved on—diving into the warm, crusty bread basket. Her new favorite.

She gleefully stuffs piece after piece into her mouth, so quickly I start to worry she might choke. I slow her down between bites. We pause to watch the seagulls arc above the water, their wings glinting in the sun. Phoenix and I exchange a quiet smile—one of those wordless moments. Of shared pride. Progress.

On a whim, I offer Ruby a bite of calamari. She hesitates but takes it. Her face scrunches. She furrows her brow like a food critic mid-review—then nods, satisfied.

"More camari?" she asks.

We laugh. We order more. Just as the sun tilts in the sky, the waiter brings out my birthday cake, aglow with candles. I close my eyes and make a wish—just this. Us. Like this. Always. Ruby helps me blow out the candles, our giggles twirling up with the cries of seabirds.

These are the moments that suspend time. The simplest ones. The ones that make ordinary feel extraordinary. I guess that's just the magic of life.

As the day winds down and the sky blushes pink, we walk back to our car, our hearts as full as our bellies.

Months pass like leaves carried along a swift river. Ruby has transitioned from the Building Bridges program into preschool. Thanks to Carolyn—and a lot of fighting with insurance—she still sees her twice a week for OT and feeding therapy. And she's thriving. She's eating now. Not everything, but more than just tofu and seaweed. After one of her sessions, Carolyn leans back against the wall. Her gaze is soft but direct.

"You know," she says, soft smile touching her lips, "I feel like we've moved past therapist and client. You guys feel more like friends now."

She leans forward, eyes bouncing between Phoenix and me. "You're actually the only couple from our whole parent group who's still together."

The statistics hang heavy in my mind. Most couples in our situation drift apart. How many divorced parents have we met at Blooming Steps? I lost count. Phoenix squeezes my hand—an acknowledgment of the hard journey we've shared, facing down the challenges that often pull others apart.

Carolyn leans forward, hands laced over her knees, her expression shifting. She's more serious now. "Can I ask you a personal question?" Her tone is soft, but behind it lives a kind of quiet wisdom—maybe even sadness. Like she's seen the unhappy story unfold too many times. Like there's a pattern we cannot escape.

"Of course," I say, bracing myself. I fidget with the drawstring on my hoodie.

"When was the last time you two went out on a date? Just the two of you."

The question stings more than I expect. Her words echo in the suddenly quiet room. I exchange a glance with Phoenix, uncertainty creeping into my voice. "When I was pregnant," I admit. It slips out like a confession. Not an answer.

Carolyn's eyes widen. "Wow. That's a long time... Ruby's five now." Her brows rise, then knit together as if she can't decide which expression to use.

The weight of those years presses down. Not with regret. Just the fact that it has been this long. Part of our lives that's been swallowed up by routines, therapy plans, and survival.

She breaks through our silence: "You know, my nineteen-year-old daughter, Cierra, would love to babysit Ruby. Of course, if you're open for it." She scans our faces. "She's fantastic with kids, and I'd come along the first few times to help her settle in."

I take a drag of air to respond, but Phoenix is quicker. "That sounds great," he says, lighting up.

The idea of an evening for just us—to peel back the layers of exhaustion and find each other again—sparks something in me I haven't felt in a long time. A slow-blooming heat. A memory of who we were.

"You're right," I say, my fingers lacing through his. "We need to nurture what we have. I'm done with survival mode. It's time to thrive."

A week later, Ruby is giggling with Cierra—her new favorite person—and I'm blindfolded in the car, heart fluttering, unsure where Phoenix is taking me.

"Okay, wifey, we're here," Phoenix says, his voice laced with mischief as he helps me out of the car. My heels tap uncertainly against what feels like concrete. The air smells musky, familiar. I hear the flick of his lighter—again and again—then feel warmth brush up my legs.

He loosens the red blindfold. My eyes blink open to a soft glow. We're surrounded by dozens of flickering candles, forming a heart on the street corner where we first met—our cherished spot. Phoenix catches my gaze, his eyes glowing with that old, untamed fire. A hint of playful conspiracy dances at the edge of his smile.

"Can I take you for a magic day?" he murmurs against my neck, his voice a velvet ribbon unspooling down my spine. His hand settles on the small of my back, drawing me close. Our lips meet. A kiss that's hungry, deep. Sparks jump between us like we're touching power lines. The years melt. The world melts. Shivers explode everywhere. He still sets me on fire without even trying.

His hand slips beneath my short black dress, gliding up my thigh like a summer wave. Our tongues tangle, slow and starved. Heat blooms in my cheeks, in my chest, everywhere. His fingers trace a line up my waist, raising a storm of goosebumps.

And then—

"I'm sorry, guys. You can't have this here."

The grating voice scrapes through the spell. We freeze. A hotel security guard stands a few feet away, eyebrows raised. He's eyeing the candles. The warmth of Phoenix's touch vanishes as he fumbles for his phone, snapping a few photos of our candlelit heart. "It's just for a photo shoot," he says, nonchalantly.

"Do you have a permit?" the guard asks, crossing his arms. I roll my eyes. Dear Lord, doesn't he have anything better to do.

Phoenix meets his eyes, trying charm. "Come on, man."

"Sorry, sir." The guard starts stomping out the candles with the heel of his boot.

"You're an asshole, you know that?" I snap, fury prickling at my skin. My gaze knife-sharp. If eyes could kill...

He starts to respond, "Ma'am, you just—"

"It was rhetorical," I cut in, deadpan.

Back in the car, Phoenix and I burst into laughter, the tension dissolving into purse hysteria. "My god!" he exclaims, doing a perfect impression of the guard: "'Do you have a permit?'" His eye roll is pure theater. Dramatic. Perfectly over the top.

I'm laughing so hard I have to clutch my sides. "Well," I gasp between giggles, "I officially lived through my most LA moment in LA."

Our laughter keeps spilling, wave after wave, shaking off years of everyday anxiety.

"Off to our next mesmerizing adventure," Phoenix says, his hand holding mine as our car glides silently toward downtown.

When we step into the Walt Disney Concert Hall, the buzz of the city fades. Everything hushes. The architectural splendor of the lobby, with its sweeping curves and reflective surfaces, casts dancing shadows around us. Our footsteps echo softly on the polished floors as we pass other concertgoers. The air feels still, filled with murmurs of people, like a chapel before a mass.

Phoenix guides us through the mostly mature crowd, his reassuring hand on the small of my back. I'm captivated. Gehry has always been one of my favorite architects. I once watched an interview where he crumpled a piece of paper and said, "This is how I design." Chaos into beauty. I wish Grandpa could see this.

Above us, soft golden light spills from sculptural fixtures, turning the lobby into something sacred. A temple made of art and music.

Our seats are in the balcony—perfect. From here, I can see everything. The way the space curves like a seashell. The anticipation. And then—my breath catches.

At the center of the hall, Refik Anadol's digital sculpture pulses in holographic motion. Layers of memory, data. Moving. Alive. His art has always felt like a mirror of my own brain: vivid, recursive, impossible to pin down. The lights dim. A breathless hush settles. And then the music begins.

Dudamel lifts his baton like it's a thread of silk. The first notes—soft, aching, alive—rise from the strings. A violin carries us forward. The melody swells, and we all rise with it, held in an invisible current of sound. Every breath in the room feels synchronized.

Phoenix's fingers intertwine with mine as the music unfolds in layers of complexity. I feel every note vibrating through me, a beautiful ache. I lean closer to him, and our shoulders meet. I feel him shiver.

Each note feels like a brushstroke of emotion—torment, yearning, triumph—painted across the air. An older man nearby dabs his eyes with a handkerchief. The music moves like fast breathing around the grandeur of the hall, and Refik Anadol's shifting lights respond almost in rhythm, flickering to the pulse of the orchestra.

During one particularly stirring passage—where strings and bass coil and rise into a crescendo—my breath catches. It's too much, almost. Or just enough. Orgasmic, in the truest sense of the word. Pure sensory overload. Phoenix notices. He squeezes my hand tighter as tears fill my eyes.

How can music do this? Open us up so deeply, so instantly? I hear Phoenix's words—Time isn't linear—and they ring true here, suspended in this cascade of sound. A sound that can reach deep into your soul. For a moment, I'm everywhere. Then. Now. Becoming. The beauty of our being. Was I here before?

The final note lingers in the air. Then fades. A breathless pause. And finally, applause explodes around us—but we stay seated, letting that last note echo somewhere inside us. We savor it for just a second longer.

Phoenix turns to me. His eyes shimmer with reflected lights from the ceiling. And he winks.

"That was incredible," I say, my heart overflowing. "Best magic day ever." I'm smiling, but my eyes are wet. He kisses my hand. The look he gives me touches my soul the same way the music just did. As we leave, I can't stop smiling. Love is a fire, I think. You just have to keep blowing gently on it to keep it alive.

We swing by the LA Phil store and pick up a little Dudamel plushie for Ruby. When we get home, she squeals at the sight of it.

"Thank you, Mommy, Daddy! I missed you!" Her little body crashes into our arms like a meteor made of our love.

"Did you have fun with Cierra, my love?" Phoenix asks.

Ruby nods with big, animated eyes. "So much fun, Daddy! We played dolls, and then I was an actress." She twirls in her Tinker Bell costume, the LED lights on her wings flickering like fireflies. Phoenix scoops her up and spins her through the living room, her giggles bouncing off the walls like music.

"I love you, Daddy," she cries between bursts of laughter.

And my entire world is weightless again, like it had never been anything else.

CHAPTER 20
LAST LETTER

"Sometimes you have to feel it before you can see it."

And here it is—the day we were told would not come. Doubts voiced by family members, some professionals, and even our own fears—What if she never speaks? What if she needs more help than you can give?—all fade into the background as we walk Ruby to her first day of first grade. A regular classroom. She's wearing a turquoise backpack (Uncle Allan's doing), a glittery tutu skirt, and oversized heart-shaped sunglasses. A walking burst of personality. Unapologetically herself. Her proud little march toward the school gate dismantles years of fears. Years of people projecting limits onto her. Onto us. Her existence is the rebuttal of what people think it means to be autistic.

Her teacher greets her with a warm smile.

"Hi, I'm Ruby, and I'm autistic," she declares, confident as California sun.

Phoenix and I glance at each other. His eyes brim, mine too. She turns to wave, and I snap a photo—frame it forever in my heart. I send it to Grandpa with a caption: Your girl made it. You were right. Love makes anything bloom. Love you.

Later, hand in hand, Phoenix and I stroll through the park, morning light casting long shadows on the path. I feel weightless, like maybe everything is going to be okay.

Then my phone rings. I glance down, expecting Grandpa. It's my dad.

He never calls out of the blue. My heart sinks with a premonition of bad news.

"Hi, Lena," he says, voice taut.

"Dad, what's wrong?" My heart is pounding.

There's a pause that lasts too many breaths.

"Grandpa passed away this morning," he says finally, his voice splintering "Mesothelioma. We've been expecting it. He was very sick the past few months... He didn't want us to tell you. Said he didn't want you to worry."

I stop walking. Stumble. Phoenix catches me by the elbow.

"What?" I whisper. No. No. I just spoke to him yesterday. We had plans. I just bought tickets. Christmas. Kraków. I pinch myself. Repeatedly. But I am not dreaming.

"Grandpa is gone, Lena," Dad says gently. "We found him in bed this morning. He passed peacefully. He was smiling...holding photos of you. Of Ruby. And Grandma."

Each word hits like an arrow to the chest. The park around us dissolves into a blur of indistinct green shapes. Grief swallows me whole. My grandpa. My poet. My philosopher. Gone. I had so hoped he'd meet Ruby. One more hug. One more lullaby in that soul-stirring voice. One last story about the nightingale's nest. But time keeps marching on. Indifferent. Merciless. Slipping through our fingers like sand. It doesn't stop for longing. Doesn't care about our sorrow.

My tears are uncontrollable as I think of my Grandpa. His gentle, selfless nature, artistic soul. His voice, rich and soothing like warm honey. I replay his voicemails over and over, clinging to the echoes. His blue eyes held galaxies. Wonder and poetry. A soul lost in so much love for others. He was the only person, besides Phoenix, who ever truly got me. He never questioned why I was the way I was. He just loved me.

In the weeks after his death, my phone fills with missed calls from Poland—numbers I don't recognize. I answer them, every time, only to be met with silence. Silence that makes me feel like I hear his voice. Then after the funeral, they stop. I like to believe it was him. Reaching out from beyond. Still close. Still speaking between the rings.

I dream of him every night. He doesn't say a word, just holds me close. No language needed. Love, in that place, is not something you speak—it's something you feel.

A few days later, Anya calls. "I had a dream," she says, breath catching. "I think it was your grandpa. He was singing. Dancing with you. So full of life. Like he wanted you to know he's okay."

I close my eyes. I can see him. Twirling me like I twirl Ruby. Reading Tom Sawyer to the quiet little girl I once was. The one just beginning to peek out of her treehouse.

His stories, his laughter, his love—none of it fades. It just becomes part of the melody underneath everything. An underpin of my life. I dab my eyes, chuckling through the sniffles. "Thank you, Anya, so much," I whisper. Then I shift us gently toward lighter things. "How's my new mama doing?"

She exhales, laughing. "Ah, you know. The baby's perfect. I'm…just doing." Her voice carries that sleep-deprived glow, equal parts joy and unraveling. "But I'm so in love with him. Being a mom—it's the most beautiful gift."

Her words warm my heart. My best friend. A mama now. She married Mark a couple years ago, back in Chicago, and gave birth just last month. Our Windy City days feel like a flickering film reel now—so vivid yet so far away. But threaded through every memory…is Grandpa.

"Sure is," I reply, my voice softening just as a newborn's cry pierces through the phone.

"Oh—speaking of the little gift, he just woke up for the boob," Anya laughs. "Gotta go."

"Hopefully we can meet up next summer at Disneyland. Take care," I say quickly, as the cries grow more urgent, the soundtrack of her new reality.

"See you soon, Lena. Love you."

I've only just plugged in my phone to charge when it rings again. Allan.

I hadn't called him yet—still holding back, remembering how his mother passed away just weeks after school started. Grief has a way of stirring up old ghosts.

"Hey," I say.

"Hey, you," he replies, his voice instantly calming. "I saw your post on Insta," he adds gently. "I'm so sorry about your grandpa."

"Thanks for calling." My voice cracks. His kindness makes my eyes mist.

"Always here for you. Your brother from another mother," he jokes as always, trying to lift the heaviness. Then, as if sensing my breaking point, he shifts gears. "How's my goddaughter?"

I smile. Back in med school in Tennessee, I'd sworn that if I ever had a daughter, he'd be the godfather. And he is (fully, truly) the best one Ruby could ever have.

"She's great. Did you see her first day of school with the backpack? The one from Uncle Allan?"

"I look at that photo every day. Warms my heart. I'm so proud of you both."

"We miss you. It's been a few months. Too long."

"I'm just a stone's throw away in San Francisco. I'd love to see you guys for Thanksgiving."

"You're the best."

"I know," he says. I feel him grinning through the phone. I smile.

When the call ends, I sit in stillness for a moment. And I wish I could call Grandpa.

My phone doesn't stop ringing those first couple weeks. Mom. Monique. Distant aunts. Cousins. A chorus of love, weaving itself into a tapestry of voices. Threads of family and friendship stretched across the aching space where Grandpa used to be.

Grief is a peculiar companion. One moment, laughter finds its way through the cracks—light, fleeting. The next, it hits like a punch to the gut. Sharp. Sudden. The shadow of loss stains every day, muting vibrancy of joy. Sometimes, on solitary hikes, I play Grandpa's saved voicemails. Or dial his number—one I still refuse to delete—just to hear his voice on the recording. Pretending he's picking up. I whisper, "I love you," into the silence.

"Hi, my love," Phoenix says, stepping into the kitchen as I sauté mushrooms for a pasta sauce. Their rich umami scent fills the air.

"Mmm, smells amazing." He playfully slaps my butt, making me giggle, before wrapping his arms around my waist.

"Can you grab the mail?" I ask, glancing at him over my shoulder.

He kisses me on the cheek.

"Sure, be right back." His hands sweep gently across my hips before he heads out.

I pour in the cashew cream and turmeric, the sauce turning golden as steam rises around me. The fusilli boils. The whole kitchen turns to vapor.

Phoenix returns with a bundle of envelopes. "That smells so freaking good! I'm starving," he says, sorting through the mail at the counter.

"What about a kiss for the cook?" I tease, waving my wooden spoon at him.

He leans in, kisses my cheek, then pauses. "Oh—there's a letter here for you."

I dry my hands, take it—and freeze. My breath catches as I see the sender. It's from Grandpa. Postmarked the day before he died.

"What's wrong?" Phoenix asks. His voice cuts through the shock as I sink into a chair, the envelope trembling in my hands.

"This letter..." I whisper. "It's from Grandpa." A gasp slips past my fingers as I try to catch it. Phoenix stares at me. His wide eyes and raised brows mirror the disbelief spreading across my face.

"Aren't you going to read it?" he asks, gently.

I meet his gaze, placing the letter gently on the table, tracing its edges with my fingers. "Not yet," I whisper.

He kneels in front of me, his hands warm against my cheeks, his forehead resting against mine. "You want to go on your hike?" he asks softly, understanding written all over his face. "I'll pick up Ruby from school. We can reheat dinner later."

A smile cracks through the fog building behind my eyes. He always hears the unsaid. How did I get so lucky?

The fall wind brushes my cheeks as I hike through Placerita Canyon. The sun plays peekaboo through fluffy clouds, casting flashes of gold across the trail. I press Grandpa's letter to my chest, its weight syncing with the rhythm of my breath.

Above me, the trees, touched by wind, whisper their old melody. The leaves flicker like memories—memories not just of Grandpa, but of Phoenix and Ruby too.

The moment Ruby was born. The look on Phoenix's face when he held her for the first time. How he asked me, in all seriousness, if her cone head was permanent. I laugh thinking about it. How he shifted—from a wild, untethered soul to the kind of father who can read her needs without a word. The kind of man Grandpa once told me to hold out for. A man who would understand the poetry of my silence.

It feels as though Phoenix has taken the baton from Grandpa—nurturing both Ruby and me. Watching the way he loves our daughter, I know now: the kind of love I once thought only existed in books is vividly, gorgeously real. The letter in my hand feels almost too light for the weight of the words I know it carries.

Each step along the trail pulls me back to hikes with Grandpa—our hands brushing against wildflowers, laughter rising into the open fields of Bieszczady. I see his linen hat flapping in the wind, his songs gently radiating along dirt paths. I carry those memories like heirlooms stitched into the lining of my life.

And still, I feel ready to let them rest.

At the mountain's peak, I inhale deeply. The air is laced with black sage. Minty and sharp. The scent blooms stronger under the heat of the midday sun.

I sit down on the trunk of a fallen oak and unfold the letter with trembling hands. The paper crackles like dry leaves. Inside, a white card. A single pink rose painted on it so vividly it seems to bloom in my lap, petals opening beneath the shimmer of my tears. A bird sings. One bright note against the quiet. I imagine it's Grandpa.

I glance up. The sky is a watercolor blue, and I swear I can see his twinkling eyes in the clouds, smiling down at me.

I blink the tears away and read:

"My Dearest Lena,

As I reach the end of my path, I have one last piece of wisdom to share.

Love is the essence and the extent of our existence; it envelops us, empowers us to climb and move mountains.

Love is you.

I will miss you, but know that I am reunited with my Maria, dancing with her in the clouds.

Do not grieve for me—I have relished every moment as your grandpa.

And you were right. Out of all the flowers that have bloomed in my presence, you are the strongest, the most beautiful. You are the flower that gave my life purpose.

Until I hold you again...

A last kiss fired from my soul's cannon.

With eternal love,

Your old flower-loving poet,

Stach."

THE DIAGNOSIS

"You're the author of your own unfolding novel."

"What a story. Can I give you a hug, Lena?" Dr. McKenna's voice rings through the thick of my vivid memories. I nod, and she pulls me into a hug—genuine, almost maternal. When she steps back, I catch a shimmer of moisture in her eyes, a small smudge of mascara catching the light just beneath her lower lid.

She returns to her desk while I blow my nose into one of the tissues from the box Phoenix placed gently on my lap. Out of the corner of my eye, I see him dabbing at his own tears.

For a beat, the office falls into such deep silence that I can hear the soft puff of the diffuser—lavender rising into the still air in slow, fragrant breaths.

Dr. McKenna leans forward, inhaling slowly, deliberately. Her gaze locks with mine. "Before I share your results, I want to ask you something. You're forty-two. Why now? Why seek a diagnosis at this point in your life?"

Her question floats between us, deceptively simple, achingly profound. I take out my phone and glance at the lock screen—Ruby's smiling face, frozen in time. My thumb traces an invisible heart around her cheek. Like the ones Phoenix always traces on my hands.

"I wanted to do this for my daughter," I say softly. Then I pause, searching for more words, but Phoenix picks up where I leave off. "Ruby's made incredible progress. She's in a regular fourth-grade class now. But back in second grade, she started getting bullied." His voice tightens. The memory bites sharply.

"Oh no. I'm so sorry she had to go through that," Dr. McKenna says, her brows drawing together. "Kids can be so cruel."

"Second grade was a nightmare," I say, each word heavy with the recollection of her struggles. "It carved deep scars in her—awakening a painful awareness of being different. She started masking. And watching her self-love start to fade..." My voice catches. I can still hear her cries, the lonely sobs that lodged themselves in my chest.

Phoenix's arms wrap around me in a comforting half-hug. He is like a shield against the pain of this unaccepting world. "Seeing her regress was heartbreaking," he murmurs, voice thick. "We had to help her understand that being different isn't something to hide."

Dr. McKenna nods. "A lot of autistic people learn to mask as a survival strategy. It's how they adapt when the world doesn't accept them."

"I feel like I have masked my whole life," I say, shifting forward. "My suspicions that I might be on the spectrum...they kept growing the deeper we went into Ruby's world," I say, drawing in a breath. Bracing myself. "Then a few months ago, she came home in tears. Couldn't tell us exactly what happened, but she broke. She said..." I pause, the words slicing through me again. "'I hate my autism. I wish I was normal—not this weirdo.'"

I look away, searching the walls for something to steady me. "That's when it all clicked." There's a tremor in my chest. And then the words pour out.

"I realized if I got a diagnosis, I could show her she's not alone. That there's nothing broken in her. That being autistic isn't something shameful—it's part of who we are. And that she's loved. Not despite her autism. With it. All of it."

Dr. McKenna leans on her elbows. "You wanted her to see herself in you."

I nod. Phoenix pulls me closer. Kisses the top of my hand. His purposeful silence is like the crowd quieting during a concert, encouraging me to continue.

"Yes. I thought that if I got diagnosed, she would no longer feel like a rare, lonely flower in a grassy field of sameness." My eyes blur. The words feel like they're meant more for Grandpa than for Dr. McKenna. She takes off her glasses and places them on her desk, the frames making a muted clunk against the worn wooden surface.

"Well," she says, lips curling into a warm smile, "I'm happy to tell you that now, officially, both of you are rare flowers."

She puts her glasses back on. Her pen scratches for a couple of seconds on the paper in my file. "Dr. Hartley," she says, lifting her eyes to mine, "you are officially diagnosed with autism spectrum disorder, level one."

Her gaze locks with mine as I let out a long exhale. With it, somehow, all the anxiety leaves my body. My shoulders lift, no longer slumped by the weight of all the years I've spent not fully understanding or loving myself. Then comes the wave—relief, thick and unstoppable, like rain finally breaking from the swollen gut of a storm. I feel tears prickling at the corners of my eyes. It's as if the scattered pieces of my identity have finally clicked into place. And I can see myself clearly. A mosaic of fragments put together...for the first time.

"Thank you," I whisper. "You have no idea what this means. To me. To us."

Phoenix lets out a breath, half laugh, half sob. "My beautiful, unique wife," he says, his eyes shining with pride.

Dr. McKenna shakes her head, smiling wide. "You know, Dr. Hartley, you're one of the most interesting cases I've had in my career. I really hope more people get to hear your story one day."

Dabbing my eyes, I let out an uncontrollable giggle. My head shakes in unison with hers.

Like a fairy with her wand, Dr. McKenna points her pen at me. "You should write a book."

Phoenix nods, lifting his brows as he throws me a side glance. His hand pulses gently against mine in that signature Phoenix way.

I meet Dr. McKenna's gaze. The eye contact feels easier than I expected, almost like it does with Phoenix. And I smile.

"I just might."

By the time we step out of her office, the rain has vanished, and the sun peeks through what's left of the June gloom. We sit in the car, quiet, letting the moment settle. It's a day I'll never forget—for more than one reason. June 9th. Grandpa's birthday. He's been gone for years, but today, he feels closer than ever. And now, this day holds something else: my rebirth.

A rebirth of a woman connecting the dots. Finding her strength. And in all the love she's poured into others—a fragment of love for her true self. I close my eyes and smile. What I've found, this understanding—it's a map. A map I can pass to Ruby so she'll never feel lost inside her own autism. The way I once did.

"How do you feel?" Phoenix finally breaks the silence. He's looking at the tree in front of us, its branches swaying gently in the early summer breeze. Then his eyes shift to me.

"At peace," I say, and press play on my iPhone shuffle.

Edith Piaf's 'La Vie en Rose' blasts into the speakers. We exchange teary looks, then burst out laughing.

"Grandpa!" I gasp. Of course it's him, sending me his favorite song like a wink from the beyond. And I see him in my mind: singing to me, arms stretched wide, mustache twitching with every "ah" as his little girl twirls barefoot on his flower-filled balcony.

Phoenix steps out of the car, his hand reaching for mine. "Come, my magician flower," he says. The music swells around us, wrapping the car in Piaf's velvet. We dance in the parking lot, tears slipping down our cheeks, laughter caught in our breath.

"Do you think he's here?" I ask, twisting Grandma's emerald ring on my finger.

"He's always with his girls," Phoenix whispers into my ear.

And I believe him. I've saved hundreds of photos—Ruby with white orbs hovering like whispers around her.

"She's going to be so proud of you," he murmurs, eyes shimmering with love. "You're showing her it's okay to be exactly who she is. That she's perfect—just the way she was born."

I nod. "You know what I realized?"

"What, mi amor?" he says, brushing my short pixie strands from my forehead.

"That strength is just love. And like a river, it flows through us to fill another soul. Grandpa gave it to me. So did you. And I get to give it to Ruby. The river of love." I lean in, our cheeks touch. "Thank you for accepting...loving all of me."

"Loving you," he says, smiling, "is the most magical thing that's ever happened to me." His soft kiss grazes my lips.

We drive back home and pick up Ruby from school. It's her last day—summer has officially begun. She sits in the back seat, window rolled down, smiling as she weaves her hand through the waves of air. Just like I do. You will never feel alone again, I think as I watch her curls whip wild in the breeze. We are two rare flowers.

I glance at Phoenix's smiling face. Then back at Ruby, vibing to the beat.

"What would you guys say," I ask, turning up the volume, "to a magic day?"

BUGLE CALL

"I see my own reflection in you."

I t's a radiant day in Kraków as Ruby, Phoenix, and I wander the streets of the old town. Sunlight shimmers off the pastel facades, and pigeons burst into flight at every sudden movement that doesn't promise breadcrumbs.

My favorite destination, Wawel Castle, stands regal with its splendid medieval architecture. Its copper domes gleam against the summer sky, like they are on fire. Inside the adjacent cathedral, we meander through chapels layered in centuries of style—Baroque, Gothic, Renaissance. It's as if every era left its fingerprints here. Poland's rich and winding history. Our footsteps tap gently on the old stone, and I wonder if the ghosts of kings and queens beneath can hear us.

When we reach the Dragon's Den by the Wisła River, Ruby gasps. The sculpture of the Wawel Dragon—frozen midroar outside the legendary cave—holds her in the same awe it once held me. The legend of Smok Wawelski was one of Grand-pa's favorite tales to tell.

"You know, Ruby," I say, pointing toward the dark mouth of the cave, memories flickering behind my eyes, "a dragon used to live right here. He terrorized the town—ate all the sheep, even demanded the king offer him a maiden."

She looks at me, wide-eyed, completely enraptured. I hesitate for a second, remembering how dark the story is. But the magic of it always outweighed the fear. So I go on.

"Many brave knights tried to fight him and failed. But then, a young shoemaker's apprentice came up with a plan," I say, kneeling beside her. "He stuffed a sheepskin with sulfur and salt from the Wieliczka mines. Left it out for the dragon like a tasty snack." I puff out my cheeks, mimicking the dragon. Ruby giggles. So does Phoenix.

"And what happened, Mommy?" Ruby asks, fists clenched, amber eyes sparkling in the sunbeams bouncing off the Wisła River.

"The dragon ate the sheepskin and got so thirsty he nearly drank the river dry," I say, stretching my arms wide like wings. "He drank and drank until—boom!—he exploded."

Right on cue, the metal Wawel Dragon sculpture lets out a burst of flame. Ruby gasps, her little hand flying to her mouth to catch it.

"Wow, Mommy. I guess cleverness wins over evil," she says. My little philosopher in pink glitter sneakers. Phoenix gives me a look: pride, awe, love, all tangled into one.

"You're so smart, my love," he tells Ruby. "Cleverness always wins."

I slow my steps as we head back toward the old town square, near Grandpa's apartment. The pull of memory tugs at me painfully. I glance around—so much is the same yet changed. The same cobblestones, the same street performers, the same scent of freshly baked pretzels in the air. People move past us like ants, each in their own world, crossing paths without ever knowing what the other carries. Joy. Grief. A story. A storm. The never-ending web of human existence. We all brush against one another like sunrays—seemingly purposeless, but somehow meaningful.

"My grandpa used to live right there," I say, pointing to the colorful three-story building above the bookstore.

Phoenix and Ruby stop to admire it—Renaissance curves meeting Art Nouveau grace, the way Kraków always does. Suddenly, Ruby slips from my hand and walks toward the building, her long curls fluttering in the warm southern wind—Halny, we call it. The windows are closed now, all of them. My heart squeezes as I search for his silhouette, knowing it's not there, still hoping. My eyes fill.

"Mommy! Look, I found a flower!" Ruby runs over, clutching what looks like one of Grandpa's old balcony pansies. She twirls it between her fingers, the purple petals catching the light. "It's for you. The flower of love," she says, placing it in my outstretched palm.

The flower is weightless—but somehow, it carries every fragment of my childhood. His smile. The way he twisted his mustache when he was about to say something profound. The songs he sang to his flowers. The kitchen, filled with aromas of dill and garlic and zurek. My eyes sting. The pansy blurs.

Phoenix's teary eyes lock with mine, reading me like a book. Then he pulls us all into a warm, breath-stealing family hug.

"He's here," Phoenix murmurs, brushing his fingers across the petals. "Saying hi."

But I can't find the words. My eyes drift to the closed windows above the square, to the balcony that once overflowed with pansies and birds. I imagine Grandpa waving me in. My heart aches with the regret of not coming sooner. I always told myself we had time. That once things settled with Ruby, we'd visit. I got lost in belief of having all the time for him in the future—but the future came without Grandpa in it.

Sometimes we go through life thinking time will wait for us. Not understanding that time is always now. And once it passes, it's gone. Forever.

"Let's make this moment last," I whisper, hugging Phoenix and Ruby tighter. "The time is now."

They hold me close. And for a breath, the time pauses. The moment engraves itself into us. Like that very first hug Phoenix gave me on the street corner in LA. Only now, it's deeper. Now, we're linked by the greatest love of our lives—our miracle child.

"Mommy? Daddy?" Ruby whispers, tilting her head up, nose crinkling into a smile. "I really, really love you."

"Love you more," Phoenix and I chorus, grinning through our tears.

She giggles. So bright and unfiltered.

We stroll through the old town square, Kraków rising around us in its full summer glory. The towers of St. Mary's Basilica stretch high into the blue. Laughter spills from open cafés. The scent of tapped beer and grilled kielbasa lingers in the air.

As we near the cathedral, my eyes scan the crowd. Searching for her—my babushka. Was this what she saw?

Phoenix always says time isn't linear. That the past and the future are always bleeding into now. Into moments like this. Maybe she saw it. Or heard whispers of it from somewhere beyond.

Stepping into the cool majesty of St. Mary's, it feels as if the babushka is here with us. I close my eyes for a beat, pressing my palm to my heart.

"Thank you, you were right," I whisper into the silence, so softly that only her spirit might hear.

"Wow," Ruby breathes out. Her gaze climbs the soaring arches, tracing the rainbows that spill across the stone from the stained glass above. We settle on a bench tucked into a quiet corner, its old wood creaking beneath us—centuries of prayers soaked into its grain.

Phoenix folds his hands, his head bowed in stillness. Around us, the cathedral is a singing bowl of whispers—a cough, the soft shuffle of an old woman's rosary, the slow burn of wax and sage rising in the air. Incense from another world. Mystical solemnity.

I lean in closer next to Ruby, brushing her curls back. "Remember when Mommy went to that evaluation a while ago?" I whisper in her ear.

She nods. "The autism evaluation?"

"Mmm-hmm, and guess what?"

Her eyes widen. Her hand flies to cover her mouth. "You're autistic?" she asks, her voice spiking with excitement—loud enough to draw a slow, disapproving glance from the rosary lady.

"I'm autistic," I say, kissing her forehead. She tilts her head up. Eyes scanning me in disbelief. Huge smile.

"Just like me?"

"Just like you." I wrap my arms around her, pulling her close. She melts into me, curling like she used to when she was a baby, her cheek tucked into my neck.

And in that moment, I feel it—wholly, deeply—I am a mother. And the river of strength doesn't just flow one way. This little girl gave me the courage to keep going. To look deeper. To find myself.

I lean back and meet her eyes. Those amber eyes sparkling beneath the muted light filtering through the Rosetta window above.

"You know," I say, more to myself than to her, "I was lost in autism all this time. And you found me."

She blinks. Silent. Watching me. And something passes between us. Beyond the gaze. There's love. So much it aches. Like her father's. Like Grandpa's. That kind of gaze that touches places within you...you could never quite reach on your own.

"You're my mommy. I didn't have to find you. You found yourself," she murmurs, her words carrying a weight far beyond her years.

"I have something for you," I say, reaching into my pocket. Her eyes light up as I slip off Grandma's ring and thread it onto a thin gold chain. She gasps when I fasten it around her neck.

"Wow, Mommy. Thank you. Now I'm a magician too," she whispers, her little fingers immediately twirling the ring the same way I always twirl hoodie strings.

Then, as if someone flipped a switch, she straightens—eyes wide with a sudden thought.

"I want ice cream!" Her voice cuts clean through the basilica's hush, drawing a flurry of turned heads and raised eyebrows. A priest stifles a chuckle nearby, and I bite my lip, trying to contain my own laughter. Phoenix opens his eyes, his prayer finished, and gives Ruby a conspiratorial wink.

She tugs gently at his hand, her grin both sheepish and mischievous. "Ice cream?" she whispers again, this time with an exaggerated innocence that almost makes me lose it.

Phoenix nods, his hand finding hers as they both turn to me. Their eyes gleam in unison.

"I'll be just a minute—go ahead. I'll meet you there," I whisper, needing one last breath of this sacred quiet. Phoenix smiles, understanding without a word, as Ruby leads him toward the doors. Just before they disappear into the light, he raises one hand and forms a half-heart with his fingers. He doesn't look back. He doesn't have to.

A smile spreads across my lips, blooming from someplace deeper. I feel it radiate through me. This warm feeling. Love.

Watching them walk hand in hand, my heart swells. I've spent years wondering what a soulmate truly is. Phoenix is it.

Still reading my mind. Still speaking without words. Maybe twin flames aren't just poetic nonsense. If we're all made of energy, maybe soulmates really are two sparks from the same star, breathed into human form. How many of us get to feel that? Sometimes, I wonder—was autism my compass? My soulmate radar? Would I have known Phoenix was the one if I wasn't autistic? Would I have recognized how our hearts vibrate to the same melody? I guess I will never know.

My eyes are closed, my thoughts scattering in all directions. From a misunderstood child dancing alone, barefoot, in the grassy fields of the Bieszczady Mountains...to a model—ambitious yet so deeply scared—chasing the dream of becoming a doctor...to a woman who found true love, her dream career, and became a mother. Every fragment has shaped who I am today.

I open my eyes. My hand slips into my pocket and pulls out a note, folded into a small, dense square. Edges softened with time. The paper is a bit yellowed from being carried all these years. Tucked inside is a tiny pencil stub—sharpened so many times it's barely there.

Late afternoon light spills through the stained glass, casting rainbow freckles across my hands. I unfold the note slowly. The soft crinkle of paper fills the sacred stillness around me.

My little girl, alone on a soft, grassy mountaintop
with the earth cool beneath your bare feet
and wild chamomile whispering to your
thoughts—I write this for you. Know that your
solitary dance won't last forever; the world
will one day catch on to your unique rhythm.
This is my offering, the understanding that
society never gave you but should have...

I smooth the paper over my lap, its frayed texture tickling my fingers. My handwriting hasn't changed much over the years. Tears blur the graphite, smearing faint lines across the paper. I steady my hands and begin to write again:

...but don't worry, one day, true love will find you.

The love that speaks without words. The love that
understands. That holds a mirror reflecting the
intricate beauty within us all, showing how your
perceived flaws can lead to an understanding of
your brilliant, luminous self. You will see it in his
walnut eyes and her smile as her curly hair whips
in the wind. And they will arrange the fragments of
your broken heart into the most beautiful mosaic.
Know that one day you will no longer dance alone.

I fold the letter one last time. My eyes linger on the gilded altar before I rise. I walk slowly toward the stand by the exit, flickering with dozens of lit candles. The Hejnal Mariacki trumpet call, so loud it reaches through ancient stone, echoes inside with each step I take. It feels as though the sound is coming from my chest as I light two candles, one for Grandpa and one for Grandma. My tears fall on the crumpled paper clutched in my hand. As I place the letter between the two candles, the trumpet vibrates through me one last time before its beautifully sad scream suddenly ends.

THE END

ABOUT THE AUTHORS

Magdalena and Ashe Stevens, affectionately nicknamed *The Author Couple* by their readers, are multi-award-winning authors based in California. Their debut, *Lost in Beirut*, captured hearts worldwide and received numerous accolades, including honors from IndieReader Discovery Awards, Readers' Favorite, and the Chanticleer International Book Awards.

Known for bold, psychologically rich narratives, their work is shaped by backgrounds in art history, fashion, writing, theatre, and medicine—as well as by their lived experiences as neurodivergent and BIPOC individuals—offering a voice both unique and urgently relevant.

Their latest novel, *Fragments*, is a deeply personal story inspired by their journey with neurodiversity.

When asked about their collaborative writing process, Ashe often says with a smile: "He is her storyteller, and she is his poet."

@theauthorcouple
theauthorcouple.com

ACKNOWLEDGMENTS

TO OUR BELOVED DAUGHTER, LUCREZIA—
You inspired this book with every "ayawoo" and every brave
step you've taken to find your voice in a world not always ready
to hear it. You are the greatest gift in our lives. Thank you for
reminding us every day to reclaim our own voices. To write.
To fight for what we believe in. To love even louder.
Fragments exists because of you. Know that Grandpa
Stach is always watching over his little flower.

TO OUR EXTRAORDINARY EDITOR, SARAH DE SOUZA—
Thank you for nurturing this manuscript with a depth of care
and brilliance that defies words. Your hundreds of tracked
changes comments made us laugh, cry, reflect… and believe
more deeply in what this book could become.
Thank you for recognizing that the message in this book is
bigger than all of us. Working with you has been pure joy.
We can't wait to create something beautiful together again.

TO MARY IZZO—
Thank you for believing in two artists with haunted
hearts and stubborn hope, and for always reminding
us that our writing is a marathon worth running.

TO XAVIER COMAS OF COVERKITCHEN—
How you designed not one, but two breathtaking covers is still
beyond us. The genius that lives in your mind is the kind of
magic we aspire to. Your vision gave *Fragments* its skin.
We are so proud to call you a friend.
Love you, guapo.

TO JAIME DILL, OUR HAWK-EYED PROOFREADER—
Thank you for your sharp, loving editorial care—and
for catching the chaos spilled from the wild mind of a
dysgraphic author. Our Zoom meetings, your dedication,
and your belief in this story made us emotional too many
times. It's been an absolute pleasure to work with you.

TO HEATHER SANGSTER AND BROOKS BECKER—
Thank you for helping us shape the early drafts of *Fragments*.
Your insights lit the first sparks that became fire.
And to Brooke Vera and Veronika Gagovic—thank you for
reading those first fragile drafts with such generosity and grace.

A special thank you to all the patient
and compassionate therapists who were there
for our daughter throughout the years—
You helped our little girl bloom. We are forever grateful
for the light and nurturing you've brought into our lives.

**TO OUR DEAREST FRIENDS WHO BREATHED LIFE
INTO THE CHARACTERS OF *FRAGMENTS*—**
Monique Chmielewska Lehman, Anca Stan, Allan Apostol,
Danny Bitar, Michelle Easter, Carolyn Thomas, Cierra
Sterling, Lindsey and Olivia Hart, Alejandro Rivera—
Your spirits are etched into these pages. You've
touched our lives so deeply, we wrote you into
the characters everyone now loves.

TO GRANDPA STACH—
Thank you for reading to me for hours before I knew
how (even Dostoyevsky, when Grandma would protest
I was too little). You taught me how to find beauty
and magic in little things... so now I find you in every
hummingbird that visits flowers in our garden. Thank
you for encouraging me to write all these years. I miss you
so much, but I know you're watching over your girls.

AND TO MOM—
You're forever my dragon. I love you.

A POETIC LOVE STORY ABOUT IDENTITY, HEALING, AND FALLING IN LOVE WITH THE PARTS OF OURSELVES WE WERE TAUGHT TO HIDE.

Lena Hartley was a runway star in her youth. Now, she's a doctor. Her beautiful mind has always made sense of the world by observing, feeling, and analyzing first, participating second. She never questioned the way she was—until now, at the age of forty-two.

As she sits in a psychiatrist's office, the past she tried to bury splits open like an overstuffed valise of memories.

First there is Paris. The flashing cameras. The cramped apartment of fashion models. The toxic relationship. Crumbling under pressure, Lena chooses to leave this glamorous life behind and start again—from scratch.

Newly single and working in a bar to fund her studies, Lena is feeling adrift—when a chance follow on MySpace changes everything. Enter Phoenix: a gorgeous, talented artist, who sees the true Lena—but is also haunted by a traumatic past.

Their love story blossoms through poetic text messages and California landscapes into a connection that feels healing, passionate...and most of all, mystically fated.

Years later, when their young daughter, Ruby, is diagnosed with autism, Lena begins to see the world differently. In Ruby's eyes, she recognizes something familiar, and starts to piece together the fragments of her own identity.

Told in lyrical flashbacks during one extraordinary psychiatric evaluation, Fragments is an emotionally raw story of love that nurtures, not destroys—and the messy, beautiful process of self-discovery.

For anyone who's ever felt like too much—or not enough. (Bring tissues.)